THE SUMMER
OF SECRETS

SARAH JASMON

LARGE
PRINT

First published in Great Britain 2015
by
Black Swan
an imprint of Transworld Publishers

First Isis Edition
published 2016
by arrangement with
Transworld Publishers
Penguin Random House

A catalogue record for this book is available
from the British Library.

ISBN 978–1–78541–173–1 (hb)
ISBN 978–1–78541–179–3 (pb)

Published by
F. A. Thorpe (Publishing)
Anstey, Leicestershire

Set by Words & Graphics Ltd.
Anstey, Leicestershire
Printed and bound in Great Britain by
T. J. International Ltd., Padstow, Cornwall

This book is printed on acid-free paper

To Fuchsia, Hatty and Gabe

THE SUMMER OF SECRETS

The ... ... next door, sixteen-year-old Helen's lonely world is at once a more thrilling place. She is infatuated with the bohemian family, especially the petulant and charming daughter Victoria. As the long, hot days stretch out in front of them, Helen and Victoria grow inseparable. But when a stranger appears, Helen begins to question whether the secretive Dover family are really what they seem. It's the kind of summer when anything seems possible — and then something goes terribly wrong . . .

Alice

1973, Greece

So much blue. From where she sat at the very back of the ferry, this was all Alice could see. The island had changed from a place to a shape to the faintest blur and now it was gone, without leaving a trace. Jakob was out there. She should have stayed. She wanted to take off, to dive into the sea and make her way back. Instead, her body pressed itself into the heated metal of the deck. How would he find her now she was gone? The gulls circled, screaming for her.

She closed her eyes. This was the same sun, she thought, giving the same heat, the heat that all summer had kept her pinned to the sand. And alongside the unnumbered days, the heat that spilled into the nights. She squeezed her eyes more tightly shut. If she concentrated hard enough, surely she could piece it back together.

There was music, and they were dancing. Jakob was telling her something she didn't want to hear. She could picture his mouth but the sounds it made were a jabber. She couldn't slow them down to make sense of the words. She remembered the light, though, flooding out from the villa as she staggered away. And his brother, holding her by the shoulders. Piet was always there when she needed him, of course, but when had this happened? The memories were slides, changing too fast. She couldn't be sure of the order any more. Think, think. Jakob, lying on the ground: her mind flashed into hiding like a gecko touched by lamplight. She forced it back, waiting for him to get back up, conjuring up the sound of the cicadas, the scent of the jasmine.

No. Her memory was playing tricks. Piet had explained it all, about Jakob leaving, and why she must take the children back to England. They would sail to Athens, and the aeroplane would take them away. Everything would be fine. She inhaled as the nausea returned, and again her hand circled on her stomach. It was the motion of the ferry, that was all.

Voices approached. She wanted them to stay away. They were her children and she loved them, of course she did. But they needed too much of her, and she had nothing to give. Even before she started taking the pills, it was as if someone had sliced her in half and scooped her out. Seth studied her with his eight-year-old eyes and seemed to understand, but Victoria's demands were insistent and shrill. She'd always been her daddy's girl. Alice allowed them to lean into her, with their golden summer skin. What would they remember?

And then Piet was crouching in front of her, his hands warm and heavy on her shoulders. Alice let him fill her mind with certainty. The water surrounded them, its ripples flattening as they stretched into the distance. Along the horizon, a pale, unbroken haze merged into the turquoise of the sky. The island was there, would always be there. One day, she would come back.

CHAPTER
ONE

Helen

2013, Manchester: 9.30 a.m.

It can't be her. I stand on the opposite pavement, waiting for the lines and curves of the lettering to shift, to resolve into another name entirely. It's happened before. I am bumped by passing bags, pushchairs, elbows, but the words remain the same: Victoria Dover.

The poster is on the wall of a new art gallery, the sort that has a café and a meeting space and a workshop programme. It's the kind of place that comes and goes a lot in this area. I must have passed it earlier as I walked off my sleeplessness, and I close my eyes, go back to the barely lit emptiness of dawn, the blankness of the shuttered windows as I headed out towards the suburbs. It wasn't there then, must have risen like the castle in the *Arabian Nights* once my back was turned. I half expect the whole place to shiver and vanish as I cross the road. It doesn't.

I look at my hands as they rest on the glass, one thumb on the V, the other to the right of the R.

In the end, I step away so I can see the whole thing. The background image is of water, water in the early morning, captured in black and white, and still supporting a dawn mist. Below the name there are smaller words, something about *photographs, awards, memory, unique*. And a date: today's date. I notice the flyer pasted to one side. Her exhibition launches tonight; all are welcome for wine. The artist will be present. Victoria is here, somewhere in the city. I could see her, tonight, in the flesh. The print wavers in front of my eyes. My chest doesn't want to let the air in and I feel my ribs and shoulders rise with the effort. I can't remember how it feels to breathe normally.

Somehow, my feet take themselves away in the direction of the bookshop. I have tried to find Victoria over the years. At first, after that summer, I was always following people. Sometimes I thought it was Seth, occasionally the twins, but mostly I saw Victoria. I would see her in the back of a head, the swing of an arm, and add it up to a whole, a composite trick of the light. The sightings diminished over time. As the Internet arrived, I also made digital sorties, but with no better luck. She remained hidden in spite of technology, and my attempts dwindled to the odd search term, her name entered more out of habit than anything.

When I reach the bookshop, I lock the door behind me and leave the shutters down. After the light and noise of the street, I feel hidden, furtive, as I slide behind the counter. The computer screen flickers, and goes into the slow dance of starting up. My fingers wait above the keys.

4

The Dovers' names are a litany of all I have lost, and so I have kept them hidden, safe. Now I close my eyes and let myself remember. I curate the memories, shuffling through them with the ease of an expert as the sun makes patterns on the surface of the canal and the heat fills the air with the dry dust of summer grass. The stills become the silent, jerky frames of a home movie. We are in Victoria's room, the heat making it too much effort to stand, the drummer looking down at us with his melancholy eyes. Or we are in the garden. Victoria sits in the lotus position before rising up on to her knees and walking on them across the scrubby lawn, her feet sticking out from her hips like an origami fold. Pippa tugs at my arm and whispers in my ear and I hear the sound of Seth's guitar. I try to see my dad, but he won't come out of the shadows. Victoria runs along the bank, daring me to follow her, always increasing the stakes.

The water shifts relentlessly over my head, distorting the pictures. I cannot allow myself to remain there for too long. My hands drop. The screen remains blank.

CHAPTER
TWO

1983

The fly kept landing on her book. Helen blew at it yet again, and tried to refocus on the print, but the sun was too bright, it made the letters blur at the edges. She let her head drop on to her arm, the book closing with her thumb trapped inside. This time the fly landed on her leg. A twitch made it bounce along, but the moment was broken. She was now lying there and waiting for it to land again. With a sigh, she rolled on to her side and pushed herself up.

It had seemed so perfect first thing, a whole day with nothing to do except lie in the heat. Her O levels were done, school was over, and there was no nagging mother around to make her do things. Who cared if there was also no one to call up, no offers of plans to be made? When she let herself remember the last weeks of term, she could feel the burning embarrassment of being stuck without an ally for lunchtimes, sports, for all those end-of-school activities that were never as optional as they made out. She let herself fall backwards on to the old beach towel, holding the book over her face to block the heat of the sun. At least there was no one watching her be alone here. July was only the beginning. If she focused on the good things, she could pretend that September would never come.

Something scuffled outside the gate. A dog, probably, on its way down to the canal for a walk. She lay where she was, motionless, waiting for the noise to go away, but it was joined by the sound of whispering voices. Helen scrambled on to her knees, unknotting her T-shirt to cover up her midriff. There wasn't anyone who was likely to drop by for a visit. She hoped not, anyway, not with her hair needing a wash and her face all red from the sun. Was there time to slip round to the back of the house and go inside? But then whoever it was would see her. With a sigh, she stood up, hoping to catch sight of whoever it was without them noticing.

It wasn't what she'd expected at all. A small girl, Helen guessed about nine or ten, was stuck in the middle of the hedge. There was no sign of whomever she'd been talking to.

"Uh, hello?" Helen took a step towards the gate. It wasn't someone she knew. Possibly she was visiting a grandparent in one of the houses back along the main road. "Have you lost something?"

The girl started up from her half-crouch. "You saw me!" She made an attempt to back out, but one of her plaits was caught on a twig. "I was trying to get to the other end of the hedge without you seeing me. It was a dare." She paused in her efforts and lifted a hand to rub at her nose. "Could you get my hair off?"

It was a long plait. As she disentangled it, Helen noticed that the girl was brown in a dusty, beach way, which meant she wasn't from round there. Even

Michelle Smith, showing off her bikini lines in PE after she'd spent three weeks in Majorca, hadn't had a tan like that. Helen waited as the girl wriggled herself out, not sure what to say.

"Are you sunbathing?" Standing upright, the child came up to Helen's shoulder. "You can go back and carry on, if you like."

Helen opened her mouth and then shut it again. The girl's accent wasn't local either. She sounded Southern, a bit posh, and Helen almost felt as if she should be thanking her. "I was reading."

"Oh. In that case." The girl followed her back across the grass. "Have you lived here for a long time?" She took her shoe off and shook it. "What's your name?"

"Helen."

"Like Helen of Troy." The girl giggled. "She was so beautiful that there was a war. But we saw a painting of her and she wasn't pretty at all." She giggled again. "My brother said she wouldn't have launched a thousand dinghies." She stopped to peer at her shoe and kicked off her other one adding, in a confidential tone, "I'll be more comfortable without."

"I'm Helen after my grandmother, actually. What's your name?"

"Well, our surname is Dover. I was going to be Persephone because I was born in the spring, but Seth kept making it PercyPhone, so Mummy changed her mind and called me Pippa because of a poem she liked, and my brother's name is really Wilfred because of a poem as well, and usually he's called Will but I've decided I'm going to call him Fred." Coming to an abrupt stop, she twisted round. "I don't know where he's gone." She lifted a hand up to her mouth and called out, "It's OK, she says we can come in."

Helen was about to say she hadn't said that at all when a boy appeared at the side of the house. She'd never seen two children more alike. Twins, surely, although they couldn't actually be identical. A fragment from a biology lesson floated into her mind. *Identical twins are monozygotic, formed from a single egg. They are genetically identical, therefore always come in same-sex sets.* These two resembled an illustration from a children's book: tilted noses, freckles, dungarees. The boy, Will, was even carrying a fishing net. He didn't come all the way across to them, but hovered by the path before dropping to his stomach, his eyes fixed on the section of the garden Helen's mother had always referred to as "the meadow".

Pippa rolled her eyes. "He's practising to be a soldier," she said. "Though we think it's just a phase." She giggled. "Seth says it wouldn't be any good him being a soldier anyway, because he doesn't believe in taking anyone's side but his own."

"Seth's your other brother?"

"Yes." Pippa had turned towards the shed. "Are those garden canes? Do you ever play horse jumping?"

They made an efficient team, Helen loosening the compacted earth with an old screwdriver, Pippa driving in the canes. The course had four jumps, ranged around in a circle, crossed canes held together with oddments of old twine, and single poles balanced across them at varying heights. Helen listened to Pippa's chatter as they worked. There was the holiday in Spain, the older brother who'd stayed behind, although he'd be back soon, the older sister who was cross a lot. Hadn't her mother said something once about the Weavers, from the big, new white house up by the crossroads, having a timeshare in Spain? Pippa and Will must be their grandchildren. The Weavers were newcomers. Helen didn't know them well, but she wasn't surprised Pippa hadn't suggested building jumps in their pristine garden.

Pippa stood up and planted her hands on her hips, surveying the course. "All right, we're ready for the competition."

Abruptly, the game became ridiculous. Helen took a breath. She couldn't galumph about pretending to be a horse, not even with Pippa as the only audience.

"I'll time you." She twisted herself round, trying to see where she'd left her watch.

"But that's no fun!"

Helen had never seen anyone actually make their lips tremble. Pippa even had tears welling up.

"Look, how about —"

Before she could finish, something jumped out from behind the shed with an ear-shattering howl. The jolt of adrenaline that kicked at her ribcage stopped Helen from saying anything.

"Will!" Pippa stamped a foot. "You spoil *everything*."

Will ignored her, going around the course with his legs thrashing out wildly, yipping at a high pitch. He caught his foot on the final jump and ended up

10

sprawled full length on the grass. He didn't seem the worse for it. "I'm having another go, that didn't count."

Pippa pushed him out of the way. "No, it's my turn."

Will pushed her back, pulling a face and imitating her in a high-pitched tone.

"Helen, tell him it's my go!" Pippa's face was red, and her eyes appealing, but the injured expression didn't stop her digging her twin hard with her elbow. "We *made* the jumps, he has to do what we say!"

Or we could stop being horses? Helen didn't say it, though. She stared at them in turn, her mind a blank. She had no experience to draw upon. It had always been only her and her parents. She sent a hurried glance to the gate, hoping for an adult, any adult. The lane was empty.

"How about Will has another go, and then you have two in a row?" Even to herself this sounded a lame compromise.

Pippa crossed her arms and turned her back on her twin. "It's not fair, and he knows it," she began. "I'm always having to give in to him because I'm the sensible one."

"Why don't I time you both together?"

Pippa thought this over, sucking on the end of one plait. "All right." She flicked the plait back over her shoulder and took a step towards the start before running back to whisper in Helen's ear. "Watch out for him, he cheats."

Will had wandered off, though, scrabbling for something in the long grass. Pippa heaved a sigh and rolled her eyes at Helen, and counted herself down. "Three, two, one . . ."

And Pippa was racing around the jumps and Will was chasing after her, a spare cane in his hand, swiping it through the air towards her legs. As Helen jumped up, ready to protest, Pippa let out a long howl, drowning out Will's cowboy whoops.

A voice from the gate broke into the noise.

"Pippa! Will!"

There was a pause in the furore and then they both burst out with their grievances.

"He hit me with that cane! It *hurt*, look at my leg!"

"I was only being a trainer. It made her go faster." Will gave Helen a sideways glance before dropping his head and scraping at the ground with his cane.

It was a girl of about her own age, but so different that she could have been dropped from another planet. She had long hair, heaped and knotted at the back of her head, and she was wearing a tie-dyed sundress, pink going through purple into blue, brown leather sandals with toe-posts, and yellow nail varnish. Helen realized she was staring, but couldn't stop herself. The girl was ignoring her anyway, addressing Pippa alone.

"I don't care what he's done, you need to get here."

This must be the twins' sister, thought Helen. She had been expecting someone older, more . . . governessy. As the girl's gaze briefly flickered over to her she knew exactly how she must look: too-tight cut-offs that were the wrong colour denim. White legs. T-shirt shapeless from being tied in a knot. Fingernails dirty and broken from digging holes for the canes. She put her hands behind her back.

"Hi." Her mind was completely blank. She sounded like a fool. The girl ignored her, anyway.

"Do we have to go?" Pippa's voice was desolate. "But we've got *horse* jumps!"

"Yes, we do. And if you go off like that again without telling me, I'm going to tie your hair to the banisters."

"I *did* tell you. I called up the *stairs*. I . . ."

"Pippa, get your shoes." She turned her back slightly. "And you, Will." She didn't look at him.

"It's Fred. We decided." Pippa folded her arms and stared into her sister's face. "And we *did* tell you."

"Pippa, shut up."

Turning to Helen, Pippa spoke with a distant dignity. "This is my sister. She thinks she's in charge but she's only fifteen. She's called Victoria. Like the Queen. Because they're both grumpy." She trailed off across the grass.

Helen cleared her throat. She couldn't work out if Victoria was angry with her. Should she have known that the twins weren't supposed to be there? Sent them back earlier? She put one hand up to fiddle with her hair, remembered the dirt under her nails and jammed both hands in her pockets. "I like your dress."

"Thanks." Victoria gave a brief smile then went back to examining the grass along the edge of the path.

"Are you staying with Mrs Weaver for long?"

Victoria glanced up. "Who's Mrs Weaver?"

There was silence.

"In the house up there." Helen lifted a hand to point but let it drop at Victoria's expression. "Isn't she, well, your grandmother?"

"Is that what Pippa's been telling you?" Victoria glanced over to where Pippa was inching into her shoes. Her face was the same as Pippa's had been when she was exasperated with Will. "What else has she said?"

"She didn't . . ." Helen tried to remember what Pippa had said. "I thought perhaps . . ."

Her sunburn prickled across her neck and shoulders as she came to a halt.

Pippa wandered up to them. She seemed to have regained her equanimity. "Can I come again, Helen?"

Helen caught an expression of what could have been annoyance or distaste flash over Victoria's face, although it was hard to read her properly.

"I . . . uh . . ." She felt bad. It had been kind of fun but, with Victoria standing there, she felt silly. "I'm — I'm not sure my dad'll want to keep the canes up."

"What she means, Pippa, is no, she's got better things to do than jump around like an idiot."

Before Helen could say more, Pippa pushed past Victoria and started off down the lane, going towards the canal. "I hate you, Victoria Dover!"

Will slid past Victoria, giving her as wide a berth as he could before setting off after Pippa, all arguments forgotten.

Victoria made to follow them. Helen's mind raced. There had to be some way of delaying her. It was one thing to make the best of an empty summer, but knowing someone like this was down the road, someone who'd never come back because of a stupid first impression: that would be unbearable. She spotted Will's fishing net.

"Do you want to take this?" She bent to pick it up. Victoria had turned, and was staring at the net as if wondering what it was. Helen kept going anyway: "And will Pippa be OK? She can come over if she wants, I didn't mean . . ." She stumbled on what she wanted to say. "You know, I didn't want to upset her."

Victoria gave an unexpected laugh. "It is what you meant, though, isn't it? I've done you a favour, believe me. She'd have taken residence, bridles and all."

Helen smiled back. "I didn't have anything else to do." She thought of something else. "Do they know about the canal down there?" She gestured in the direction Pippa and Will had gone. "Only, it's quite deep."

"Yeah." Victoria passed through the gate and shut it behind her with a bang. "We're living in a cottage on the bank."

Helen waited for Victoria to look back as she followed the path of the twins, to wave, or make some acknowledgement of leaving, but she sauntered away with no sign, already in another world. Then, at the last moment, she seemed to lift the fishing net in a kind of salute. Helen raised a hand in response. The scent of the privet hedge was rising, as it always did at this time of day. It was an odd smell, coming from nowhere and setting off a tingle in the pit of her belly. Only last night, as she'd leaned out of her window, it had surrounded her with melancholy, reminding her of everything she hadn't got. Now it promised excitement instead, the world outside, some half-acknowledged dream. Helen rested her forearms on top of the gate and dropped her chin down on them as she gazed out at the empty lane. A new summer seemed to be spread out in front of her, but it was still beyond her reach. If only Victoria would come back, then perhaps it would happen.

CHAPTER
THREE

A handful of letters slithered down on to the doormat as Helen came down the stairs the next morning. She knew without looking that they'd mostly be junk. There was already a heap of them on the hallstand now that her mother wasn't there to sort and bin. Helen thought about adding the fresh arrivals to the pile, but she couldn't be bothered to bend down and collect them up. She carried on to the kitchen instead, pausing as she always did to assess her father's mood. If he was even a bit cheerful, it would validate her own feeling of lightness, meaning her anticipations were strong enough to be rubbing off.

He sat at the table, dressed but unshaven, his hair rumpled and greasy. There was an empty mug and a full ashtray at one elbow and he'd pushed the mess on the table aside to make room for the newspaper. Helen pictured the kitchen as she'd always known it: ordered, shiny, nothing ever out of place. It wasn't big, and the layout made no pretensions to an efficient use of the space, one of her mother's running complaints. It was too much to expect her to manage in such an impractical room, she said. She'd been promised a new kitchen and she wasn't going to put up with this matchbox any longer. Helen packed the arguments back into their box and slammed the lid. She hated remembering the trickle of helplessness as she'd watched them brew and the sick fear of what was to come. She didn't want to feel sorry for her dad, either. His back wasn't giving much away, but the air was free from any noticeable tension. She was an expert at spotting that.

He turned another page of the paper, and then picked up his mug, holding it out to one side. "Make me one, will you?"

"If you'll let me get by."

He squeezed himself in a fraction, eyes fixed on the paper. "You're up early today. Got a plane to catch?"

Helen pulled the kettle to the length of its cord and tilted it to fit under the tap. The sky was as blue as on the previous day, warm air pooling through the open window. She smiled inwardly as she spotted the garden canes scattered over the grass. Pippa was so sweet. The thought prompted her to lean over the sink so she could see the gate. Not that she was expecting to see anyone, of course. She held her breath anyway.

Water overflowed from the spout of the kettle, soaking the front of her T-shirt and spraying over the floor.

"Damn!" She let go of the kettle, grabbed at a tea towel to dry herself. "Shit!" The tea towel had left a streak of grease down the white front of her top.

She had yet to get out of the habit of expecting a rebuke for clumsiness. There was something relaxing in the way Mick didn't notice. Helen emptied some of the water out of the kettle and put it back down on the counter, flicking the switch and looking for the dishcloth. It was crumpled up behind the tap. She soaked up some of the puddle with it and then pulled at her T-shirt, wondering if rubbing at the mark would make things worse. Maybe her dad could help. She glanced at him dubiously. He did surprise her sometimes with things he knew, and she didn't have another clean top. "How do you get grease out of clothes?"

"Washing-up liquid." Mick turned another page. "Where's my tea?"

Helen ignored the question and opened a cupboard door. There was an empty packet of cornflakes, and a tin of custard.

"There's nothing for breakfast." It was Mick's turn to ignore her. She crossed to the other side of the table and peered in the fridge. "And we're out of milk."

Mick leaned back and stretched, nodding his head towards the door.

"Doorstep. I haven't brought it in." He rubbed at his temples. "Got a bloody headache again. Must be the sun."

Or the whisky. She tried not to notice the empty bottle standing by the toaster. Saying anything made it worse. The milk was on the back doorstep, the foil top of one bottle pecked out by a bird. The milkman had left a note. She brought it in with the bottles, and dropped it by her dad's elbow.

"Dad . . ." She was stopped by the sound of the kettle. A plume of steam was bouncing against the wall, making wet runnels on the paint. There weren't any clean mugs in the cupboard, so she made do with rinsing one from the crowded sink. "Dad, you know those cottages?" She put the tea on the table.

"What cottages?" Mick turned another page of the paper, leaning in to study an advert.

"The ones down on the canal."

"What about them?" He put the paper down and reached for his tea. "Where are my cigarettes?"

Helen could see the tobacco tin under the edge of the newspaper. She sat down on the other side of the table and picked up her own tea. "Does anyone live there?"

Mick wasn't listening. "I had it a minute ago. Mess every-bloody-where."

He swept a hand through the piles of paper in front of him, and the tin fell to the floor. His belly got in the way of him bending, and he couldn't quite reach it. She gave in and leaned down to pick it up for him.

"Dad? The cottages?"

"What?" He flicked the lid of the tin up with a thumbnail, pulled out the packet of papers. "Nearly out." He glanced up at last, fingers separating the strands of tobacco and rolling them up in the paper without him needing to concentrate. "They're only at the bottom of the lane, go and see for yourself."

Helen took a sip of tea. "I wondered if anyone lives there, that's all. I thought they were empty."

She could picture them: a row of three or four in a brick terrace, with front gardens right up to the towpath. Surely they'd had missing tiles, broken glass

20

in the windows? She hadn't been down to the canal for such a long time, and they probably weren't as bad as she thought. A tiny, clear memory popped into her head, of herself on the bank, holding her dad's hand. That must have been years ago, definitely before they'd bought this house. It had been one of their special places, where he'd taught her to skim stones and explained about the locks. They'd had a game where they chose a boat, and her dad would tell her a story about how they'd sail away to where the water was carried across a valley on a bridge as high as the sky. Had it been real? She turned to ask him, half-expecting the man from that time to be sitting there. He'd finished making the cigarette, and was tapping the end against the folded newspaper, searching for something. Helen picked up his lighter and held it out. Mick sat back in his chair, the roll-up in his mouth, and held the flame to its tip. When he was done, Helen picked the lighter up, even though she knew the engraving on the side by heart. The letters curled into each other: *Not all who wander are lost.* She flicked the top open, spun the wheel, watched the flame rise steadily. She could remember the moment when she managed to light it by herself for the first time.

"There's the old lady, she still lives down there. What's her name, Taylor? Tyler?" Mick's voice came as a surprise, and it took her a moment to catch up with what he was talking about. "She must be getting on a bit, though."

"So they're liveable?"

"More or less." Mick pushed his chair back with purpose and stood up, patting at his pockets. "Right, I'm going into Southport. Someone's having a sale of boat stuff. One of the old shrimpers." He pushed the stub of his cigarette into the pile on the ashtray.

"Can you get some shopping?" Helen scrabbled in the mess on the table for a pen and an old envelope.

"Only if you're quick." He picked up the newspaper and folded it twice more before shoving it in his back pocket. "Not too much, mind, I don't want to be all day."

After Mick left, Helen sat at the table gazing into her half-empty mug. The sense that something was going to happen, the mild fizz that had woken her up and driven her out of bed, was fading away. The mess seemed to have taken over, and she could never decide where to start. It wasn't fair that she was left to do it all. She let out her breath in a long sigh, tipped the rest of her tea into the sink. She wasn't going to do any tidying up now, anyway. At least the sun was out. If nothing else, she might as well see if she could get a tan this year.

The leaves from the tree danced shadows across her eyelids. There was a lump digging into her back, from a root going under the ground, she supposed. It was too much effort to find another spot, so she wriggled around until she was more or less comfortable. How long had she been lying there? Long enough to check for any colour change? She took a quick peek. In her mind, she was already turning brown, and the pale reality made her close her eyes with a sigh. She was considering whether it was time to turn over when she heard the gate squeak. From some vague superstitious impulse, she kept her eyes shut. If she didn't look, she wouldn't be disappointed. Instead, she strained her senses to pick up clues. She was almost sure someone was there, but didn't realize how close they'd come until a shower of grass seeds fell on her face. She sat up in a hurry to see Victoria collapsing down next to her.

"Are you busy?" She was wearing exaggeratedly baggy trousers, held up on her hips with a drawstring and tightening at her ankles so the fine cotton ballooned around her as she sat, and a white sleeveless blouse with elaborate pintucking down the front. It looked like an antique. "I had to get out of the house. I painted my room this morning and now, of course, the twins want to paint the attic, and they expect me to help them." She felt around in a pocket, pulling out a squashed bag of jelly babies. "Do you want one?"

"Thanks." Helen took a moment to choose, in lieu of any speech. A blackbird called out from the hedge into the silence. Victoria bit the head off a green baby and impaled the body on a twig. She reached out a hand and picked up the book from where Helen had dropped it on the grass.

"Are you enjoying this?" She put on a voice of exaggerated drama. "'A stirring tale of passion and betrayal, sweeping from the courts of the French kings to the conquest of the New World.' Sounds like total crap to me." Without waiting for an answer, she flopped back on to the grass, and seemed to be addressing the top of the tree. "I've got a reading list for the summer. All the books people complain about."

"All of them?" Helen felt like kicking herself. Why did she have to sound so sceptical? Victoria didn't seem to mind, though. She threw a jelly baby into the air and caught it neatly in her mouth before holding out the bag.

"It was in the paper. I'll give it to you too, and we can share the books. I've not really started yet, so you haven't got loads to catch up on."

"OK." Helen reached for the paperback and studied the cover. "I was working on a system of random choice. Closed my eyes and had to read the one I touched first." She discarded it. "If you think that one's bad you should have seen the last one."

Victoria laughed, catching at a daisy on the grass above her head and shredding off the petals.

"Come and try that at our house." She threw the remains of the flower at the trunk of the tree. "We carry all these books round with us in boxes and none of them are worth reading. I had to go to the library to get the books on my list, and the twins wanted to come along, of course. They caused havoc on the bus."

Helen sat up and wrapped her arms around her knees.

"How long have you been here? Only . . . I mean, I haven't noticed any removals van or anything."

Victoria raised her eyebrows.

"Removals? Hardly." She held out the bag, but there was only one left, so Helen shook her head. Victoria bit into it, and then screwed up the paper bag. "A friend of

Alice's brought some stuff round in his van. And there's a bit more coming next week."

Helen tried to place the name from Pippa's chatter the day before. She couldn't remember hearing it.

"Is Alice your sister?"

Victoria pushed herself up on her elbows. She squinted slightly, and aimed the paper bag at an empty flowerpot.

"No, my mum."

Helen waited for more, but Victoria didn't expand.

"What's it like around here, anyway?" She asked the question without any great enthusiasm, examining the immediate area with a world-weary expression.

"Oh, you know." Helen bent to scratch at a bite on her ankle to gain time. It wasn't something she thought about. It was just home, with the wind beating across the flat expanse of the fields behind and the sky that had reminded her of the prairies ever since she'd been given *My Ántonia* for Christmas years before. And, when her mother left, it was a place where she'd been surprised to find she'd needed to stay. "Quiet. Not much happens."

"Oh." Victoria sat up and crossed her legs. "Is it only you living here?"

"Well, and my dad." Helen waited for the enquiring look which meant, *And what about your mother?* But it didn't come.

"It's a lot of house."

Helen tried to see it through Victoria's eyes. Grey pebbledash on the walls, stains running down from the overflow pipes. It was quite big, she supposed. She'd never thought of it like that. Victoria hadn't finished with her questions.

"Are you staying home for the summer? Or do you go away?"

Helen leaned over to pick up her glass of squash but there was a wasp floating in it. She didn't want to lie, but she hated having to admit that holidays mostly revolved around air shows and vintage car rallies. She'd never been abroad, unless you counted the Isle of Wight. It was one of the other things her mother had always gone on about: never going anywhere, how other people rented gîtes or toured the Italian lakes. There had been talk of hiring a boat on the Norfolk Broads this year, but that was out the window now.

"Probably here." She tipped the glass up, letting the squash trickle into the dry earth at the base of the tree. The wasp twitched. "My dad's got plans to fix his boat up."

That was stretching the truth. Mick had been fixing his boat for most of Helen's life.

They both turned at the sound of an engine. It slowed as it reached the house, the car pulling into the drive on the far side. The engine cut off, a door opened and slammed shut, and there were footsteps on the gravel path. A minute or two later, Mick walked up the side of the garage and disappeared inside.

Victoria checked her watch. "I should go. Alice'll be waking up soon, and she doesn't know anything about the painting. I want to see her face when the twins come down. It'll be hilarious."

26

Alice again. Helen had an odd feeling of swimming into uncharted water, her feet scrabbling to find a foothold. Victoria's family gave her no reference points, and she wasn't sure how to navigate without appearing completely stupid. It was exhilarating, all the same. All she needed now was a proper invitation to visit, a gesture showing that she would be allowed further in.

"Was Pippa all right? You know, after . . ." She waved a hand towards the garden canes. Anything to keep the conversation going.

"What?" Victoria followed her gesture with a puzzled expression.

"You know, when she ran off." Helen could feel her cheeks burning.

Victoria still looked puzzled. She stood up.

"Yeah, she was all right."

"Oh, OK." Helen scrambled to her feet as well, but wasn't sure what to do next. Victoria bent down to brush some dirt from her trousers before she straightened up and set off towards the gate.

"I'll see you," Helen called after her.

"Yeah." Victoria lifted a hand in farewell. "I'll bring that list of books round."

"Books?" Then Helen remembered. "Oh, the list. I'll look forward to it." She bent in confusion to rub at the imprints the grass had left on her leg. Victoria was talking again.

"It might be a couple of days. There's . . . stuff." There was a pause, as if she was about to say more, but her next words seemed unrelated. "My brother's going to be back soon."

"The one who's been hitch-hiking?"

"How did you know?" Victoria's voice was almost accusing. Then she grinned. "Pippa, right?" She shook her head. "That girl yacks like a leaking tap. See you around, anyway."

She drifted rather than walked, not looking back or making a gesture of farewell. Her hair was in a long French plait today, haphazardly messy with loose ends that looked as if they were meant to be there, and threads of a lighter colour weaving in and out. It reached almost to her waist. Helen put her hand up to feel her own hair. She could never get it to stay up in any style. If she got to know her properly, she could ask Victoria to show her.

"Who was that?" Mick came out of the garage, beer can in his hand. He didn't wait for an answer. "Shopping's in the car. Get it out, will you?"

Helen stayed where she was, following Victoria's progress until she was out of sight.

CHAPTER
FOUR

The lane had been surfaced at some distant point, but what remained was cracked and dusty, the space reclaimed by the thrusting growth of dandelions and grasses. Helen stopped, pinching a grass stem between finger and thumb and sliding up, so the seeds gathered in a neat bunch. *April showers*, she thought, as she tossed them away. The sky was cloudless and the air heavy, the heat a dense curtain she had to push her way through. She couldn't imagine ever being cold. She looked down at herself, at the big white shirt she'd unearthed in the airing cupboard. Her skin was the slightest bit browner, and her bare feet looked nice. She placed them carefully. There were nettles here as well, and the odd thistle.

When she reached the water, she sat on the bank at first, picking up small stones and tossing them in. Again, she remembered walking along a path like this with Mick. There had been ducks, and a boat that had sunk, with only the cabin poking up. Had there been more boats in those days, or was she imagining it? The ducks were still here, a scattered group dabbing at the water like busy shoppers until, at some hidden signal, they paddled off downstream.

Two days had passed with no further sign of Victoria, the twins or the book list. Helen couldn't settle. She had tried to read, but the books she had now seemed somehow ridiculous, and when she sat in the garden all she could do was listen for footsteps coming to the gate. The same dialogue circled her head. She should go down to the canal. But she hadn't been asked, and there was the "stuff" Victoria had mentioned that was going to get in the way. If she pushed in when she wasn't wanted, they would never be friends. But the canal didn't belong to anyone, and she'd be out on a walk, that's all. By the middle of the afternoon on the third day, she'd had enough of her own company. Anything was better than waiting. Even so, she got halfway down and turned back more than once. It was the sound of a car turning down from the main road that pushed her on. She didn't look back, but it sounded as if it had gone into the Weavers' driveway.

The far side of the canal was hidden by a spread of reeds. As Helen looked across, a dart of blue shot out of the growth and sped across the surface. She stood up in a hurry, trying to track it. Was it a kingfisher? She'd never been fast enough to follow Mick's pointing finger, had been left pretending she'd seen one. It was gone, anyway. Probably she'd imagined it. Since she was up, she carried on walking, still keeping half an eye out.

The cottages were set back from the canal's edge and fronted with gardens partly concealed by a thick and overgrown hedge. Beyond them, a minor road crossed the canal by way of a small hump-backed bridge, the

30

rough grey stonework supporting long strands of trailing moss and a burst of pink and white flowers. The sound of an engine broke the quiet, changing gear with a wrench on the approach to the bridge. Helen edged closer to the cottage hedges as the car went over. She heard a spurt of gravel as it sped up on the far side. At the same moment, she saw again the flash of the kingfisher. This time it landed on a branch near to the bridge; she took a step that way, her eyes fixed on the compact shape. It was bigger than she'd imagined, and motionless on its perch, almost all beak from this angle.

"They're good luck, they are."

The voice came from behind the hedge, a sound so unexpected that Helen started. She turned to see the top of an old woman's head. It nodded towards the bridge.

"Good luck and prosperity."

Helen smiled uncertainly at her.

"That's what they symbolize." The woman gave a grim smile. "Good luck and prosperity, if you believe in it."

Helen looked away in time to see the kingfisher launch itself and disappear from sight. "I've never seen one before."

The woman gave another nod, and started to shuffle along to the gate at the end of the row of cottages. There were four in all, the gardens in various degrees of wildness, separated from one another by the remains of wooden fences. They all joined up to the one path, which ran parallel to the canal, bordered by the hedge and ending at a gate going through to the lane. Helen watched the woman bend over to place an empty milk bottle on the ground. In spite of the day's heat, she was wearing an assortment of cardigans, and thick tights under her misshapen grey skirt. When she drew level again, she paused.

"If you're here after that lot at the end, they're not in." She gave a sniff. "Proper crew, they are. Music and shouting at all hours."

She carried on towards the second cottage. Helen opened her mouth in a question, but before it came she changed her mind. Instead she lifted a hand and called out.

"Thank you." She wasn't sure what she was thanking her for, but still. "Thank you, Mrs —"

"Tyler." The woman went through the door without a backwards glance. "For sixty years and not many to go." The door shut behind her.

There didn't seem much point in hanging about, but Helen stayed to throw a few more stones before heading home, taking her time in case they came by. When she got home, something was wedged in the letter box, a fat book, the pages slightly spread and wrinkled. Had it been there all along? Surely she'd have noticed? It took some minutes of wiggling to get it free. *Ulysses.* Wasn't he Greek? Something was scribbled on the inside cover. "*Had this lying around. Thought it would make a good start.*" The letters were small and tight, and Victoria hadn't signed her name. Helen turned to the first page, doubts starting to flicker as she tried to work out what was going on. It wasn't her usual thing, but it gave her a connection, anyway. She needed to try, that was all.

In the garden again, she tried to get comfortable. The book was thick enough to need both hands to keep it open, and doing that lying down made her back hurt. She wriggled into a sitting position and leaned against the tree, with her knees propping the book's weight.

Stately, plump Buck Mulligan came from the stairhead, bearing a bowl of lather on which a mirror and a razor lay crossed.

She riffled through the pages. Seven hundred to go. And she hadn't understood a word so far. With a groan, she turned the page and flattened it down. She had to do it. But first she might let her eyes close for a second.

A lean, golden-skinned boy was standing above her. He used his foot to turn the book over from where it had fallen face down.

"*Ulysses*, huh?" He grinned. "Joyce always makes me go to sleep too. How are you getting on with it?"

Helen's neck ached. How long had she been asleep? She had a hideous vision of herself with her mouth open, snoring in the sun. Sitting up, she fiddled her hair straight. What were you supposed to say in a situation like this, anyway? He answered for her by holding out a hand.

"Seth."

His hair was the same brown as Victoria's, but curly, standing out from his face and falling a good few inches below his shoulders. Helen remembered his hand, and held her own out. He took it in a firm grasp and then dropped to the ground beside her. With an air of being completely at home, he let himself fall back and tilted his face up towards the sun, his eyes closed.

"I've only been back for an hour, and I've spent most of that trying to round people up. The twins were up a tree in someone's garden, and now Victoria has disappeared again. I thought she might be here." He opened one eye in joke consternation. "You are Helen, aren't you? Pippa's horse-riding friend?"

So someone had been talking about her. "Yes." She felt her tongue begin to tangle already. "Though I don't actually ride them at all. I mean, real horses. It was Pippa, she got really keen."

He laughed, but it was a warm sound, comfortable somehow.

"Pippa and her ponies. She has me leading them out to grass on a regular basis. It's those pony club books she keeps reading." He had both eyes closed again. "So tell me: why are you out here on this beautiful day reading *Ulysses?* Can't be for exams."

Helen hoped he wouldn't ask what she thought of it. "It's for Victoria's reading list."

He gave her a sideways glance.

"Victoria's?"

"Yes." Helen picked the book up and riffled the pages under her thumb. "She's got a list of books, ones that no one ever finishes or something, and we're going to read them all and compare . . ." Her voice trailed off. She wasn't sure it was making sense now she was saying it out loud. "She must have finished this one already."

"Did she tell you that? Because she's having you on." Seth lifted a hand to shade his face. "Victoria's never read anything longer than Enid Blyton."

"But . . ." Helen stopped.

Seth's voice interrupted the worry before it could take root.

"She gets these schemes into her head sometimes. She'll have big plans but never get past the first page. Ask her to explain the role of the main antagonist."

Helen was unsure herself what he meant. They sat without talking, a faint buzz wavering in the background. Mr Weaver at his endless lawn-mowing, probably. For a mad moment Helen thought about telling him her mistake, how she'd actually wondered if they were related to people as boring as the Weavers. It would only turn into a rambling mess, though. The silence was making her feel uneasy, clumsy, and she turned to Seth in relief when he spoke.

"I take it she's not here, then?"

"What?" Helen scrambled to follow what he meant. "Oh, Victoria? No, I haven't seen her today."

"In that case —" Seth sprang up into a squat and balanced on the balls of his feet, arms stretched out for balance — "I'd better carry on with my search." He continued into a stand and paused before spinning round on one toe and heading towards the gate. She thought she heard him say something over his shoulder.

She thought it was, "Come over later, if you like," but she couldn't be sure. He was gone before she could ask him to say it again.

CHAPTER
FIVE

She got to the cottage with the uncomfortable feeling of arriving at a party at the wrong time. What had Seth meant by "later'? What if she walked in and they were in the middle of tea? She played for time by looking at the other cottages. The first in the row was more or less derelict. Tiles were missing from the roof, the windows were covered with boards, and the front door hung at an angle from one hinge. The next one in was Mrs Tyler's. Clean windows, here, hung with spotless lace curtains. The door was painted green and, though the paint was peeling at the bottom, the brass knocker shone. The third in the row was in better condition than the first but seemed to be empty, the curtainless panes shadowed inside their brick edging. Beyond the Dovers' cottage she could see the beginning of the bridge. Helen edged closer. There were boxes piled up against the front wall, and what appeared to be an old-fashioned car horn hanging from the door handle, the black rubber bulb twisted around with string.

She was about to go on when she saw something from the corner of her eye. One of the lace curtains in the second house had twitched, but it dropped back down again straight away. What if Mrs Tyler came out and started going on about noise again? The path carried on around the corner to what must be the back garden, where she could hear voices. As she was starting down it, Pippa came flying round, coming to a halt just in time, grabbing her hand and pulling her down behind the pile of boxes.

"Sshhh, hide." Pippa buried her face in Helen's shoulder, and Helen found herself closing her own eyes tightly in the long-forgotten "then you won't see me" response. She could smell Pippa's hair, a mix of biscuit and something pungent and smoky. Not tobacco, more a hint of fragrance, something like the privet. One of her hands had ended up around Pippa's back and, as footsteps approached, she tightened her grasp, mirroring Pippa's hold on her own wrist. The footsteps came to a stop, and Helen could barely hold in the tension. Had hide and seek always been like this? She felt Pippa quiver as the sound of the feet retreated, and opened one eye. The sun seemed very bright, and she was aware of the rough wall against her back, the tingling of her folded knees. Beside her, Pippa shifted so her mouth was against Helen's ear, but before the whisper took shape, a shadow leapt over them.

"Boo!" It was Seth, appearing like a genie from the other side of the boxes. Helen shrieked in spite of herself, and followed Pippa at a run down the side of the house.

It was shadowy inside, dusty glass obscuring what sunlight there was on this side. There was an old-fashioned sink, square and white, a wooden draining board piled high with plates. One wall was taken up with a sideboard, the shelves stacked with oddities. A line of teapots. A small gold statue of a seated figure holding out multiple arms in a fan shape. Bottles layered over with swirls of candle wax.

Pippa tugged at her arm. "We're making real pizza. I'm having the one with peppers. Seth brought the olives back from Spain."

Helen's eyes were beginning to adjust to the change of light. Jars and boxes crowded every surface and Will was sprawled on the floor, building a complicated structure around the table legs. She tried to take everything in. Vintage tins balanced in a row along a narrow shelf, next to a rusted sign for soap. On the opposite wall, an embroidered panel glowed, what light there was reflected from hundreds of circular mirrors sewn into it. A stack of books was ready to topple at one end of the table, and she could see a pan of something involving tomatoes bubbling on the stove. Their heady, sharp smell filled the space around her. Seth came in from behind her and crossed to the other side, disappearing behind the printed fabric curtain which hung in the doorway. Victoria appeared immediately after, as if she was swapping with him, stopping at the far end of the table and not seeming to notice Helen's presence. She opened a jar, scooped something out and popped it into her mouth. Then she held it out.

"Olive?"

Helen had never tried an olive before. It was firmer than she'd expected, with green skin that didn't give under the pressure of her fingers. She nibbled a tiny bit from the end, expecting the sourness of an unripe plum. It was salty, though, followed by a not unpleasant taste, as if she was nibbling on the end of a grass stalk. She couldn't decide if she liked it or not, but it seemed rude not to finish so she carried on, scraping fragments away from the stone with the edge of her front teeth.

The jar was nearly empty. Victoria angled it to get at the last few, offering them to Helen again. This time she shook her head. Victoria tipped them all into her own mouth and threw the spoon across the table. As it clattered into the sink, she spoke through the mouthful of olives:

"Let's go upstairs. The dough won't be ready for ages."

Helen stood in the doorway, wondering where she was supposed to go. There were clothes everywhere, in silted heaps on the floor and spilling out of drawers in tangled chaos. Something that could have been a chair stood by the window, but she felt shy about pushing stuff off to uncover it. Victoria showed no signs of unease. She flopped on to the bed, wriggling herself more comfortably into the folds of the thrown-back blankets.

"Come on, sit down." She gestured to the other end of the bed.

Helen perched on the edge. "Should I take my shoes off?"

Victoria looked down at her own faded baseball boots, crossed in front of her on the bed sheets. She shrugged. "If you want to."

"But what if your mum . . . I mean . . ."

Victoria made a sound that was almost a laugh.

"Believe me, she'd be the last person to notice."

Helen took her shoes off anyway.

The walls of the room had been painted a streaky pale purple, and were covered in an overlapping patchwork of posters: classic movie adverts, pop groups and arty prints. The smell of new paint hung in the air. An image of her own room — neat and pink, with no pinholes allowed in the wallpaper — went across Helen's mind. It wasn't as if her mother ever saw it now anyway, so why did she still keep it so tidy? She felt like going home and tearing big chunks out of the walls.

"Where do you get your posters from?" She pushed herself further back across the bed, so she could lean against the wall. "I've never seen any that big."

"London, mostly." Victoria reached to push a drawing pin in more securely. "There was a great shop down the road from our last house. And my uncle gives me them sometimes."

The showpiece hung at the head of the bed, old and battered and thin along the crease lines. The corners rolled over the drawing pins and the pink and orange background colours were faded and beautiful. The main figure was caught in three-quarter profile, the colours blocked in varying shades of yellow and brown: it was a man like a side-burned lion, his arms holding drumsticks triumphantly aloft and his knees splayed out behind a drum kit. The circle of the bass drum was filled with a landscape, a crazed country cottage at the side of a winding road headed for the mountains. The drummer's feet, planted firmly in a two-and-ten position, seemed at first sight to be wearing odd shoes, but closer inspection revealed that the foot on the right was hidden behind a highly decorated snail. Snail and man had matching, heavily ringed eyes.

"That's my dad." Victoria had twisted to follow Helen's gaze. "My uncle did the artwork."

Helen read out the words beneath the figure. "Isle of Wight Festival, 1970." She turned to speak over her shoulder. "We went to the Isle of Wight once. I can't remember it really, except we had to walk everywhere." Her eyes returned to the poster and she started to read the list of names. "What sort of festival was it? There was a street parade in Cowes when we were there."

Victoria fell back on the bed, holding her stomach as she let out a howl of disbelief.

"A parade in Cowes? This was the Isle of Wight festival! Six hundred thousand people and Jimi Hendrix!"

Helen's face was a single hot flush.

"I've never heard of it." She looked back at the list of names. It was no use; she didn't know any of them. "Was your dad in a band?"

Victoria pushed herself up again, and ran a finger down the poster.

"Here — Cumulus. My dad was the drummer." She put a hand up towards the poster. "Well, obviously."

"Oh." Helen did a quick calculation. "So were you there too?"

Victoria nodded. "I don't really remember it. I was only, what, two? Three?"

"Is he in a band now?" Helen scanned the walls, trying to find him there.

"My dad? Dunno." Victoria stared at the poster. "We haven't seen him for a long time." Her face had darkened, as if clouds really were passing over. "But my uncle's usually around in the summer. The artist one."

"Does he see your dad?"

"Nobody does." Victoria stretched to her full length along the bed, keeping her fingers in touch with the wall and reaching for the far end with her toes. "The last we heard, he was in South America. He was fighting with the MIR in Chile." She turned her head and regarded Helen through half-closed eyes before sending her gaze back to the ceiling and giving a small sigh. Her voice was patient, explaining to an idiot: "*Movimiento de Izquierda Revolucionaria*. In English, it's the Revolutionary Left Movement."

"Oh." Helen paused, not sure if this was a good thing to have your father do or not. "My mum left in the spring." It was a relief to be able to say it to someone who might understand. She'd been the only one in her class with parents who didn't live together.

"Oh yeah? Where'd she go?"

"Only to Southport." It sounded so commonplace. "I don't see her, though."

Victoria said nothing. She was right, Helen thought. It wasn't much of a story. Trust her mum to leave in the dullest way possible. Her leg gave a twinge from the position it was in and she stole a glance down. Victoria was lying inches from her feet, fencing her in. She tried to shift into a more comfortable place without making too much of it, though Victoria seemed oblivious. On the windowsill, she could see a half-eaten apple, the bitten surface brown and curling inwards. A fly had come through the window, and now circled briefly before resting beside the stalk. She watched it shift, pause, and take off as the silence was broken by a shout from downstairs. Victoria jumped off the bed and ran out on to the landing. Helen could hear her calling something back down; a moment later her head came around the edge of the door.

"Pizza time!"

Helen glanced at the poster again as she stood up to follow Victoria. The melancholy eyes of the drummer followed her out of the room. As she reached the top of the stairs Victoria, a few steps down, paused and fixed her with an intense expression on her face.

"You can't ever talk about it, what I told you about my dad." She took another couple of steps, before stopping again. "You have to promise."

"Of course I won't." Helen stayed where she was for a few seconds, watching as Victoria carried on down, jumping the last section in one go. Was this all a massive wind-up? She recalled the expression on Victoria's face as they'd studied the poster. If a story like that could happen to anyone, it would be this family. She'd just have to keep quiet and hope for more.

The pizzas were a communal affair, with everyone elbowing for space around the end of the table.

"Do you do this often?" Helen asked, shoving at her hair with the back of her wrist.

"Only when someone can be bothered to get it started." Seth grinned at her as he dumped another ball of dough on the table. "We'll end up picking bits off the furniture for weeks."

Helen's dough didn't want to go into a pizza shape; it thickened and bulged, fighting back against the heels of her hands. She stood back for a rest, taking in the scene around her. The flour dusting the table rose up in the slanting light to settle in a fine layer over books, noses and hair. Victoria was adding arms and legs to her bases, and Seth was showing Pippa how to spin hers out on her fingertips. From under the table, she could hear Will banging something on the floor while giving a running commentary. It was, she thought, like being in a slightly weird dream. Cooking was something she'd been made to do at school, or tried with her mother standing there and telling her she was doing it all wrong. And with her dad, food was ready meals or stuff out of tins. Pizzas came in frozen stacks, to be heated in the microwave into a floppy fold. She would never be like that when she grew up and left home. As she let her mind wander to a future where she had a life full of colour, where exotic flavours and beautiful possessions were taken for granted, something hit the side of her face.

"Earth calling Helen, we're doing the toppings." Victoria was poised to throw another olive from the far side of the table.

"Don't waste them." Seth was bringing the saucepan over. "How about making some space?"

The sauce was still warm, and doing the toppings turned into a battle, getting spoons into the saucepan before it all went, grabbing the olives and cheese to layer on top. There were other odd ingredients as well, things Helen had never seen: a jar of soft peppers that slid through her fingers; anchovies; a long, mouldy-looking cylinder of salami.

They ate the pizzas in the sitting room, helping themselves from a huge tray in the middle of the worn carpet. To begin with, Helen slipped some of the more unfamiliar ingredients to one side, but bits kept getting mixed up and they didn't taste too bad anyway. She gave up and tried not to worry about the trails of flour and tomato sauce and oil leading in from the kitchen. It didn't seem to be bothering anyone else, and it wasn't as if there were any adults to worry about. Dimly she could hear her mother's voice in her head, fussing about fingers and crumbs; it seemed to come from another world entirely. Even so, her stomach tightened with anxiety when she heard voices at the door. She braced for the storm that must be about to erupt.

But the woman in the doorway was oblivious to the pizza on the floor and the sauce that had found its way into one twin's hair and across the other twin's T-shirt. She tapped them both on the head as she crossed the room to get to the stairs, but otherwise ignored them.

Anyway, this couldn't be anyone's mother. Helen had never seen such a beautiful face; the pale, delicate oval seemed to float against the peeling wallpaper, remote in

46

some way, and calm. Helen gazed at the swathe of hair cascading over the woman's shoulders, each strand a different shade, ranging from buttered toast to the most fragile baby white. She was wearing the same voluminous Eastern trousers that Victoria had, but in deep purple and with heavy embroidery at the ankles and waist. As she reached the corner she stopped, as if considering something. Helen eased herself back behind the cover of the sofa's edge, and looked from one face to another. Pippa was leaning against Seth's arm. Victoria's head was down, and her fingers held the remains of a pizza crust, which she pinched and ripped into crumbs. Will was taking no notice of anyone, lying flat on his front and driving a toy car around the legs of the armchair.

Seth's voice broke the silence. Disentangling himself from Pippa, he gave her cheek a gentle stroke before putting her to one side and standing up.

"Was it good?" He reached the woman and took her bag and her coat. "Come on, you need to go to bed."

The woman's eyes rested on him. The pause went on for a fraction too long.

"Yes," she said. "Yes, it was good. But there were too many people."

As Seth steered her with a gentle hand towards the stairs, Victoria finally looked up. Her face was in the shadows and hard to read.

"Night, Alice."

CHAPTER
SIX

Helen peered through the window of the oven door. The recipe book said twenty minutes, but she didn't want to burn them. The glass was dark with the scorched brown of old meals, though, and she couldn't see through. She reached for the handle and paused. Wasn't it supposed to be bad for cakes if you let air in? Everyone laughing in Home Economics at someone's disaster? She cracked it open a tiny bit but changed her mind. The warm, sweet smell wafted up towards her face as she checked the timer again. She'd better leave it a few more minutes.

The good weather had rolled out like a red carpet, one day of sunshine and blue sky after another. No, like a yellow brick road. She thought back to the emptiness of the time before the Dovers had come. Had it only been a week? She'd have died, spending the whole summer by herself. And the Helen from then floated through her mind, pale and wobbly. She rubbed her hands down her bare legs, now unmistakeably starting to turn brown, to reassure herself she was real, that this was happening. The timer started to ping, and she opened the oven door.

The cakes down one half of the tray were golden, well risen and firm. The others had fallen away a bit, with the ones in the last row barely reaching the top of their paper cases. They were a much darker brown as well, but not, she hoped, actually burned. The previous day, she and Victoria had discussed their favourite cakes. Hers was Battenberg, something remembered as a special childhood treat, to be picked apart and eaten in constituent order. Victoria had scoffed at cakes that you bought in packets, and instead described freshly cooked doughnuts from roadside stalls, and pastry shops where the shelves were stacked with delicate squares glazed with fruit. The stories of Victoria's travels coiled through most of their conversations, until Helen could almost imagine being there as well.

Seth's voice had broken into this particular thread: "They never taste as good as they look, though."

"Didn't stop you eating them," Victoria had said.

"Wouldn't have them going to waste." He'd given Helen a sideways grin to make her feel included. "If you ask me, the best cakes are those butterfly ones, like you get at school fêtes."

So these were for Seth. Over the week, she'd eaten all sorts of new things that the Dover children took for granted. Spaghetti from a long paper packet with nothing added but oil and herbs. Things from tins with French names: ratatouille, cassoulet. A sort of grain you had to pour hot water on, which they mixed with a fiery paste. She'd joined in, clumsily chopping onions, or stirring when directed. Once or twice, Seth had taken a plateful upstairs, but more often it was as if Alice didn't exist. Sometimes Helen would find herself looking at the stairs and wondering if Alice was up there or not. She couldn't decide on the right way to ask, and in the end, stopped noticing.

The cakes were also a way of proving she could do something of her own, and she'd found Seth's choice in the only recipe book her mother had left behind. She pulled the book over now to check again on the butter-cream filling. There was no icing sugar, so she'd had to make do with a bag of hardened caster sugar that had been hidden away at the back of the cupboard. As she pushed the wooden spoon into the block of butter, the crystal edges of sugar began to break, with a satisfying crunch. She let her mind drift, picturing Seth taking a cake, smiling at her, saying how nice it was.

She'd barely finished scooping the last of the butter-cream into its hollow when Pippa burst through the door.

"Victoria needs you to come over!" She was panting from her run. "Ooh, those are pretty. Can I have one?"

It was good to hear. The cakes didn't look much like the picture in the book. Helen broke the flattest one in half.

"Here you are. We'll take the others with us." She'd spent enough time with Pippa to guess the summons wasn't as urgent as it sounded. "What's she doing?"

Pippa shrugged her shoulders.

"I'm going to have that one next. The one with three wings."

★   ★   ★

The cottage kitchen was full of steam. Helen paused on the step, wondering if Victoria had been baking as well.

"About time." Victoria turned from her position in front of the stove and pointed to the saucepan on the gas ring. "Stir!"

Helen squeezed her plate of cakes into a space on the dresser and did as she was told.

"Is it supposed to look like this?"

The pan was half-full of a lumpy grey mass with a slowly erupting surface.

Victoria was kneeling on the sink, trying to open the window. It had been sealed with years of repainting, though, and she didn't seem to be having much luck. She gave the frame another bang with the heel of her hand and it jerked out a few inches, one of the panes of glass falling loose. They both stopped to listen as it shattered on the stones outside.

"Oh well." Victoria manoeuvred herself down from her perch. "At least we'll get some air in."

Helen looked back at her saucepan.

"What is it?"

Victoria came back and, lifting the wooden spoon, let the mixture drip off.

"That's about right." She carried the saucepan across to the table, then took an empty one across to the tap. "But we're going to need loads more. Pass me the flour."

"Need it for what?" Helen went to the cardboard box in the corner where they kept their stores. "Dinner?"

"Mmm, yes, does it tempt you?" Victoria dumped the new pan on the stovetop and held out a hand for the flour. "It's glue, actually. We're going to paper my ceiling."

"With this? Really?" Helen dipped the tip of a finger into the mass. "How do you know it'll work?"

"It always has before." Victoria emptied the entire bag into the water and turned the heat up under the saucepan. "Except once when we ran out of white flour and Alice said to use wholemeal. The walls went mouldy that time."

Alice. It was hard to imagine her involved in anything so messy.

"I suppose if she does it . . ." Helen's voice tailed off as Victoria turned round.

"Alice?" Victoria gave a short laugh. "Alice doesn't do things. She waits for other people to do them for her."

She gave the mixture a vigorous stir. Drops of floury water flew out across the table and splattered down the front of Helen's T-shirt.

"Careful!" Helen wiped some from her cheek.

"It won't kill you."

Victoria went back to her stirring and they were silent for a time. The weather had changed today. The air felt sticky and slow, and clouds, low and dark, had been building up as Helen had walked down to the cottage after breakfast. Now, the kitchen was full of shadows.

"OK, it's ready." Victoria turned off the gas and picked up the saucepan with both hands. She nodded towards the table. "You bring that one."

As Helen went after her towards the stairs, there came a rumble from the sky outside. Helen stopped to count the seconds before the lightning. It was a long way off yet. Victoria lifted her saucepan above her head and glanced over her shoulder.

"It looks as if we've cooked up some magic," she said, and broke into a run.

Victoria had discovered the wallpaper in an outhouse. It had been partly used at some point, the end edges left roughly cut and the tightness of the rolls finishing in a loose furl. There was no sign of its pattern inside the cottage, which Helen could understand. She thought it was horrible, the huge brown and orange flowers reaching out with nightmare tendrils towards each other. Now, putting her saucepan down inside Victoria's bedroom door, she leaned her head to one side. Spread out in long strips on the floor, it wasn't any nicer than she remembered.

"And you're sure you want this on your ceiling?" She spoke to Victoria's back. "It'd give me nightmares."

Victoria was gathering armfuls of clothes from the floor and piling them on to the bed.

"It's brilliant." She didn't look round, but nodded towards a plastic washing-up bowl. "Can you fill that with water?"

A louder crack of thunder sounded. Helen turned, but was too late to see the lightning flash.

"It's going to rain any minute. Do you want to close the window?"

"Not really." Victoria dragged a bedspread over the pile she had made and waved a hand towards the bowl. "Water!"

Helen bent to pick it up as the next roll of thunder came. This time she was quick enough to see the forks of light stand out behind the network of trees on the far bank. She felt the air holding itself ready for the rain, but none came.

"Hello! I need it over here!" Victoria's voice was sharp, but still Helen lingered by the window. The sky beyond the trees was a smooth metal plate, reflecting darkness with menace. "Helen!"

She jumped at the tone, and dragged herself away.

The flour-and-water glue turned out to be less sticky on the ceiling than it felt on their hands and arms. As Victoria pushed one end of the wallpaper against the corner of the wall, Helen pressed with her hands along its length. By the time she reached the end, though, the middle section was bellying off. She saw Victoria take a step forwards and, in that instant, the far end fell away.

"Quick, it's coming down, behind you, behind you!" She let go of her own piece to pat ineffectually further along, but her hand went straight through.

"It's got me!" Victoria's voice rose up in a shriek as her head and shoulders disappeared under the collapsing paper.

Laughing, Helen forgot to keep an eye on her own end. Seconds later, it came down as well. There were acres of it, the clinging sodden folds wrapping themselves around her as if the flowers had come to life. The paper felt soft, but she couldn't break through.

54

Slime filled her mouth as another bolt of thunder cracked. Her breath was coming in gasps, and she couldn't inhale. Just as panic was about to win, she felt the paper being pulled away. Victoria's head, covered in wallpaper with holes torn for eyes and mouth, loomed over her.

"Whooo!" She was waving her arms, and laughing so hard that her ghost noise trembled and ran out. Her expression changed as Helen rolled to one side and began to cough. "Are you all right?"

Helen peeled more paper away from her head and let out a shaky giggle.

"I think so." The remembered sense of cloying dark brushed through her mind again and was gone. It didn't seem so bad now. Something cool landed on her cheek. Rain, coming down in huge slanting drops and bouncing over the sill. "You might want to close the window."

Victoria glanced over her shoulder, then shrugged.

"Let it rain." She peeled a long strip away from her hair. "It might work better if we put the paste straight on to the ceiling."

"You want to carry on?" Helen spat glue out as she stared up with what she hoped looked like dismay.

"Well, we're already covered in it. No point in cleaning up before the job's done." She held out a hand. "Come on."

The second method worked better, although they had to use drawing pins to hold the paper in place. The rain stopped as abruptly as it had come, tailing off into a slow continuous mizzle. The bedroom felt humid and sticky, but Victoria looked around with a satisfied expression.

"OK, now I need to wash it out of my hair." She stepped over the piles of discarded wallpaper, pausing when she reached the door. "Are you coming?"

Helen poked at the chaos on the floor with one foot.

"Don't you want to clear this away first?"

"We can bung it on the landing for now. Come on."

Helen followed, only wondering once she was in the bathroom why Victoria wanted her there. She stood in the doorway, watching the bath fill with water and feeling more uncomfortable by the second.

"I'll wait in your room."

Victoria had already stepped out of her jeans and was leaning into the mirror examining the clumps of paste drying in her hair.

"What for? You can sit and talk to me." She crossed to the bath and dipped a hand in before shaking salts under the stream of water. A delicate scent of lavender drifted up with the heat. "The water's nice and hot, anyway. Shut the door." She was pulling her shirt off now. At least she'd turned away. Helen slid down to the floor, keeping her back to the bath. Water sloshed as Victoria got in. She was still talking. "Last week the boiler stopped working but I didn't realize until I got in. It was freezing. And this bath takes for ever to fill."

It was huge, the taps bellying out beneath their handles like fat barrels instead of coming out at the normal angle. Helen could feel the heat through the side of the tub. The walls were tiled with an odd pattern in sage green, the lines reminding her of tree bark. If she half-closed her eyes, they shimmied, stretching and contracting in an odd optical quirk. Victoria's voice echoed from the inside of the bath.

"Why do you never have friends round? Were you at boarding school or something?"

Helen turned involuntarily before remembering where Victoria was, but it was OK. She could only see her head.

"No, I was at the high school."

"Oh." Victoria slid down under the water. It was strange to hear it lapping from the outside. Then her head appeared over the side, hair slicked back like paint. "So go on, why nobody coming round?"

"Well . . ." Helen hesitated. Abruptly, she was back there with the smell of the corridors sharp in her nose. They were always cold, even in the summer term, but she'd taken to walking them, slowly, to avoid being outside. Everyone else was sitting in knots on the playing field, lounging in the aftermath of exam tension. Sometimes a teacher would chase her out. It was amazing how many hidden spaces there were if you were desperate enough to search them out. Anything was better than sitting alone. "No one lives that close." She wasn't about to admit the truth.

"What I hate at school is when everyone stops talking to you." Victoria stood up, sending water ricocheting around inside the bath. "Pass me the towel."

Helen reached out for it, forgetting to turn away.

"Did it happen to you as well?" She realized she was staring and dropped her eyes in confusion. The relief of Victoria understanding was making her feel breathless. "I don't even know what I did, but one day everyone was laughing at me in registration, as if I'd got my skirt caught up in my knickers."

"I found a Tampax in my pencil case." Victoria pulled a clean, oversized T-shirt over her head. "They'd coloured it in with red felt-tip."

"No! What did you do?"

Victoria's voice was muffled as she rubbed at her hair with the towel.

"Went and shoved it down this girl's shirt. Bitch. She was the worst one. They left me alone after that." She gave her head a last shake, and dropped the towel on the floor. "Are you getting in?"

"Well, I —" Helen stopped. The glue had started to go hard in her hair, and she could feel it tightening on the skin of her arms. "Yeah, I guess so." She rolled on to her knees and leaned across to the tap end of the bath, reaching for the plug chain.

"There won't be enough hot water." Victoria stopped at the door. "That's why I left it in."

"OK." Helen stayed where she was. What was she supposed to do? Getting into someone else's bathwater felt wrong, like touching their skin or . . . She made her mind stop. She could wait until Victoria had gone, and rinse her hair in the sink. Unless Victoria was planning to stay and talk while she got in the bath. Helen felt her fingers grip on to the smooth edge of the tub. She couldn't do it.

"I'll go and find you something to wear." Victoria spoke over her shoulder as she went out to the landing.

Helen dipped the ends of her fingers into the water. It was warm enough, and the bath salts left an oily smoothness on her skin. And she didn't want to come across as snotty . . . Before she could think about it any more, she stripped off her clothes and got in. The water closed over her skin like a gossamer tickle and she felt herself shiver. She let her head sink under the surface. She always used the shower at home, and had forgotten how luxurious a bath could feel. And, after all, this was no different to being in a swimming pool where other people had been. She let the water burble against her ears. The air was cool where her skin was exposed, and she shifted herself to make the water ripple across. She couldn't let herself enjoy it too much, though. There was no lock on the door, anyone could come in. The thought made her plunge into hasty washing, and she was already wrapped in the towel when Victoria's head appeared around the door.

"The paper's staying up," she reported, thrusting an arm in to drop clothes on to the floor. "I'm putting the kettle on. You'd better hurry up before the twins eat all those cakes."

"You've got to save one . . ." Helen began, but Victoria was gone. "For Seth," she finished.

CHAPTER
SEVEN

The thunderstorm ended the run of fine weather. Almost immediately, it was as if the heatwave had never happened, and the overcast skies and drizzle might as well have been there for ever. Mick's mood went down with the barometer. He stopped scouring the paper for auctions or making trips for boat parts, instead spending hours in the gloom of the garage, contemplating the bare structure of the hull. His mood permeated the house and Helen found herself tracking his movements to avoid him. In the evenings, she'd stop in the hallway when she came back from the cottage, gauging his frame of mind from the volume of the television, the number of beer bottles lined up by the sofa. He was often asleep. One evening, she stood and watched him, head back against the chair, his mouth open as he snored. If it hadn't been for Victoria, she thought, this would be her only entertainment. So it was with relief that she'd slip out every morning, calling behind to let him know she'd be back later, and ignoring the confused sense of abandonment she felt towards him.

Even though the cooler weather showed no signs of ending, she was happier than she'd ever been in the world they created in the confines of Victoria's bedroom. By the time the two of them had got bored of lying around swapping daft stories and making elaborate travel plans for the future, Victoria had resurrected the book list.

"All that, and she follows him to Siberia!" Victoria didn't look up as Helen came into her room, but stared at the book in her hand, her face wrinkled in disgust.

"All what?" Helen flopped down on to the bed, flipping open her own book where she'd folded down the corner of the page, and immediately closing it. She was having trouble keeping the characters straight in her head, and she knew she'd lose track if Victoria was talking.

"This book." Victoria waved it in front of Helen's nose, but too fast for her to read the title. "First of all it's like reading . . . treacle." She threw the book in the air, hitting it with the palm of her hand so it flew across the bedroom, landing face down and open on the floor. "And her dad drinks all the money away, her mum makes her be a prostitute, and this nutter who axed someone and thinks way too much is in love with her and she follows him to prison. In Siberia." She wandered across to the window. "How are you getting on?"

"OK, actually." In fact, Helen hadn't been able to sleep the night before until she'd found out whether Natasha had broken off her engagement. "But I'm skipping the battles."

"So what you're reading is actually *And Peace*." Victoria pulled herself up on the sill. "You can only get half points. No prizes for missing bits out."

"Not fair!" Helen protested. "It's at least twice as long as yours."

"Rules of the game." Victoria pulled up her knees and picked at a loose thread on her jeans. "And I get extra because everyone in mine was so incredibly miserable." She grinned at Helen, daring her to disagree.

Helen joined her at the window. The rain somehow made everything the same: tree green merging into grass green before the dimpled surface of the canal absorbed all of the differing shades in subtle, swaying streaks.

"My dad and me used to play a game with the raindrops," she said, following one down the glass with a light fingertip chase. "We used to choose one each and race them down."

"Nice story, Grandma."

Victoria's tone was cutting, and Helen felt her face heat up. She went back to the bed and picked up her book, but she'd lost the thread, and the names floated, faceless, on the page. A corner of wallpaper hanging down from the ceiling caught her eye. The twins must be up in the attic, jumping off boxes again if the noise was anything to go by. The hanging paper gave a surprised jerk every time one of them landed.

Victoria added big feet to the figure she had drawn in the condensation on the window before sweeping a palm across it and pressing her face to the glass.

"I'm so *bored*."

"You could start the next book?"

Victoria groaned and mooched across to the bed. "No, anything but that! I don't ever want to read anything ever again." She started to flick at Helen's hand, trying to dislodge her book. "Do something, amuse me!"

An extra-loud crash from above made them both look up, waiting for shrieks. Instead there was a brief silence, followed by the sound of something heavy scraping across the floor.

Victoria flopped over, letting herself slide off the bed, and crawled on her hands and knees to a pile of boxes stacked in one corner.

"We always used to make up plays. We could put on a Russian drama."

Helen let her book fall to her knees as she watched her rummage.

"Dressing-up stuff!" Victoria pulled one of the boxes out, making the rest wobble. "Come and see."

Helen went and knelt on the floor next to her. The box held a motley collection. She could see a moulting fox-fur stole tied up with some old dresses, a handful of tangled beads, a pair of satin shoes with pin-thin heels and long pointed toes. It all smelled old and, what was the word her mother used? Fousty. Fusty. Helen fingered a brightly patterned shift, breathing through her mouth to keep out the waft of mothball.

"Where do you get all this stuff from?"

"What, isn't it good enough for you?"

Helen was taken aback by Victoria's tone. She hadn't meant to be rude, and opened her mouth to explain but

Victoria had already turned away and was digging into the box. She scrambled to retrieve the situation.

"I only meant, well . . ." She struggled to come up with a better way of saying it. "I mean, it's all really cool, but you have all these boxes of clothes and stuff you have to take with you when you go somewhere new, but you don't have things like, I don't know, knives and forks."

Victoria shrugged.

"There's always that sort of stuff in wherever we end up. It's not important."

"Don't you mind? Having to keep on packing up and starting again?"

There was silence, and Helen held her breath. When she spoke, Victoria's voice was remote.

"As long as you can take the important things with you, it doesn't matter where you are." She bent forwards, sweeping a hand through a litter of scarves. "And are you happy with where you are, even with all your knives and forks?"

Helen let the dress drop. She visualized her home, with its beige walls and blank spaces. Her mother's influence lingered beneath the surface clutter that had built up in her absence. At least they always knew where the cutlery was.

"I suppose I can't imagine living anywhere else."

"Not being able to imagine something doesn't make it impossible." Victoria was ramming the clothes back into the box now. "We go where people offer to let us stay, or Piet finds us somewhere. It's like the universe gives it to us." She turned to look at Helen. "And we've been in some fab places as well, they're not all like this." She waved a hand around the room.

"No, I didn't mean . . ." Helen tried to find the right words. "It's lovely here, it's the best house I've ever been in."

Victoria gave a wicked grin, and the atmosphere cleared.

"It's a shithole, and you know it. It's only for the summer, though. We won't be around any longer than that."

The words, thudding like rocks into sand, brought Helen to a halt. She split in two, one Helen sitting on the floor being part of Victoria's world, the other floating above them, knowing she could never truly belong. The summer would end, the Dovers would go, and the new Helen would slide back into her grey life where nothing ever happened. Victoria wasn't even showing any signs of regret. Helen would be one of those ghosts from the past, a vague recollection half-recalled: *"Do you remember that girl who never went anywhere?"* She was nothing but an episode. Somehow, that felt worse than anything. Victoria was staring at her now, but it was all too difficult to explain.

"Where's the best place you've ever lived?" Her voice caught in the back of her throat, as if that was where the tears had piled up, taking up all the space.

Victoria pushed on her hands to swing her legs into a squat. That was one of Seth's tricks, and Helen remembered him doing it in the garden the first day she met him. Victoria's voice recalled her back to the room. "I'll show you."

She pulled another box across, this one jammed full of snaps of all sizes. A lot were small black-and-white prints, curling at the corners, although Helen spotted studio portraits of a baby and a serious-faced toddler. Victoria started sorting through a stack of colour ones, each a square with a thick white border. Helen glimpsed pictures of a small Seth standing on an immense pile of sand; Victoria wearing a buttoned coat with a velvet collar, clinging to a hand as a giraffe's head came down at her over a fence at the zoo. She picked up a few herself, stopping at one showing Seth and Victoria together, older now, standing on a hillside. The sea was ridiculously blue in the background and square white houses were dotted up the slopes. Both of them had sun-bleached blond hair, the strands blowing across brown faces.

"How old are you here?" She turned it round so Victoria could see.

"That was when we were in Greece, so I'd be about six, and Seth's eight. We were living on Andros." Victoria reached out a hand to take the photograph. "It's a Cycladic island." She gave it back.

It's all Greek to me. Helen laughed inwardly at her silent joke, and put the photo down.

"Was it a holiday?"

"No."

Helen waited for Victoria to go on, but she'd come to a stop, staring ahead, as if her mind was in another country.

"So, how long were you there for?"

Victoria gazed blankly at her as if she didn't know who she was. After a moment, she gave her head a shake.

"Five, six months. Dunno." She shuffled through the prints she was holding. "It was the last time I saw my dad, actually."

The words were casual, as if seeing your dad for the last time was a perfectly normal thing to happen, but they couldn't cover up the tightness of her voice. Helen glanced up at the drummer on the wall, wanting to ask for details but not sure how to start. Then Victoria threw the handful of snaps to one side and reached in the box for more before continuing.

"We went there with the band, they were working on an album." She discarded that pile as well, and grabbed for more. "My dad and the other guys were in this villa with a pool, and Alice, me and Seth had a sort of donkey hut." She glanced up. "Converted, you know, we didn't sleep in hay. It was brilliant, actually. We had this beach all to ourselves and there were these old ladies on donkeys and they gave us figs and stuff." Her voice tailed off. "Anyway. We were there, and my uncle Piet had come out to join us. Then one night there was a massive row." She stopped sorting and leaned back against the bed, her eyes closed. "Me and Seth, we got up to see what was going on. They were all off their heads, chucking stuff in the pool. And in the morning, they were gone."

Again, Helen waited for her to carry on, but there was silence. She couldn't leave it like that. Helen leaned closer and prompted her.

"Was this when your dad went off to South America?"

There was a pause.

"Yeah, round about." Victoria sat staring at the photos in her hand as if she wasn't sure where they'd come from. She gave her head an impatient shake and carried on. "Though we didn't know about it at the time, of course. We found Alice in the villa, but we couldn't wake her up."

The room seemed to be holding its breath along with Helen. She could feel the heat as the two blond children walked hand in hand through an empty courtyard, a dry wind blowing through the surrounding trees. It made her think of Mary Lennox after the cholera.

"You must have been terrified." Her voice came out as a whisper, but Victoria's reply was matter-of-fact enough to bring her back to the bedroom.

"Not really. There was a house down the hill, an old Greek farmer and his wife. They took us in."

"And didn't ask any questions?"

"They didn't speak English. Just fed us bread and olives until Piet turned up and brought us all back to England."

Helen picked the photo of Seth and Victoria up again. Behind them, the tangle of shrubbery seemed to shift, and she imagined a sharp, exotic fragrance. Momentarily, she tasted the sharp juiciness of an olive, felt the heat of the sun against her back. The children looked back at her, their gaze unwavering. No wonder

Victoria was a bit odd about her mother. She tried to come up with something neutral by way of response.

"It's like something out of a novel."

"Better than this Russian crap." Victoria leaned sideways to grab at *War and Peace*, lying forgotten on the bed, and held it away as Helen tried to reach for it. Helen lunged at her and they toppled over, Victoria squirming until she was free and scrambling on to the bed. Helen began to make a half-hearted chase but let it go. The photos were more interesting. Victoria came back to join her, and plucked one out of the spread on the floor.

"Here's a picture of him, anyway."

Helen leaned across.

"Your dad?"

She glanced up at the poster on the wall again before studying the photo. It was definitely him, minus the sideburns. He was wearing a long sheepskin coat, his hair curly and touching his shoulders, like Seth's did now. On his face was a broad grin, and each arm was wrapped around the shoulders of a beautiful woman. Helen pointed at one of them.

"Alice?" She didn't need to ask. Alice was gazing up, a thick fringe shadowing her eyes, but her mouth full and joyous.

"Yeah." Victoria held out another picture. "And here he is again. Daddy Jakob with Uncle Piet."

Jakob was withdrawing from this shot, his eyes narrowed against the sun. Piet was taller than his brother, leaner, propped against a wall, head tilted towards the camera. Something about him seemed

69

familiar. Helen held the photo away, trying to recall. He should be wearing a Stetson. She searched around Victoria's walls.

"He's exactly like him," she said, pointing at the poster of James Dean, the shy cowboy avoiding eye contact.

"You reckon?" Victoria sounded sceptical. "He's not much like him now." She took the photo back and held it up to compare it to the film poster. "Must be the way he's standing."

She flicked the photo into the box, before suddenly bending to scoop up a huge armful, pressing them down into the box.

"Careful!" Helen tried to help. "You're going to crease them."

"And that would matter why?" Victoria turned and left the room. For a while Helen stayed there, cross-legged, rearranging the pictures in the box so that they all lay flat. There were shots of landscapes, buildings, more and more faces. She stopped at one showing a group of young men on banquette seating arranged around a table. One of them was Victoria's dad. The other faces were vaguely familiar, but she couldn't pin down why. One smiled, another had been caught mid-grimace. They had long hair, ruffled shirts printed in floral designs, cigarette smoke coiling up in the air before them. A woman's hand rested on the table, but her body was out of the shot. Helen gazed up at the poster of the drummer. Where was he now?

She became aware of the silence in the house. She'd felt that she should wait until Victoria came back, but

70

now she wasn't sure. After returning the rest of the photos to the box, she stood up and went over to the window. A mirror had been propped at one side and Helen bent to look into it. There was a scatter of cosmetics in front of it, and she spent some minutes smudging kohl under her eyes. The faces in the posters on the walls seemed to burn into her, asking what she thought she was doing, and she leaned in again and rubbed it off, until it was the faintest grey shadow. She wasn't sure she liked how the room felt any more.

Downstairs, the cottage was empty. She crossed through the sitting room and stopped inside the kitchen door. There was no sound other than the drip of water from the tap, but through the window she could just see the back of Victoria's head. Holding her breath, she edged around the table, careful to keep out of view.

Alice was sitting in a chair on the patch of gravel that widened out to where the grass began. Her hair and face were wet from the rain, her blouse a clinging second skin. Victoria was standing behind the chair, massaging Alice's shoulders, but they didn't seem to be talking. The sun was out now, a swathe of light catching the two of them against the red brick of the wall. The colours around them, on them, were rich and somehow golden. Helen felt her throat close up again. Poor Alice. She was so beautiful, so . . . other. A picture came into her mind of her own mother, fussing about things being tidy, always asking what she, Helen, had been doing. Victoria was so lucky.

Helen swiped a hand across her eyes, wishing she could go and join them. It would be like breaking through a spider's web, though. She felt too large, too solid, the sort of clodhopping peasant who crashed into fairy stories and got turned into stone. Instead, she retreated into the sitting room but the front door was locked and there was no sign of the key. The windows were no use to her either, their frames sealed with many years' worth of thick, white paint. For a brief second she felt a lack of air, the walls closing around her in a dizzy rush. The house was silent, with even the twins upstairs making no sound. She tried to think. She could join the twins. She could go back up to Victoria's room. She could wait where she was, pretending to read or something. Or she could go home, giving a casual wave as she passed by, as if this sort of thing happened every day. There was only one option, really, and she made her way with slow steps back to the kitchen. It turned out that she needn't have worried. As she sidled down the side of the cottage towards the path, one hand lifted, neither Victoria nor Alice noticed her go.

CHAPTER
EIGHT

The feeling of being an intruder lingered overnight, and Helen found herself searching for things to do around the house. As she kicked mess into corners and behind furniture, she went over the previous afternoon, replaying the conversation to work out what had happened. Perhaps she'd asked too many questions. She tried taking pictures down from the sitting-room walls with the vague idea of making the house more Dover-like, but there was nothing to put up in their place, and the pale squares they left behind made the rest of the walls seem dirty. She hung them back up in a different order, but they were still boring. The dream of having a home like the Dovers' seemed a long way off. Dissatisfied, she drifted back to the kitchen. The dirty washing-up water still hadn't gone down the drain. She'd have to tell her dad.

As if on cue, Mick came out from the back of the garage. She watched him shamble along the path to the house and waited for the kitchen door to swing open.

"Dad, the sink's blocked."

Mick didn't answer, but sank down on a chair and started to roll a cigarette. He seemed tired, the pouches heavy under his eyes and rough stubble covering his chin. The ribbing around the V of his jumper was loose, the wool unravelling in a curly spring. Helen felt a twist of love for him in her stomach. It wasn't fair. Mum had been so mean, always going on about what he didn't do. She'd make it up to him somehow. Leaving the sink, she crossed to the chair on the other side of the table.

"Have you been doing something to the boat?"

He lit up; closed his eyes.

"It's too much for one person." His eyes stayed closed. "I've missed my time."

"No you haven't." She tried to remember the names of friends he'd had, people he could contact. "How about Ken? You know, he used to be interested in it."

"Too busy with his wife and kids." Mick blew out a gush of smoke and opened his eyes to study the glowing end of the roll-up. "There's not enough maintenance done on the canal, anyway. The locks are falling apart, the bottom's filling up. Won't be anywhere left to take the boat at this rate."

"You could always go to sea." Helen forced a smile into her voice. "I'll get you a captain's hat for Christmas."

They sat in silence for a while, the weight of Mick's thoughts an almost palpable mass. Helen made a decision.

"I'll be down at the cottage."

Mick lifted a hand slightly as if in assent. As she went outside and through the gate, her feet picked up speed, lightened by relief at her escape.

74

The hedges bordering the lane seemed to have doubled in size from the rain. Even the fringe of cow parsley had lifted up into another burst of creaminess. She couldn't help but feel the optimism. As she reached the end, the sight of the canal made her stop in her tracks. The morning sun had risen into a perfectly clear sky, and the surface of the water was as smooth as she'd ever seen it. It reflected back the blueness without even the hint of a ripple, and the inverted trees stretched downwards with every detail as sharp in the mirror image as it was in the original. Maybe the canal wasn't really a channel of water, dug out by humans; perhaps it was a portal, the upside-down world as real as the one she stood in.

The thought of what the Helen below ground might be doing took her round the corner and into the garden. She couldn't remember why she'd been worried about coming back. There was a book lying on the grass beneath the apple tree, and she went over to pick it up. *Little Women*. A tiny unripe apple landed on her head.

"About time you got here. I dropped that ages ago."

Victoria was sprawling along the length of the lowest branch, one hand out towards her. Helen stopped, caught between her private story and the reality of Victoria being so normal. The sense of something unfinished floated around her like a mote in the sun before disappearing in among the shade of the branches. She made a show of studying the cover.

"I don't think this is on the list."

"I know." Victoria yawned. "I needed something easy to make up for that other one you made me read."

"I've nearly finished *War and Peace*. You can have that."

Victoria groaned as she swung herself down, arms laced around the branch, and landed neatly on the ground.

"More Russians, that's what I need." She took the book from Helen's hand and turned it over to examine the picture of the four girls. "You know, I didn't enjoy this as much as I remembered." She flicked through the pages, stopping to study one of the illustrations before slamming it shut. "It does make me want to make something, though. They're always being creative. Painting pictures and sewing things. I feel like being an artist." She chucked the book back down on the grass. "You can be my model."

They were in the sitting room. Helen sat as still as possible, head side on to Victoria. Seth was in the kitchen, beyond the looped-up curtain in the doorway, his head bent over a large sketchbook. He frowned in concentration at whatever he was working on as she studied him, trying to decide who he resembled. Victoria, definitely, though neither of them was noticeably like Alice. She pictured the face of their father from the poster. They had the same nose, even the same jaw if you ignored the drummer's sideburns.

Seth sat back to examine what he had done, his hand tapping the tabletop. He had long fingers, the square nails blunt and oddly pleasing, and she had a rush of feeling as she noticed other details: a tiny mole below his ear, the slight difference in the colour of his skin where he shaved. What would it be like to run her fingertips along the edge of his face?

He shifted his head as if he sensed her gaze and she felt her cheeks grow warm, but his eyes travelled past her. He stood up, and came through, walking round to see Victoria's sketch.

"You're making her into a Roman centurion. She's not got a right angle on her nose."

Victoria ripped the page from her pad, screwing it up and throwing it into the corner.

"It won't go right. The shadowing is all wrong."

Helen started to move, but Seth gestured to her to stay.

"Give me the pencil. Helen's got a really individual profile, I'll do it."

This time, she focused straight ahead, intensely aware of Seth's hand inches away, tracing around the edges of her face. It was as if the line of the pencil was on her skin, riffling through her hair; he made Victoria gather it up into a chignon so her neck would be clear. He didn't call it a chignon, but that was what she pictured, something coiled and tendrilled and elegant, nothing like her own messy attempts in the mirror at home. She imagined the pencil lines carrying on, tracing her shoulder blades, the hollow at the base of her neck. He was making her feel almost pretty.

From another world, she heard the kitchen door crash open, and the sound of footsteps approaching. In the second before her mind began to wonder who might be coming, the scene she was in floated before her eyes, perfect and untouchable. If she stayed exactly where she was, perhaps the moment would continue anyway. She willed Seth to ignore the interruption, to keep on drawing, but almost immediately he was standing, leaving. A man's voice sounded behind her.

"Afternoon, everyone. I found these two outside, does anyone want them?"

Nobody would have noticed her pause before she turned. Seth and Victoria had forgotten her anyway. The man was tall and thin, the twins clinging on to him like burrs. Seth was already doing the man thing of slapping shoulders, but Helen could tell from the length of time they left their arms resting how pleased they were to see each other.

Then Victoria leapt past with a shriek of "Uncle Piet!" Her extra weight sent them all staggering back, almost into the sink. Uncle Piet, of course it was, the special uncle, the one who had found the house and paid the bills. It was a bit like seeing someone from the TV. Victoria was right, he didn't look much like James Dean any more, but he was a cowboy nonetheless; an older, tougher cowboy, with a lined face and greying hair, his eyes slightly narrowed, even inside the house. He wore boots, faded jeans. Helen wondered if he saw it himself, played up to it. She stood by her chair, fiddling with Seth's abandoned pencil. His sketch was lying there, and she edged it closer. What had he called her? "Really individual." She wasn't quite sure if that was praise, but the drawing did make her look nice. She pulled it away from the pad and folded it into her pocket as the others barged past her into the sitting room.

Piet went straight over to the stairs. Alice, Helen thought, up there in her secret world. Pippa tried to follow him up, and Helen watched Seth distract her with a question. Pippa swung round to whisper in Will's ear, and they both ran out through the kitchen, followed by Seth, their voices fading into the garden. Victoria had propped herself against the windowsill and her head was bent over as she picked at the varnish on her nails. The room felt stuffy, dust hovering lazily in the light from the window. At this time of day, it came through in a wedge as the sun hit the furthest edge of the glass. Helen traced the raised fabric pattern on the arm of the chair, wondering if she could follow the others outside. She heard one of them call out, and there was the sound of a ball being hit. French cricket, the twins' latest passion. She pushed herself up and took a step towards the door, but Victoria put out a hand to stop her.

"Come on." She didn't wait for an answer, but set off up the staircase, beckoning Helen to follow.

She came to a stop by Alice's door. Helen, expecting to go straight on to Victoria's room, fell into her.

"Ssh." Victoria pressed her ear up to the wood, holding on to Helen's arm. Helen held her breath, unable to hear anything to begin with, other than the blood rushing past her eardrums. Then, slowly, noises began to float through: a low voice, the creak of feet across the floorboards.

"They're coming out," she whispered, the sound too loud in the waiting air.

Victoria took a tighter grip of her arm. "In a minute."

It was easier to stay than make a fuss by pulling away, but Helen kept her gaze fixed on a dusty cobweb swinging from the corner of the ceiling, trying not to listen. Finally, Victoria turned around.

"He might even get her out of there. He usually can."

There was a pause, as if she was about to go on, but Piet's voice sounded right next to them, and they tumbled into Victoria's room, stifling each other's laughter. It wasn't funny, though. Helen felt Victoria's hand over her mouth as Piet spoke again.

"See you in a few minutes, sweetheart."

Alice did join them, sitting at the table by Piet, sometimes leaning her head on his shoulder. As the colours leached out of the day, Seth lit candles and shadows filled the corners. They'd had party food: crisps and sausage rolls, a bowl of jelly mixed with mandarin pieces, chocolate fingers. Following the rules of the food, they should all be overexcited and feeling sick by this time, but then again, they hadn't had pass the parcel or musical statues so it wasn't actually a party. Helen giggled to herself, wondering if she'd had too much of the golden French cider. Her head felt light, as if it wasn't entirely real. She leaned it on one hand and picked at fragments as laughter swirled around her. Piet's face was long in the dusk, his eyes retreating into the sockets as he turned to listen to Seth. Victoria butted in and made Piet laugh and Helen tuned in to hear what was clearly a family story, the punchline chorused by Pippa and, from under the table, Will. The stories grew wilder and funnier, Alice and Piet missing a train connection, bucketing across Istanbul in the back of a car with blacked-out windows in the company of men in dark glasses; a small Victoria in Italy, running away to join a goatherd and his flock in the mountains; Seth falling asleep on a ferry on the way to Mykonos and finding himself back in Athens.

In a lull, Piet turned to Helen.

"I'm sorry about this, Helen. Listening to other people reminisce gets very dull." His eyes crinkled at her. "Come on, it's your turn. Tell us about your family."

She felt her cheeks grow red as they all turned to her.

"Mum got locked in the toilet on a cross-country train once, but that's about it." She lifted both hands in the air. "Honestly, those sorts of things don't happen to us."

"Tell Piet about your dad's boat," said Victoria, her chair wobbling under her as she tried to pull her feet up into the lotus position.

The atmosphere of the evening inspired her. The story of the day Mick had bought the boat had never seemed so funny. There was Mick, madly pumping away in midstream to stop the boat from sinking, while various passing dog walkers and cyclists hauled on the ropes to bring her into the bank. In reality, Helen had been too small to have any real memories of the event, but it was a tale Mick liked to tell, and she embroidered without shame. It was liberating to laugh at the boat that had signalled the beginning of the end of her parents' marriage, now landlocked in a garage with her father the only crew member, sitting in his chair down in the hull, a crate of beer the only ballast.

"So he's been working on it all this time?" asked Seth. "What a waste, with the canal practically at the bottom of the garden."

"It's why they bought the house, because of the canal. Dad always wanted to live by water. But Mum hated it. And now . . ."

"Aluminium hull, you say?" asked Piet.

Helen nodded. "You have to be careful what you build on to it, other metal eats away at it or something."

"I spent a few years in Holland once, worked in a boatyard for a bit, learning the trade." He turned towards Alice. "Do you remember? The family business, building boats. I almost stayed there." Alice made no response; her face was expressionless again, withdrawn. He turned back to Helen. "I'll have to come and meet your dad. Be good to have another try."

It was late when Helen left, and dark enough to make her want to run fast, to outpace the shadowy threats behind the hedges. She forced herself to walk, not wanting to misjudge the water's edge even though she knew the towpath ran some distance up from the bank. There was only a tiny sliver of moon, but it somehow gave enough light to silver the water while leaving the edges blank and formless. Dark tree shadows trembled on the surface and she remembered her fancy of the mirror land beneath the water. It felt ominous tonight, hands waiting to grab her feet. A splash made her stop, heart pounding. It was a moorhen or a duck. Telling herself this didn't make the rustles along the lane any easier to ignore as she headed to the house. She broke into a run.

There was no light from the garage, so Dad must already be back in the house but, she reassured herself, he'd be asleep in front of the television. It wasn't as if he noticed her lately anyway. It had always been her mum who had cared about curfews and homework. All the same, she tried to tread lightly as she went down the side of the house.

He wasn't asleep. He was sitting at the table in the kitchen, a whisky bottle in front of him. The fluorescent light was playing up again, the tube flickering at one end. Helen's stomach tightened; she closed the door.

"Your mother called." His voice was steady, but each word was pronounced with a touch too much care. Helen's eyes went to the bottle on the table, then back to his face. "She wanted to talk to you, and I had to say I didn't know where you were."

His head slumped down on to the table. Helen began to sidle around him. If she could get to the hall, she could leave him to calm down. Before she reached the door, though, his hand slammed down flat on the tabletop, and both she and the whisky bottle jumped. He turned around.

"Do you know how stupid that made me sound?"

And she was back to last Christmas, the screamed accusations, the broken glass, the anger in the air turning her insides to water. Arguments raced through her head. She *had* said where she was going, and he *couldn't* have said that to Mum because she'd have had the police in. And he knew where she was anyway because where else would she be? The words rolled helplessly around in her head, crossed paths and confused her. She should have left a note, or double-checked. The memory of the candlelit cottage hovered in her mind and was snuffed out as if it had never been.

"I'm sorry, Dad, I thought you knew, I thought . . ." The words came out by themselves; she was finding it hard to orientate herself. She focused on the door handle, solid and real in the small of her back; a remote part of her brain was pointing out that he wasn't listening anyway. The table tilted as her father lurched to his feet, the bottle smashing unheeded to the floor.

She had never seen him like this before, even in the weeks before her mother left. She wanted to scream at him, make him stop, but her mouth wouldn't do it. He was pacing, pulling his head from side to side holding great handfuls of his hair. Instinct told her to be small, hidden, and she slid down to the floor, wrapping herself tightly in her arms and pressing her eye sockets against her knees. She heard the table turn over, tried not to see as this man who wasn't like her father any more slammed his fist into a cupboard door then swung around to pick up a pile of plates from beside the sink and hurl them across the kitchen.

She was staring at a smear of egg and ketchup on the wall. It reminded her of a bloodstain, the sort of thing a detective would examine in the aftermath of a crime. The house was silent now; she felt as if she had been holding her breath for a very long time. She watched her father as he pushed himself upright and stood with his head bent, one hand resting on the kitchen counter; he seemed about to speak, but eventually turned and went in slow motion out of the back door, knocking into the frame on the way.

The shaking started in her arms. It was autonomous, out of her control. It pushed itself through her tightly wrapped body, down her legs, over the back of her skull. Then came tears, and with the tears a great sweep of rage, ballooning out from her chest, forcing her breath into heaving gasps. This was pain that wanted to be howled out, to be scored into the walls of the house. She could feel her skin stretch with the pressure, ready to split at the slightest touch.

The despair and anger lifted her up from the floor in the end, taking her round the room, feet crunching on glass, fists beating on the sink. It dropped her in a chair, where she wanted to put her head in her arms and weep it all out, but she couldn't because the table was over there on its side so she sat with her hands on her knees and rocked backwards and forwards and cried out for someone, anyone, to come and put it all back together. It felt as if hours had passed when the telephone rang. The glass of the window was black, reflecting the mundane ordinariness of the kitchen, but it had been dark when she'd got back, hadn't it? She was no longer sure about anything.

The ringing was insistent. It clamoured round and round her head, urging her up, but she couldn't do it. There were a few minutes of silence before it began to ring again. This time she pushed herself upright and forced herself towards the hall. Her legs felt as though they weren't going to work, as if her thighs were too short to keep her upright, and her feet didn't belong to her. She reached the hall table.

"Hello?"

"Helen, it's Mum." Her mother's voice rang out, sounding too loud against her ear. It was unfamiliar, harsh. "I called earlier but you were out. Your father didn't seem to know when you'd be back, I was worried."

"I'm fine."

The emptiness of the telephone line stretched between them. Helen wished she'd go away. Her voice was the outside world, it was everything Helen wanted to forget about. Why couldn't she leave them alone?

"I was wondering . . ." Her mother's voice tailed off. There was silence on the line, then she continued briskly: "I wondered if you'd like to come to stay for a night or two. In my flat."

"No." It wasn't hard to say. Helen could feel more words bulging at her throat, shapeless and incoherent. In the end it seemed easier to simply put the phone down.

It was strange to be there, in the silent house. The conversation with her mother already seemed unlikely.

Maybe none of it was real. In a daze, she found herself back in the kitchen, her hand on the switch to turn out the light. There was the proof it had happened, crunching under her feet.

CHAPTER
NINE

2013, Manchester: 11 a.m.

There's someone at the door. I journey up through layers of sleep too fast, identifying the sound as knocking the second after it stops. By the time I am conscious, I have lost hold of the dream where the sound had been — what? The dislocation of the moment opens up a space too big to contemplate, the sort of space nightmares create.

I'm on Larry's sofa, in the small room behind the shop. It will always be Larry's sofa. The curtains are full length and heavy, there to shut out the world. It's the room where he cut telephone deals with collectors, shuffled orders and invoices. It's where he slept, and where I found him slumped sideways after he had the first stroke. It's one of the few places where I feel safe. I don't want to open my eyes. I could have been asleep for one hour; I could have been asleep for twelve. This is how it must feel to emerge from stasis, with vision and consciousness struggling to align with where the body is in space. If I could stay here, I would, resisting the siren call of the past, closing my ears and letting the current drag me beyond its reach. Everything I have lost is buried so well that I can no longer be sure what

I will find if I go looking. I'm not sure I have the strength to try. But the gallery is there. Victoria is there. It will happen whether I choose to act or not. The weight of this knowledge sits on my pelvis, reaches up and under my ribs.

Sounds sharpen into focus: a reversing delivery truck, a sudden shout, the low hum of the computer. I separate the levels of dust, the dry age of books from the shop, the heaviness of old upholstery, the cold notes coming from the unused rooms upstairs. Over the years, I have imagined the path of the Dovers through life. Victoria travelling the world, a chameleon equally at home in a sealskin tent or an Eastern palace. Seth would have a band, successful in a non-mainstream way, but he became a writer, or perhaps an architect, always surrounded by beautiful women but never finding a soulmate. Will and Piet build boats together, smoothing the wood with practised hands while Alice watches with her otherworldly smile. To Pippa, I give children, dressed in corduroy pinafores and hand-knitted jumpers. She has a husband who loves her and a dog that runs after a ball in a sunny garden. From her shabby, comfortable kitchen, with walls covered in children's drawings, she smiles at me.

If I see Victoria, my imaginary Dovers will melt away. By letting them go, perhaps I will find their solid replacements. The risk is that I will lose them for ever. The problem chases round my head with no answer in sight. I do what I've done ever since I got here when things get too much for me. I go up to the roof.

The first flight of stairs lead up to the kitchen, a cramped box of Formica and chipped enamel unchanged since the forties. The pipes bang and shudder as I run the tap. Up again is a storage room, stacked with misshapen cardboard boxes. At the top, right under the roof, is my bedroom. There's a single iron bed made up with blankets and a blue candlewick spread, the pillows covered in pink striped ticking. The books are the only mark I have made. Piles of them, filling the space between bed and wall, stacked on the chest of drawers, spilling out on the tiny landing. Most have been siphoned up from the shop, but sometimes I've had to go further afield to complete whichever list I've been reading through. One hundred books to read before you die. Books to create a perfect library, or change your life, or see out a prison term, or make you want to live. The ten best books in translation; the longest ever written or the shortest, the most depressing or obscure or wrongfully lauded. A dusty, stacked record of the person I have tried to be.

When I first arrived at the shop, Larry took me on a tour, finishing in this room. Leaning in the doorway, wheezing for breath, he told me his heart couldn't take the stairs. When he half offered to let me have it as a sort of bedsit, I jumped at the chance. I wonder if he knew what it meant to me, how grateful I was. The room has been mine ever since, even though sometimes I feel like ghosts are clogging up the space so much it's as if there's no room left for me. Other people's ghosts. It's not as if I need them. I am my own ghost. Out through the window, on the square of roof space, was where I found my place to be. Going there now is an automatic response.

I always sit with my back against the wall, so that the only thing I can see is the sky above the low surrounding wall, and the chimney pots and TV aerials. I've never brought anything up here, no pots or plants, no candles or cushions or jingling wind chimes. I like it the way it is. I'm a character in a nineteenth-century novel: the child in the garret, the prisoner of circumstance. The escapee, even. I ran away from home and landed here. I suppose I was luckier than most.

Were the Dovers running away? Once I asked Victoria how they'd ended up in the cottage by the canal. She shrugged. Piet knew someone, it was empty, and they'd had to get out of the place they'd been in in London. The cottage had been a wreck, with bulging walls and dodgy electrics. A boatman's house, damp, dark and leaky. But it was summer after all; it only rained enough for the drips to be funny and it didn't matter that the doors all stuck because they were never closed. It would be renovated now, along with the rest of the row, extended and polished and desirable. The Dover summer will have been washed away as if it had never been. There are only the tidemarks in my head to show that it ever existed. I meant to be like them one day. Victoria hadn't had to work hard to convince me that change was good for its own sake.

I see the other side now, though, the chanciness, the chasms of not knowing what will happen, and I've never been able to trust in Providence. Or perhaps I knew that finding Larry was my quota and I was too tired to try for more.

The roofing is rough beneath my legs. I lean my head back and reach for the stash of tobacco I keep here. This is the only place where I smoke. It's what I need right now. I roll a cigarette. It's not a good one. I'm out of practice, and the tobacco is so dry that it's on the edge of breaking through the paper. My hands are shaking as well and I give up and start again. A picture pops into my head: an afternoon by the canal with Victoria, a shared smoke leaving shreds of tobacco sticking to my lip, and then it is gone. I try to bring it back, to pin down where we were, recall what was happening around us, but the moment has gone. It takes until the third go to achieve a useable cigarette. The draw, the smoke in my lungs, is vicious.

The morning's events begin to settle into a pattern I can negotiate. If I am careful, I will be able to manage this. One thing I am certain of: I cannot believe the photographs in Victoria's exhibition will be unconnected to me. I close my eyes to picture it again: the poster, with the photograph, the name. And in the darkness behind my eyes I can hear their voices, always beyond earshot. Victoria swings from a branch. Pippa holds out a bunch of daisies. Piet's laugh rumbles as he ruffles someone's hair. The summer had never had much hold on reality and its abrupt end, that total, final, underlining cut-off, has left it floating there, a fairy story so enclosed that I am never quite certain what was real and what I have created for myself. Except that I have been on the outside ever since.

* * *

I am light, too light, my head expanding like a dandelion clock in the second before it explodes and floats away. I am glad of the feel of the wall at my back.

CHAPTER
TEN

1983

Helen woke early, a headache pressing her skull back into the pillow and pushing out behind her eyes. The events from the previous evening started running across her mind, figures spreading and shouting, sliding into the surreal. She was being interrogated by a voice on the phone and at the same time had to hold a weight. She couldn't see it, but she knew it was there, knew something terrible would happen if she let it slip. The voice grew louder and the shape she was holding grew with it, until it was bigger than space. And she couldn't do anything about it, even though she knew something awful was going to happen if she didn't get there. Then she was awake again and the sun was in the room, cleaning out the shadows, even while the echoes from the dream lay superimposed on her consciousness. Part of her mind was waiting for something to jump out; her nerves were tautly ready, her fists clenched. Then it was gone, as if it had never been, a door slamming on her subconscious and leaving her momentarily fragmented. Outside, a bird sang a flurry of notes.

She lay there for a long time, needing a drink and the bathroom, but unwilling to get up, because that would signify that the day was happening. What was she going to say? Do? Would her dad even remember last night? Would he want to talk about it? The thought made her long to burrow under the covers and stay there for ever. Instead, she strained to hear sounds, to work out where her dad was. She reached out into the atmosphere of the house, but it gave nothing back to her. The quietness wasn't comforting, though. Anger could be quiet, and worse still, so could awkwardness. In the end, the need to wee drove her out. The door to her dad's room was open, the bed empty. Even so, she agonized over flushing the toilet and drawing attention to herself. She could go back to her room and pretend to be asleep, and the day would disappear. But, as she crossed the landing, she heard a door being opened downstairs, followed by the sound of footsteps from more than one person. Leaning over the banister, she tried to decipher the voices. They were cheerful, normal. Mugs chinked, the fridge was opened. Who was it down there? She tiptoed back to her room to get dressed.

Helen stopped at the door to the kitchen. They were sitting at the table, mugs of tea on the table, glass swept into a pile in the corner by the bin. The smell of whisky was almost unnoticeable. Mick was unshaven, his shirt from yesterday rucked into creases from sleep, but his face was animated, his hands busy as he illustrated some point. It felt weird, juxtaposing the man from last night with the man at the table. Opposite him, so she could only see the back of his head, was Piet. He slouched in his chair as if he'd been there a while. He was nodding in response to Mick's ideas, waiting for him to stop before he responded.

". . . So the superstructure can be half ply and half canvas, using the original bars."

Piet had a rough sketch on the table in front of him, and he was adding pencil lines to it as he talked, transforming the skeleton of the hull into a finished boat. Helen squeezed past to get to the kettle, taking a peek on her way past, keeping her eyes away from her dad. She had known, of course, that Piet was an artist, but the drawing made her catch her breath as the lines took off from the page, making the graceless shape that had been in the garage for as long as she could recall swell into a thing of beauty, her rounded base balanced with cabin and tiller.

"And she's how long?" Piet tilted his head to smile at Helen, giving his mug a nudge in silent request. She picked it up. She hadn't made eye contact with her dad yet, and didn't have a clue what she was going to say to him. The words came by themselves, although her throat felt reluctant to let them out. She coughed to clear the way and tried again.

"Dad, do you want one?"

"Yes, all right, tea." He appeared to notice her for the first time, pushing the mug across the table and continuing with the boat. "Thirty-eight foot, near enough." He reached for the sketch and drew a thick, black line through it, bisecting the delicate image with the one downwards stroke. "This is where the engine needs to be. Takes up a bit of space. I've got a line on an old Perkins, classic piece of machinery."

She was fishing teabags out and pouring milk when Victoria's head appeared at the window. Helen put two of the mugs on to the table, grabbed the third and eased herself round to the door.

"Piet came by, then?" Victoria took another glance through the window, and pointed to the mug in Helen's hand. "Give me a mouthful." She didn't wait for an answer. "Ugh, sugar!"

"He was here when I came down." Helen took the mug back and had a cautious sip of the tea herself. She was glad to leave the kitchen, have something else to think about. "Do you want me to make you some?"

Victoria shook her head.

"Don't want to go disturbing them." She gestured to the garage. "Is it open? Let's have a look."

The boat took up most of the garage, the sides curving out above their heads. How long had it been since she had come out here? Months? No, longer. Helen felt a sense of shock at how big it was, as if it ought to have shrunk in the time she'd ignored it. She could never see it without picturing how it should be forcing the sea or canal or river down into a boat-shaped space, displacing that exactitude of gallons. It was her dad's kingdom, his refuge, the millstone around his neck. Victoria didn't stop to look. She was up the ladder and swinging her leg over the gunwale before Helen had crossed the garage floor towards it. Helen heard her jump down into the base of the boat, and started up the ladder herself. She stopped at the top and peered down at Victoria.

"Why is there an office chair in here?" Victoria was sitting in it, spinning herself around.

"Dad likes to sit down there. He says it's peaceful." The boat was grimy, bare apart from the chair, no longer the dream on Piet's sheet of paper. She found it hard to imagine that it would ever look any different.

"And how long have you had it?" Victoria's voice jolted Helen out of her thoughts.

"The boat? As long as we've had the house." Helen lowered herself on to one of the crosspieces that might one day support the flooring. "Dad found it right before we moved. It was the first thing in." She sometimes thought that was when it had started to go wrong, when Dad had done nothing but bring the boat over, leaving her mother to deal with the removal men. They'd never heard the end of it, anyway.

Victoria spun again on the chair, using the side of the boat to kick herself round. There was a slight shift in the boat's balance, and she stuck her foot out to slow down, catching it on a strut.

"It won't fall over, will it?" She was holding both arms out, as if she could keep it steady by mind power.

"It shouldn't do. It's set up so my dad can get in."

"Phew." Victoria flexed her foot with care. "Don't want to go capsizing before it even hits the water." She began to swing again, but with caution. "Especially when Piet's getting interested. He'll stay for longer if he's got a project . . ." Her voice tailed away.

They sat in silence for a while. Helen's mind went back to the previous night. Out here, in the quiet of the boat, the whole event seemed so unlikely. Again, she replayed it: Mick's shouting, the smashed plates, the late phone call from her mother, and they retreated another step towards unreality. Opposite, Victoria sat with her eyes fixed on some distant point, and Helen felt an urge to tell her about it. She was trying to work out how to phrase it when Victoria's voice broke in on her thoughts, and it was as if she was mindreading.

"What does your dad do, anyway?"

Helen paused before answering. "Not much these days." A picture flashed through her head: Mick sitting here, in the boat, for hours on end. That wasn't what Victoria had asked, though. "He was made redundant."

She was instantly glad she hadn't let on about anything else. That was her dad's business, not hers to blab about. She remembered people telling her how redundancy was hard for someone like her dad, how he was likely to be a bit depressed. Especially with her mother leaving as well. She was swamped by a surge of emotion. Guilt about how she wanted to escape from him sometimes, a tenderness that she was the one who understood, relief that she hadn't said anything about last night. That wasn't him. He needed someone to be interested in his plans, to help him get on with it. He'd be OK then.

"How come you stayed with him?" Victoria was shifting on to her knees, arms held out for balance. "I mean, children usually go with their mother, don't they?" The chair wobbled under her as she carried on upwards, first on to one foot then the other. Her head was now level with the top edge of the hull. "You don't have to say if you don't want to."

"I don't mind." It was true. This seemed like safe ground. "It was all a bit sudden, actually."

Victoria raised one foot, held on to a downwards strut and lifted her leg out behind her.

"Did your mum do a midnight flit?"

"No. It wasn't like that." She fished back through her memory to the events leading up to it. Time had smoothed them, and they now seemed equally as unlikely as last night's outburst. Had her mother been so unhappy? Everything had been normal until something was missed. A birthday? Or was it an anniversary? She screwed the memory back down into its hiding place. She wasn't going to think about it. "Mum went to stay with a friend at first, so there wasn't room. And then I had exams coming up." It had been a convenient reason and one, she realized, she'd need to reinforce with something now her exams were done. She remembered how the phone call last night had ended. It would be awful if her mother turned up, telling her off about being rude. She pushed the thought away.

The conversation lapsed once more. Victoria seemed engrossed in her balancing act, and Helen let her mind drift. The air in the garage always had a smell of being kept in the dark. The big double doors at the front were never opened, so the only new oxygen was what came through the side door. And if the garage air wasn't changed enough, what about the air in the boat? She imagined it briefly as a separate atmosphere, heavy, settling within the confines of the hull like gas in a mine. From above, it would have a surface, lapping against the inside edge with little opaque waves. It was as if the two of them were caught in their own world, sitting at the bottom of this pool of heavy air. She imagined knives pressing against the soles of her feet. Who would come to rescue them? Suddenly it was hard to breathe.

"We're like mermaids in a cave." She hadn't meant to say it out loud.

"What?"

"Never mind." It was like a bubble bursting, letting in a breath of pure oxygen. Victoria felt very real, standing across from her on the spinning chair, somehow more solid than she had been before. Not easy to explain. "I was thinking about air."

"And this has something to do with mermaids because . . .?" Victoria jumped down from her chair, freezing in position at another shift from the boat. "I keep forgetting where I am!"

She relaxed her arms and edged herself with cautious steps to the other end. Helen followed her progress.

"Why do you call your mum by her name?" Again, she surprised herself by saying it out loud.

Victoria glanced over her shoulder. "Well, it's her name, for a start."

"My mum would go mad if I called her Barbara."

"I'd go mad if someone called me Barbara." Victoria shrugged. "She's left anyway. You can call her whatever you like."

The boat's sides were painted in a thick cream paint, overlaid by a slightly oily layer of dust. Helen's finger slid along it, gathering up a layer of black and leaving a clean-edged trail. High up in the front end, where the edges narrowed and darkened as they came together, there was already something drawn into the dust. It was a sketch of a man's head coming over a wall, his big nose hanging down. A familiar image, one her dad used to draw everywhere: birthday cards, steamed-up car windows. Somewhere on a beach, him dragging a stick in the sand, trying to finish before the tide came in, her mother holding a pile of towels and picnic bags and rain bouncing off the concrete steps up to the promenade. Victoria's voice broke in.

"Do you ever go and stay? With your mum?"

"She keeps suggesting it. But I don't want to."

"Is she that awful?" Victoria wasn't giving up. "Did you have to do all the housework and sleep under the stairs?"

"No." Helen stopped and thought about the tidying up and constant buzz of vacuuming that had been the backdrop to her mother's day. Another picture flashed up, her dad standing there with his head down while her mum shouted at him. "Dad never knew what to do. Mum would get angry and he didn't know why. It made me sad."

The words ground to a halt. She couldn't explain it, how she wanted to make a forcefield around him, stop him having to listen.

"I sometimes think I might go and find my dad." Victoria's voice was casual, matter-of-fact.

Helen tried to remember where he'd gone. Was it South America? She imagined Victoria galloping across some dusty plain, accompanied by men with heavy moustaches. They would cross in front of the sunset, reach a wooden homestead and behind the door would be the drummer, his sideburns flecked with grey now, and his eyes narrowed by the sun. She took a breath in readiness to speak, but her words were interrupted by the sound of the garage door scraping on the concrete floor as it swung open. The boat wobbled again and Mick's head appeared over the side.

"Come on you two, out." He was more cheerful than Helen had seen him in weeks. "We've got some measuring up to do."

CHAPTER
ELEVEN

Helen dawdled over her breakfast the next day, enjoying the sense of the sunshine waiting outside, the settled blue of the sky and the air warm through the open window. She had *War and Peace* in front of her, propped up against a pile of newspapers so she could finish the last few pages. The book was too thick to stay open by itself, so she had to eat with one hand and keep it flat with the other. And she read about Prince Andrei's death, Natasha's grief, her toast cold on the plate in front of her, and the pages turned faster as she rushed towards the end, needing to discover what happened to those left alive, the survivors of the mud and the dark and the battles.

She swam up through the layers of words, almost surprised to find herself in the kitchen, her bare toes curled around the rung of her chair and the slant of the sun hot against her forearm. She read the final lines again. Surely that wasn't it? He couldn't end it on that half-line, with Natasha drained of her sparkle and stuck forever with fat, boring Pierre. The epilogue was all about Napoleon, but she leafed through it anyway, desperate for more. Names sprang out. Natasha and Princess Marie, smug in the countryside, poor Sonya, pretending to be happy. She let the book close. That was it. She felt drained, unable to make a decision on what to do next. The sound of a blackbird singing floated in from the garden, and she stared at her half-finished mug of tea, wondering if she could be bothered to pick it up.

As if the thought of tea had called him, the back door opened and Mick came in. He swept the newspapers to one side, sending Helen's book flying. His presence, solid and impatient, brought her back to life.

"Are you looking for something?"

"Bit of paper. Might be in the car." He picked up her abandoned tea and drained it. "I'll see you later."

The house seemed lighter, from the sun, from Mick, the atmosphere bouncing up as if a weight had been lifted. The warm feeling it gave her increased as she walked along to the canal. It was a particular summer feeling, she thought: everything was possible, all things within reach. She stopped for a minute to relish the sense of it, gathering her hair up into a bundle behind her head. That made her think of Seth, his eyes on her as he sketched, and a rush of excitement spread across her chest. The whole world was present inside her, expanding into an infinite space. She wanted to cartwheel, or spin round in circles. If her dad's boat could make it on to the water, who knew what else could happen? She picked up her pace and ran down the lane.

At the cottage, though, it wasn't Seth or Victoria that she found. She was hovering by the door, waiting for a response to her call, when a voice answered her from the sitting room.

"In here." It was deep and croaky, as if the owner had only that moment woken up. Helen stepped through slowly, unsure of what she would find. But Piet was sitting on the sofa, a tall china coffee pot on the low table in front of him. He smiled up at Helen.

"Get yourself a cup and join me for a coffee. None of your instant rubbish."

She picked one up from the sideboard and came through, perching on the edge of the armchair. Piet didn't say anything as he poured for her, stirring in sugar without asking if she wanted it. She took a cautious sip. It was strong and sweet, and Piet hadn't offered any milk. After pouring some for himself, he had fallen back into the sofa and was drinking with his eyes shut. The silence spread out. Helen could hear the low hum of the fridge and some distant, unidentifiable birdsong. A car came along the road, crested the bridge, died away.

"So." Piet's voice made her start. "What do you think of it?"

Helen had no idea what he was talking about.

"The coffee?" He held up his cup.

"I've not had it as strong as this before." She took another sip. The taste was better this time. "It's nice."

Piet's laugh was rough with smoke.

"Teach your palate to enjoy good coffee and good whisky, and you won't go far wrong."

Helen felt her mouth smile. She liked him, this lean cowboy with the lined face, but he was so different to any other grown-up she knew. She wasn't sure how to talk to him. He didn't wait for a response anyway.

"When I was your age, you couldn't get coffee worth drinking over here. I'd go to stay with my grandparents, and my grandmother would have me grinding the beans before breakfast." He gave a rasping cough. "While it was brewing, she'd send me out for the fresh rolls. Man, I'd come back to England and feel like giving up food altogether."

His expression made her laugh. "Where did your grandparents live?"

"On the outskirts of Amsterdam. But we spent the summer on the Waddenzee. You ever heard of that?"

Helen shook her head.

"Miles of nothing. The tide goes out and you have the mudflats, and the sea is in channels, you don't see anything but the mud and the seals. And the birds, all the birds." He laughed, shaking his head in wonderment. "Me and Jakob —" he stopped to explain, "my brother, you know, Victoria's dad?" It was strange, hearing his name said out loud. Other than the odd reference dropped by Victoria, nobody ever mentioned him, and she always had the feeling he was hidden, secret. It was as if Piet was breaking a taboo. She realized he was waiting for her to respond, so she gave a quick nod. "We were boys, no bigger than Will, and we'd go off in a canoe, spend all day exploring . . ." His voice tailed off, lost in the memory.

Helen studied him, trying not to be obvious in case he wasn't as abstracted as he seemed. His face had the tanned, leathery look of someone who had spent their life outside in the sun. She wondered how it felt to lose touch with a sibling, tried to imagine what it would be like to grow up with another person always there. Did he know where his brother was? Here was a chance to fill in the gaps left by Victoria's titbits of information.

"I heard that he disappeared. Jakob, I mean."

Piet shifted slightly, and she felt his gaze rest on her with interest.

"Victoria been telling you stories, has she?"

"Well . . ." She'd gone too far. "A bit. She said about his band."

"Ha, Cumulus." He shook his head. "Good on their day, they were. But it so often wasn't their day."

He was motionless now, his eyes distant, focused on something out of sight. The silence seemed to stretch out for ever. Helen found herself holding her breath, hoping none of the others would turn up. There were so many secrets hidden among the Dover tales. What had made Alice who she was? Would Jakob come back? She'd forgotten how old Victoria had said she was when he disappeared. Six, she thought. And in the summer. So Jakob had been gone for ten years. She remembered Pippa saying she and Will had been born in the spring. So they'd be ten on their next birthday. They would never have seen their father. But weren't twins usually born early? She seemed to remember something like that coming up in biology. Surreptitiously, she began to calculate on her fingers. Depending on when you said spring began, and if they had been early, she couldn't see how Jakob could have been there for, well . . . She felt herself blush. That definitely wasn't a question for Piet. But she tucked it away to think about later.

Piet suddenly leaned forwards and slapped his hands on his knees.

"As you're here, you can give me a hand." He stood up. "Have you finished your coffee?"

Helen tipped back the last mouthful, caught out by the sludgy thickness of the sugar.

"Yes."

"Come on, then." He smiled.

He led the way out to the back garden, and through the gap in the fence to where he parked his van in the field. He searched in his pockets for keys, and swung open the back doors. Inside was a large, flat package, wrapped in sacking. It took up the whole length of the van, and had been padded with blankets and secured in place with a criss-cross of rope. Helen could see bubble wrap underneath.

"Here we go." Piet flicked off the rope and took the near edge of the sacking in both hands. "It's a painting, right? I'm going to slide this out, and you're going to hold it while I go to the other end." He smiled at her. "It's not heavy, but it's a bit awkward. OK?"

Helen nodded.

Once it was out, they held it upright between them and Piet led the way back to the cottage and into the sitting room, walking backwards on sure feet.

He pointed to the wall behind the sofa. "It's going up there."

The front of the painting faced away from her as she stood holding it upright. Piet stripped off the protective coverings and then, following his directions, she helped him to lift it. Her face was too close to the canvas for her to make sense of any shape within the colours.

"There." Piet stepped back. "Do you like it?"

It was an oil painting, a nude stretched out across a bed. Alice, thought Helen; a young and joyous Alice lying on her back with one leg bent up, her arms spread out wide as she laughed at the painter. It was beautiful. And then, immediately, she thought of sitting here with Alice in the room. How would it feel, knowing that everyone could see you like that? It was strange enough to be looking at it with Piet, almost as if her own clothes were gone. She could feel herself lying there, with the painter's eyes gazing at her skin, at her . . . She closed her eyes, blood thumping in her ears, horrified at herself. Piet seemed to be very close. She took a tiny step away, uncomfortable.

He was talking again, though.

"It was one of the first ones I did. Sold every single one from the first exhibition."

"I didn't know that." She took a deep breath. This was normal to him. She needed to stop being such a prude. What would it be like to have a painting of her mother on the smooth beige wall of their sitting room at home? The thought made her want to laugh.

"She's very beautiful."

Piet sat on the armchair, studying the painting as he reached for his tin of tobacco. "Isn't she?" He licked the edge of his cigarette paper and smoothed it down with one thumb. "Chuck the lighter across."

110

She picked it up from the arm of the sofa, unnerved by the slight thrill it gave her to be touching something personal to him. Their fingers brushed as he took it, and she backed hurriedly on to the sofa. His voice came almost as a surprise, and she realized she was staring at his hands. The one holding the cigarette was gesturing towards the wall, and she turned to look up.

"I did that straight out of art college, spent a month with no sleep I was painting so much." He shook his head, as if feeling again the effects of so many sleepless nights. "I found her on the doorstep of a nightclub with nowhere to go, so I took her back to my rooms. I was young, I was painting like this." He waved the cigarette up towards the painting. "Life was good." He closed his eyes. "Life was good." There was a long pause. "And then Jake rolled up and turned her head." He took another draw on the cigarette.

There didn't seem to be anything to say, although the pause in the conversation suggested it was her turn. The thought of Piet and Alice as a couple had never crossed her mind, and she was grappling with it when Piet spoke again.

"So, what about your dad's boat?"

"It's been there a long time." The transition to something she could make sense of came as a relief. "It would mean a lot to my dad to finish it."

Piet nodded.

"It's a nice hull. We'll see what we can do." He sat up, leaning forwards with his elbows on his knees. "It can't be easy for you, your mum leaving. Means a lot to your dad, having you there with him."

Helen felt her eyes sting, and she stared down at the floor, wondering if Mick had said something, or if Piet was just being nice. Light from the window pooled by her foot, the circling motes lifting up, weightless, from the frayed carpet.

"So, where are we? August, hey? What are you and Victoria planning for the rest of the summer?"

The whirl of conversation had shifted again, this time on to firmer ground. Even so, she fumbled for something to say.

"Hanging out, mostly. There's not much to do. We've got a pile of books to read through." Said out loud, it sounded a bit pathetic, but Piet seemed interested, as if this was a valid summer activity. "I had to give up on *Ulysses*, but I've finished *War and Peace*."

He laughed.

"Going for the heavy reads, are you? Well, it's one way. *Ulysses* will last you the rest of your life." He ground the end of his cigarette into the ashtray. "What did you make of the Tolstoy?"

"It was OK." Her rush through the final pages felt as if it had happened a long time ago. "I mean, it was hard to begin with, but once I got sucked in it didn't take as long as I thought it would." She stopped, experiencing again the thrill she'd felt as Anatole held Natasha's arm, the prickling tears as Prince Andrei died. Piet was watching her, waiting for her to carry on, as if what she was saying was actually interesting. She tried to work out what she wanted to get across. "I liked the changes, you know, how it was all so much fun at the beginning, and then everyone was dying, and Moscow burns and

112

they all have to run away." She could see Piet nodding his head. "The end was a bit of a let-down, though. How he paired them up and they all got boring." She broke off again, wondering if she could explain what she meant. "Don't you hate it when the heroine ends up with the dull guy because the one she really loves is dead?"

An odd expression flickered across Piet's face, gone almost before she had a chance to register it. He let out his rasping laugh.

"That's romance for you. There'd be no story if they hooked up at the start. What else have you got on the list?"

Her mind went blank. She couldn't remember any of the other names. She tried to visualize them, piled up by her bed.

"Oh, *Animal Farm* . . . And *Lolita*. And there was one by somebody called Faulkner, but the library didn't have it." She ground to a halt. "We're doing other things as well as reading." She cast about for examples. "Like cutting our hair short."

Piet got up, leaning backwards with his hands in the small of his back before stooping to pick up his tobacco tin and lighter.

"Victoria, perhaps. She's got a bit of the gamine about her." He straightened up and, as he walked past, he picked up a strand of her hair on one finger, grazing her cheek as he did. It was the lightest touch but she felt it all the way up her spine. "I'd keep yours long. Beautiful colours in there."

She found herself waiting for more, but he ruffled the top of her head, and carried on towards the doorway, pausing on the threshold. "Go for longer. Lady Godiva, Rapunzel." He stood in contemplation as if she were a painting. Again, she had the sensation of nakedness. She didn't realize she was holding her breath until after he'd gone.

She stayed where she was, feeling the pressure of his hand on her head. Alice in the picture, Lady Godiva. From a great distance, she heard a car pulling up. Vaguely she was aware of an engine idling, followed by a clamour of noise building up around the side of the house and the car pulling away again. Will fell through the door with Pippa at his heels.

"Helen, Helen, guess what we got?" Pippa pulled at her hand. "Guess, guess!"

Outside, Will was doing a mad dance, waving oars over his head. Victoria backed around the corner, dragging an unwieldy shape behind her.

"Will, come and give me a hand, why don't you?" She pushed her hair away from her forehead and caught sight of Helen. "Oh good, you're here. Grab that handle."

Helen took a step towards her before stopping as another figure came around the corner. It was Alice, who also paused, as if she was aware of the picture she made and was consciously posing for everyone to enjoy it. It was like the cover of a magazine, the shaded laurels and the grey tones of the pathway the perfect background for her pale skin and the wave of her blonde hair. She was wearing a sundress, white with

114

black polka dots, the skirt nipped at the waist and widening to an extravagance of folds. Helen had the strangest feeling that she was play-acting, but there was no humour on her face. Then she lifted a hand to take off her sunglasses, and waved them vaguely towards the bundle in front of Victoria.

"Be careful with it, darlings. I'm feeling a bit tired." As she drifted by, Helen couldn't help recalling the naked arms and stomach of the woman in the painting, her face so full of life as she turned to smile at the artist. Victoria's voice broke into her thoughts, and she was jerked back to the present.

". . . Piet knew had a dinghy. We went to see him, and he gave us a lift." Victoria, the handle twisted around her fingers, was looking up at her. "Are you going to give me a hand?"

Together, they pulled it as far as the door, and the twins fell on to it, tugging at the red and blue rubber inside. Victoria knelt down.

"He said it might need some repairs, and it's going to take a hell of a lot of blowing up, but this is where we get to be Huckleberry Finn." She grinned at Helen. "Has your dad got any rubber glue?"

CHAPTER
TWELVE

Each day followed the next, with no more interruption to their tempo than there was to the run of unbroken sunshine. It felt as if the weather had always been like this, and would never change, the temperature outside matching her blood, so it was like being absorbed into the atmosphere. With no appointments to keep or places to be, Helen found herself stopping to wonder where she was in the week. August began to roll by, and there was never any question that, every morning, she would go and join the Dovers down at the cottage, though, if anyone had asked her what they spent their time doing, she would have struggled to answer. They fiddled with the dinghy every so often, finding the holes but getting no further. The boat in the garage was making better progress. Unlike her father, with his plans permanently stuck in sometime or never, Piet made things happen. The heat seemed to energize him, and Mick was determined to keep up. She would pass the open door of the garage and hear the rumble of voices from inside the boat. As she climbed over the stile at the end of the lane, the sunlight on the canal was a living, breathing Monet, and she would let the grasses that overhung the towpath slip through her fingers so she could pinch off the seeds in a neat bouquet and throw them over the water like an offering.

"Helen!" Pippa was kneeling on the edge of the grass in the garden behind the cottage. "Come and see!"

She had cleared a space in the tangled mass of weeds that filled the border by the wall, and was building a miniature garden of her own. A winding path of stones made its way through the middle, and she was trying to make some daisies stand up in the earth on either side. Helen crouched down next to her to take a closer look.

"You need trees." She looked around for something within reach, and broke off a handful of twigs from a straggling shrub with small yellow flowers. "Do you want them in a clump at the back or in a line down the side?"

Pippa sat back to consider. "Over there." She pointed at the far corner.

For a few minutes they worked in companionable silence. "Can you help me make a house?"

Her question reminded Helen of her younger self crouching in a garden and building a tiny log cabin from sticks, setting up a table of bark with leaf plates. Where had that been? Their old house? She squeezed her eyes shut, trying to remember who she'd been with. They'd picked raspberries as well, and hidden in a tunnel of runner beans.

"Hey, what are you doing?" Victoria's voice came from overhead. Helen squinted as she looked up to see her hanging out of the bathroom window, hair in wet strands on either side of her face.

"Nothing much." Helen stood up, brushing dirt from her hands.

Pippa tugged at her shirt.

"Don't go, I need you to help me." She had a streak of earth running down one cheek, and a twig caught in her hair. Helen reached for a discarded daisy and stuck it behind Pippa's ear.

"I'll help you for a bit."

Above them, Victoria was squeezing at the ends of her hair, sending water dripping on to the path below. "I'll be down in a sec."

They had made the walls of the house by the time Victoria joined them, with twigs broken to the right length and pushed into the soil. Victoria extended a bare foot and poked at the earth to one side of it.

"You should have a pond there."

"Don't! You'll knock it over!" Pippa gave Victoria's foot a sideways swipe. Victoria swung her arms in a wide circle, in a show of trying to balance, and ended with both hands against the wall and her foot inches above Pippa's little stand of trees. She let it hover, keeping her eyes on Pippa's face.

"I can't keep it up, I'm losing my balance . . ." and she let it drop a fraction. "Oh, oh, it's going . . ."

"Leave her alone." Helen too was watching Pippa's expression. "You're going to ruin it."

The noise of Piet's van distracted Victoria from her teasing. He was coming up the rough track that cut across from the lane to the back wall of the cottage gardens. Piet had to take his time, bumping around the holes and, seeing Victoria's attention was diverted, Pippa gave her a shove, which sent her to the ground.

"I'm going to get you!" With one of her swift changes, Victoria jumped up and began chasing Pippa round in a manic game of tig. Helen knelt to put the trees straight in Pippa's garden. Victoria had Pippa down on the grass and was tickling her. As Helen stood up, the engine cut out and she heard the van door open. Pippa's giggles stopped.

A girl was getting out of the passenger side. She was young, twenty or so, with dirty blonde hair reaching to the waistband of her jeans. Wearing heavy army boots and a battered leather jacket, she stood by the van, her eyes sweeping past them with an air of detached interest. Her fingers flicked at the strap of her canvas satchel.

"This is Moira. She didn't have anywhere to stay tonight, so I offered her the sofa." Piet had come up to the gap in the brick wall, his arms loaded down with plastic bags. He stopped next to Victoria and tilted his head towards the van. "There's a box in the back. Can you bring it in?"

Victoria threw one leg over the wall and sat there, watching them go down the garden. "Where did you find her?"

Piet didn't seem to hear, and carried on, but Moira glanced over her shoulder, letting her gaze rest on Helen, as if she thought she was the one who had spoken. Her voice was cool and mocking.

"Where do you think he found me, in the bargain bin?"

Helen felt herself colour, her mouth opening and closing in mute protest. Victoria swung her second leg across and went over to the van.

"Bitch."

Helen heard the softly spoken curse, but Victoria didn't seem to be inviting any opinion. She reached into the van for the box and headed towards the house without saying anything more. Helen could sense her animosity, though, imprinted on the air. It was disturbing, as if there was some kind of history playing out. For a second, Moira reminded her of the older girls at school, the tough ones who rolled up their skirts to unofficial shortness and smoked more or less openly at break times. But she had the gut feeling this was between Moira and Victoria; although Moira had been looking at her, she hadn't *seen* her. She followed Victoria into the cottage, pushing against her own reluctance.

Piet and Moira were in the sitting room, both leaning back in their chairs, both with a foot crossed up on their other knee. Victoria was over by the window, fiddling with a group of small animal figures left there by Pippa. Helen had followed Victoria to the doorway, but hung back from entering. She watched as Moira studied the painting, and felt her fingers grip the door curtain with dislike. Who did she think she was, curling her lip like that?

"Have you told Alice that we have a *guest?*" Victoria's voice was almost normal.

Again, Piet ignored her, taking his time in rolling a cigarette before passing the tin to Moira. Then he flicked his lighter, inhaled, and reached down for a cardboard tube on the floor next to him.

"For you." He tossed it to Victoria. "I found a poster stall at the market, every girl needs Che Guevara on her wall."

Victoria slid the poster out and unrolled it. Intense, shadowed eyes burned out from a red background. She didn't say anything, but with one finger, she touched the red star on the man's beret.

"Helen, here's something to broaden your reading list."

Dumb with surprise. Helen held out her hands in time to catch the books he threw over to her. There were two of them, both battered paperbacks. She tilted them sideways to read the titles along the spines. *The French Lieutenant's Woman* and *Bonjour Tristesse*.

"Thank you!" She looked up, saw his uneven smile. She took a deep breath. "I don't read French, though."

"Don't panic, I got you the English version." He winked at her and she smiled back.

"Did you get me anything?" Pippa, who had been standing behind Helen, pushed her way past in a hurry, and leaned against the arm of Piet's chair. Piet looked up at her and pulled at a pigtail.

"They didn't have anything for your wall, trouble. But I might have found something in the sweet shop." He levered himself up slightly, and felt in his back pocket. "Here you go. Share them with Fred, mind."

121

Pippa grabbed the bag and gave him a hug. Helen was watching their faces, so close together, when a sudden realization flooded her mind. Piet had been in Greece when Victoria's dad had vanished. She remembered her calculations about birthdays. If Piet was the twins' father, it would explain why he took care of everyone. Piet's voice interrupted her thoughts.

"And Victoria." He was holding out a small box. "Repair kit for the dinghy."

Victoria had let the poster roll back on itself. Her eyes were on Piet as she reached out to take it, but she spoke to Helen.

"Come and help me put it up."

Helen gave Moira a wide berth as she crossed over to the stairs, but she couldn't help a quick glance before she followed Victoria up. The older girl was relaxed in her seat, taking no apparent interest in what was going on around her. One hand held a cigarette, the other lay motionless on the armrest. It was all wrong. Instead of gratitude, she gave off an air of being in her rightful place. As if tuning in to her thoughts, Moira lifted her eyes to return Helen's inspection. They rested on her with no expression, leaving Helen to turn away hurriedly, feeling she'd failed some kind of test.

When she got to the bedroom, Victoria was lying on the bed staring at the poster of her dad behind the drums. Helen put her books on top of the piled surface of the chest of drawers and took in the crowded walls.

"Which one do you want to take down?"

Victoria gave a dismissive wave. "It can go on top of the others." She rolled on to her side, propping her chin

122

up on one hand, the other one picking at the fringe of the bedspread. "What did you make of her?"

"Dunno." Helen wasn't sure what Victoria herself thought. "She'd be prettier if she washed."

"You're so bourgeois sometimes." Victoria had one of the strands of the bedspread wrapped around her finger. She gave a vicious tug downwards, but the threads refused to break, digging into her skin instead. She let them unravel and inspected the white and red grooves left behind. "I don't trust her."

"Why?"

"She had that look."

They were silent for a while. Helen could hear the twins running in the garden and Seth in his room playing his guitar. Either it was something new he was making up, or he didn't know the chords too well. He would start with a run of single notes spilling over each other, but when he tried to add the chords underneath he had trouble keeping them straight. Over and over, he stumbled on the same section. Part of Helen's mind was following his attempts, willing him on, the other half was preoccupied with Moira and Alice.

"Will she stay for long?"

Victoria glanced up.

"Who, Moira? Shouldn't wonder. I reckon she'll be hard to shift." She pulled at the thread again, and this time it snapped. "It's something Piet does. Sometimes he paints them."

Helen imagined Moira lying on the sofa, Alice forced to watch from her picture frame above. In her mental picture, Moira was wearing her boots, the cool, assessing expression on her face. She shook her head as if that would get rid of the image, but she didn't seem to have a stop button. Her mind turned its viewfinder, with helpless clarity, so she could see Piet standing there, holding a brush and studying both women.

"If your mum . . .?"

Victoria interrupted with a snort. "Seriously? Alice? Anyway, Piet pays the rent."

She went back to picking at the bedspread. Helen stayed where she was, perched on the edge of the chest of drawers, and feeling somehow in the way. The books from Piet were next to her, but it felt as if reaching for them would send a signal saying she wasn't involved in this, that she didn't care. The silence stretched out, broken only by the sound of Seth's guitar. He finally got the run of notes in the right order. Victoria lifted her head and yelled through the wall.

"Play something with a tune!"

Seth's reply was brief and profane.

CHAPTER
THIRTEEN

Moira's presence changed everything. She didn't have to do anything; it was the mere fact of her that made the difference. On the day following her arrival, Helen stayed at home, reluctant to face the cottage while Moira was there. She expected Victoria to come and find her, secretly looking forward to another session of complaining about Piet's unwanted guest. When Victoria didn't show up, Helen finally made herself go and see for herself what was happening, only to find the cottage silent, the doors locked and unwelcoming. There was no reason why the family couldn't go out, of course, no law that said they had to tell her where they were. But it hadn't happened before, not like this, and she felt as if a layer of her skin had been stripped away.

There'd been no sign of anyone today, either, so here she was, in the garden by herself again, transported back to the beginning of the summer but with the emptiness doubled. The same roots were pressing against the small of her back and the same light flickered over her closed eyes. She couldn't bring herself to make the walk down the lane, though. If no one came, at least they wouldn't know how much she cared.

The sun itself felt stale, its tricks exhausted. She tried to relax, to let her mind float away, but she couldn't find a comfortable position, and there were ants and tickling grass. The sound of an engine trickled through the air and she sat up to listen, waiting for it to turn down the lane and bump over the track in the field, but it faded away. She gave up on the garden and wandered inside, flicking the television on and then off. Nothing. In her bedroom, the curtains were drawn and the air was fusty. How long had it been since her bed had been changed? Doing anything about it was too much effort, though. Finding sheets, tucking in corners . . . She pushed the idea away, and sat at her desk, pushing over the pile of books that waited on its otherwise clear surface. What if they didn't come back? They'd arrived so suddenly. What was there to stop them leaving in the same way?

The wall in front of her was covered in rosebuds, tight and complacent on their white background. They wobbled, vibrating slightly as if to say they'd warned her nothing good would come of having friends like the Dovers. She'd always hated those rosebuds, she realized, sitting in the background with their endless conformity and pink smugness. There was a zipped-up case of felt-tips in the desk drawer. She started off with black. The first rosebud disappeared behind a neat, black circle. As she went along, changing colour at random, the circles grew bigger and the colouring-in less exact. When the whole area in front of her was complete, she drew a breath. It was a start.

She was in the kitchen when she heard Mick's car. As she waited for him to reach the door, she felt herself tense, picking up something, either anger or frustration. There was a feeling of excess in the air, something she hadn't been aware of since Piet had started working on the boat with him. Had he noticed Piet's absence as well? It was a different emotion, though, that pushed in with him.

"Get some newspaper on the table quick, before I drop it!" Her dad had the door open and was coming in backwards. She automatically went to close it behind him, her hands trembling with reaction. "Newspaper, girl, hurry!"

The surfaces were all clear for a change.

"I don't . . ."

"Box, cupboard, open your eyes!"

His voice was impatient. There was newspaper in the box, but it was covered in a layer of slimy potato peelings and tea leaves.

"This is the compost . . ."

"I don't bloody care if it's the crown bloody jewels, get it on the table."

With the extreme ends of her fingertips, Helen shook loose the lower sections and spread them out, and he dropped his armload with a grunt and a thud.

"How about that, then?"

It was a propeller that must have been underwater for a long time. The flaring edges of the blades were thickened with what appeared to be shellfish, and the rank smell of water and weed hung over the tabletop.

"It looks . . . old."

"Quality engineering, this." Mick ran a palm along the length of the shaft. "Needs a bit of work to get it back into condition, that's all. Nothing that can't be fixed."

"Where did you get it from?"

"I told you about the shrimpers, didn't I? Saw it the other week, but they had someone else interested. Fell through, though."

"Are you planning to work on it in here?" It was as if her mother were in the room. She fished around for a palliative. "Because I could find you some more newspaper."

He wasn't listening anyway. "I'll take it through to the garage." He heaved the propeller up from the table and gestured with his head for her to open the door. "Bring me out a sandwich, will you?"

Helen held the door wide, making sure she was out of range as he sidled through.

"Will cheese and pickle be OK?"

"Yes, fine, anything." He crossed the path to the side door of the garage and stopped. Belatedly realizing he was waiting for her, Helen ran to open it for him. As she went back to the house, he called something after her.

"What was that?"

"That youngster was round earlier." His voice sounded impatient. "Her and another one."

"Who was it with her?" Not Moira, she thought. Please not Moira. She gripped the door handle, willing him to make the right answer.

Mick's reply was muffled.

"What was that?" she called again.

There was a heavy thump from the garage, and Mick's head came back out.

"Don't go setting me up as your social bloody secretary." He was cleaning grease from his hands with what looked like one of her mother's old blouses. "Go and find her yourself."

Victoria was sitting on the canal bank, throwing stones across the water, as if she'd never been gone. She was wearing her tie-dyed sundress as well, the one she'd worn on the first day. It was an omen, a good one, but Helen paused, trying to hold down the bubbles of hope saying everything could go back to normal. A pair of seagulls swooped down, screeching in their oddly seaside way, and the noise sent her onwards.

"Hey, what're you doing?" She'd already decided not to ask where they'd been. Much better to pretend not to have noticed.

Victoria skimmed another stone out with a practised flick of her wrist. It bounced four times before sinking below the surface, and she scooped up the rest of her pile in one hand, throwing them out in a wide arc.

"Nothing." Victoria stood up, reaching her arms over her head and leaning back into the stretch. "I'm so bored."

Did that mean Moira had already left? Helen waited for Victoria to say something about her, but she remained silent, her face turned to the water, her expression dissatisfied and closed off. Helen had an unsettling thought: what if Seth had gone somewhere with Moira? She could imagine the conversation only too well: the dropping of a remark about a place to visit, a shared interest, then rucksacks packed and buses taken. Victoria would be angry at being left behind. Or perhaps the empty day could be explained by a trip to a port, the waving off of the ferry. Had there been enough time? Helen tried to remember where the ports were. Liverpool? And wasn't there one in Wales? At the back of her mind was the dull weight of never seeing Seth again. She tried to think of ways to ask without giving herself away, but whatever she came up with seemed to have a big red flag waving her intentions. The silence stretched out, and she heard herself babbling.

"Dad got a propeller for the boat. They'll have it all done soon and we can go sailing."

Victoria's face turned, her expression briefly engaged. "Will he let us take it out?"

Helen felt the tangles of opposing loyalties grab at her again. Could she say yes? She pictured her dad's face, heard the lengthy reasons why he would never agree.

"I doubt it, not by ourselves."

"A lot of fun that'll be." Victoria scratched at her ankle. "We need a boat of our own."

"What about the dinghy?"

"Still needs fixing."

Victoria tossed another stone before making an abrupt turn. After a moment, Helen followed her under the bridge. There was a small ledge on the inside and, if they sat down, they could edge along sideways into the shadows. Victoria scooped up some more stones and started to throw them at a patch of hanging moss where the bridge curved down on the opposite side.

"Where does it go, anyway?"

"The canal?" Helen slid her thumbnail under a bloom of lichen. "Along there," she nodded to the right, "it takes you to Liverpool. And the other way is Leeds."

"How come you don't know more about it? I mean, how long have you lived here for?"

Helen shrugged. "Took it for granted, I suppose."

"But you must have wondered?"

"No."

Victoria made a disapproving teacher's face. "What's the good of an expensive education if you don't think?"

"It was a comprehensive!" Helen gave her a shove, forgetting their precarious position. Victoria grabbed at her in mock terror before speaking again.

"Shall I tell you what I know?"

"Can I stop you?"

Victoria started to shuffle along to the far side of the bridge. She waited for Helen to catch up, then led the way around the wall to clamber up on to the bridge itself. At the top she stopped, and swung herself up to sit on the rough stonework, her legs hanging down above the water. Helen leaned out. It wasn't particularly high, but even so, the drop made her stomach clench.

"So." Victoria pointed back over her shoulder. "Down there is Liverpool, but when you get there you're stuck in a dock. This way," she pointed ahead, "goes, as you said, to Leeds, which means, technically, you can sail from the sea on one side of the country to the sea on the other."

And reach ports and ferries. Helen couldn't bring herself to ask. Instead she fell in with Victoria's mock solemnity. "Very handy, if you don't have a car. And why did you ask me if you already knew?"

Victoria held a finger to her lips. "I haven't finished. A short distance along, there's a branch that connects with the Ribble and therefore with the sea. Which makes the sea, quite literally, within our reach." She swung her legs back over the wall and jumped lightly on to the road. "Which Uncle Piet says would be foolhardy in our dinghy, especially if we can't fix it. But your dad's boat . . ."

"You'll have trouble convincing him."

"We'll see." Victoria ran down the bridge. "Let's see how far we can get down the bank."

The towpath on the far side of the bridge was well trodden at first, the grass flattened by walkers, most of them with dogs. Here, the canal swung round in a slow curve before straightening out next to open, flat fields. It wasn't long, though, before the track petered out and was lost under a swell of brambles.

"Do you suppose the path got covered in weeds because there were no walkers, or did the walkers stop walking because of the brambles?" Helen crouched down at a point where the bank had collapsed, forming a bite-shaped hollow. The water was hidden beneath a thicket of reeds and a rustling sound caught her ear.

132

She turned, but whatever it was swam away too fast to be seen, a ring of ripples the only sign left.

"What?" Victoria glanced up from her contemplation of the overgrown path, then resumed her scrutiny. "If we cut through the field we can get round this, after that it's clear for a bit."

"Why are we doing this?" Helen stood up with a sigh.

"Because we can. Come on." Victoria put one foot on the top strand of barbed wire which made up the boundary of the field. "You first."

The path did open up and, once they were back on it, Victoria picked up her pace. Helen had a scratch on her arm from the wire and nettle stings on her legs. She was thirsty too. It was a shame the canal was so dirty. She picked a dock leaf and rubbed it hopefully on the rash. It didn't do much.

Victoria had vanished around another wide bend. When Helen caught sight of her again, she had stopped and was squatting by the water, studying an old boat tied up on the far bank.

"How can we get across?" She didn't look around and, without waiting for an answer, suggested, "Swim?"

Helen sat down next to her and pulled at a stalk of grass. The green moss spreading out along the sides and over the windows made the boat look abandoned. She slid the joints of the grass stem apart, nibbling at the white centre.

"You can get diseases from the water if you swim in it." She threw the nibbled stem to one side, and picked another.

Victoria snorted. "You can get diseases from everything, according to you." She fell silent, considering options. "If we go back to the bridge we can get to it from the other side. The bank over there's not too bad."

"I'm not fighting my way through another lot of brambles." Helen had tingles running up both legs from the nettles they'd come through. "It's empty, anyway."

"That's it — carry on being positive." Victoria's head had sunk between her shoulders like a cross tortoise.

"Why do you want to get to it, anyway?"

Victoria stayed in the same position, not answering. Then, with her usual single motion, she stood up. "I'm going to carry on down. There's probably another bridge or something." She looked back at Helen. "You can come too, if you think you can manage it." She didn't wait for an answer.

The boat's name was partially visible. Was it an I? Or an R? Helen pushed herself up with a sigh and followed in Victoria's wake.

CHAPTER
FOURTEEN

The lock was around the next bend, sitting like a secret under a canopy of trees.

"When do you reckon these were used last?" Victoria went up to the nearest gate and gave its heavy wooden beam a shove, first with one arm and then with her whole bodyweight. It didn't budge.

"No idea." Helen crouched to read the graffiti scrawled along the stonework. "But Kev was here in 1979."

"Lucky him."

They made their way to the lower gates. The far one was tilted, the timbers at the base crumbling away from their frame, and the remains of a footbridge sending skeleton shadows across the mottled stone walls. The water level in the lock was low, and a steady leak pushed its way down from the upper gates, a constant running sound into the fern-filled chamber. Their approach had disturbed a cloud of midges.

Victoria drifted further up.

"Not much point putting your dad's boat in the water if he can only get to here."

Helen stood gazing at the water, heavy and dark under its ceiling of greenery. She was trying to remember if they had ever walked down this far, her and her dad, back when they used to come here for their boat-spotting expeditions. She was sure she could remember boats travelling up and down, and they'd definitely watched a lock working. Could it have been this one? It didn't seem possible. She visualized time passing in fast-forward, like a nature programme, the lock disintegrating while she stood beside it, in a progress of birth and death.

"He must know about this. It might not be as bad as it looks." She followed Victoria up to the other gates, and they both stared at the V-shape of the massive frame, pushing against the water to hold it back. Unmoved by the dereliction behind them and unmoveable. Helen leaned against the arm, as Victoria had done on the other set, bracing her feet against the old stone grips underfoot. It was like pushing against a house.

"Dad wants to go the other way, anyhow."

She wandered across to a stack of wood, piled between rusted metal supports.

"What do you suppose these are for?" They were the size of railway sleepers, all the same dimensions, their ends crumbling in the same way as the lock gates. The sun was directly on them and, checking the top layer for insects first, she climbed up, the warmth pleasing under her legs.

"Dunno." Victoria hopped up too, stretching herself to one side to reach into a pocket. She drew out a cigarette, bent from being in her pocket, a roll-up like one of Piet's, but thicker and longer.

"Never seen you smoking before."

"All right, Granny." Victoria had pulled out a small box of matches as well. She took her time straightening the cigarette before putting it in the corner of her mouth, then she struck a match. She leaned forwards so the end of the cigarette was directly over the flame. It took a couple of attempts to get it going, and the match burned down to her fingers. She dropped it to the ground with a shake.

Helen watched her lie down on her back, knees bent and feet flat on the wood. The line of smoke curling up from the cigarette's end smelled sweeter than the tobacco Piet and her dad used. Stronger, too, when it was this close. When Victoria held it out to her, she reached for it without giving herself time to think. For a second, she felt the cool surface of Victoria's nails under her fingertips as the cigarette was passed across.

"You have to get on with it or it'll go out." Victoria tilted her head up, shading her eyes with her hand.

"I know." Helen carried on studying it. "Did you get it from Piet? I thought he was always telling you not to start."

"No." Victoria kept her face to the sun. "I got it from Moira, actually. She taught me how to make them."

It felt like a challenge. The paper end was soggy, and Helen hesitated before tearing a bit off with her thumbnail. It was harder to tidy up than she had imagined, strands of tobacco pulling out like ends from a holey jumper. Giving up, she put it in her mouth, and drew in a cautious breath. It was easier than she expected, and on the second inhalation, she leaned back and let the smoke out slowly, watching it curl and spread. Suddenly a feeling of tightness took over, she couldn't catch her breath, and she spoiled it by coughing. She handed the cigarette back to Victoria. It was no good. She was going to have to ask.

"Is Moira still staying with you?"

"No." Victoria blew out another stream of smoke. "She only needed a couple of nights to get sorted." She held out the cigarette again.

Helen forced herself to sound casual: "And? What was she like in the end?"

The smoke had sent a light tingle down to her fingers, and her heartbeat had speeded up. She let herself drop back and closed her eyes, but everything started to spin. When she opened them, Victoria was blurry.

"OK, actually. She was telling us about all the places she's lived in." Victoria hugged her knees. "She was at Greenham Common, you know. Cutting through the wires and blocking the roads." Her voice had become high and fast and, as if suddenly aware of it, she leaned back on her elbows and slowed down to a nonchalant drawl. "She was telling us about last winter, living in tents with no heating. It was like being in the Middle Ages, she said."

"Sounds interesting." Helen struggled for something more to say. Thinking about Moira made her feel like she was one end of a magnet being pushed against the polar opposite of another. "Why isn't she there now?"

"Oh." Victoria's voice was casual. "It wasn't radical enough. All the holding hands and stuff."

Helen forced a laugh. "Wasn't that the point? Holding hands instead of bombs, I mean."

"Yeah, but it doesn't work, does it?" Victoria met her eye, challenging her to disagree. "Moira says that sometimes direct action is the only course."

They sat for a time in silence. Helen had the cigarette again, but the smell was making her nauseous. She handed it back to Victoria, but it had gone out. Victoria threw the end into the grass and stood up.

"I want to cross over," she said. She swung herself up on to the top of the lock gate and edged out to where it angled against the other one of the pair. "Come on! It'll take more than us to make it collapse." As if to prove the point, she turned a neat cartwheel along the remaining length of the narrow beam.

Following slowly, Helen gripped the scored and flaking wood of the gate. She didn't like balancing at the best of times, and right now her head felt unreliable even on solid ground. But Victoria was off. She thought about Moira, about the emptiness of the long days without the Dovers, and she hauled herself up.

The ground on the far side was less overgrown than on the towpath, with fields reaching down to the canal. The bank had been trodden into mud by cows. Several were standing there, noses dipping towards the water. As one they all turned their heads towards the girls. The nearest cow took a clumsy step forwards and Helen lost her balance, splashing ankle-deep into a brown-skinned pool. Victoria's laughter rang out in the quietness.

"It's not funny!" Helen hopped around, trying to find a patch she could safely stand on. But soon she couldn't stop giggling either. She reached the fence on the far side and stood on one foot, trying to decide if it would be worse to keep the shoe on or walk barefoot.

"Dip your whole foot into the canal." Victoria tried and failed to restrain a snort. "It'll be OK, dry out in no time."

There wasn't anything else for it. The mud had squeezed its way right inside, and she had to take the plimsoll off to wash it out.

"I should step in with the other one, too. At least they'd be the same colour." It seemed like the funniest idea she'd ever had. As if attracted by the noise, the cow started coming towards her again. "Vic, help me!"

She stumbled, windmilling for balance. At the last minute, Victoria grabbed at her flailing arm, getting a tight hold of her wrist. A tug got her started, and she came up the bank at a run, cannoning into Victoria and almost sending them both over. They swayed together for balance, and Helen smelled lavender and coconut and the sweet smokiness of the cigarette. She dropped her eyes.

"Look at my shoes. They'll never be the same again."

Victoria pulled away, wiping the edge of her own sandal on the grass. "You can bung them in the washing machine. It's what I always do." She carried on towards the edge of the field. "Come on!"

Helen paused to brush off the worst of the mud before jogging slowly after Victoria. She could feel the cows' eyes following her.

Somehow, the narrowboat was there as she rounded the corner. She hadn't thought they'd come that far along. It looked in even worse shape close up, the red-and-blue paintwork faded and peeling, and green mould encroaching on the portholes. Victoria was already next to it and, before Helen could say anything, she knocked on the boat's side.

"Vic, what are you doing?" Helen's voice automatically dropped to a whisper.

Victoria ignored her and knocked again. Helen could see food tins that could only have been on the bank for a short time. "We should go. I think someone's living here."

"Why are you always running away?" Victoria peered into one of the grimy windows before knocking for a third time.

A hatch was pushed open in the side of the boat and a man stuck his head out. Helen waited for a shout, but he said something that made Victoria laugh and set off for the far end of the boat. It rocked as she stepped on. She didn't look back at Helen.

Helen stayed where she was for a few minutes, irresolute, listening to the sound of voices inside. She couldn't make anything out, so she went closer until she could see in through the hatch.

The interior of the boat was dark, and the air coming out was heavy with the staleness of a small space and laced with the same sweet smell as the cigarette they'd shared by the lock. She could make out a narrow sofa against one wall with blankets tumbled along it; plastic bags spilling out their contents; glasses lined up on the floor. Something shifted in the gloom, and a naked foot appeared. Helen jumped back, her cheeks heating up in embarrassment.

The man's face appeared at the hatch again.

"Are you coming in or not?" He had broken teeth, and dark creases dragging at the skin of his face.

"No, no, I'm fine." Helen gave him a quick smile. "My feet are wet, I'm OK out here."

Victoria joined him. "Come on, don't be rude."

The man retreated, leaving space for someone else.

"Hey." Moira was rubbing her eyes, as if she'd only that minute woken up. "Come and join us."

If Moira was here, Helen realized she could stop wondering about Seth. She wished that made getting on the boat easier to take.

Helen smiled, keeping her lips pressed together. The muscles on her face ached from being kept in an interested expression. She was sitting on the top step so that she could stick her head out every so often, although the air above deck reeked of petrol.

"So we ended up down by the harbour, but the *poli* found us. They kicked us awake." Moira reached down to tap the ash from her cigarette into a can on the floor, then leaned back again, one leg tucked under herself, the other stretched along the sofa. She had pushed the covers up to one end, and Victoria was perched on top of them, her face turned towards Moira, hanging on to every word. "This guy, Jose Luis, he'd been in the original protest, and we were all pretending to be thick

142

English hitch-hikers, you know, not understanding what they were saying, and he was hiding at the back."

"Wow." Victoria sounded breathless.

Moira reached down again, picked up the can and peered inside it. Helen thought she was going to drink from it, but she took one last draw from the cigarette and dropped the stub in through the hole. "Are there any more, Dave?"

The man had been sitting on a high stool the whole time, one elbow propped on the open edge of the side hatch, also watching Moira talk, but with an expression that was more difficult to read than Victoria's. It might have been amusement. He gave a belch, not bothering to cover his mouth, then slid down to get another can from a box on the floor.

"Last one." Helen felt his eyes flicker over her before returning to Moira. He stepped across to give Moira the beer. "We'll have to hitch into town if you want any more."

"Yeah, in a minute."

"And what happened next? How did you get away?" Victoria sounded impatient.

"Oh, us girls got to the front, gave them a bit of attention. They went off happy." Moira detached a pair of jeans from a bundle of clothes on the floor, and started to pull them up over her pyjama shorts. "They wouldn't have been so happy the next night."

"Why, what happened?"

Moira grasped the bottom edge of her T-shirt with her hands crossed over, and pulled it over her head, so her voice was slightly muffled by the fabric. "We petrol-bombed the bar where the police hung out after hours."

Moira didn't have anything on underneath. A frisson of shock ran across Helen's skin and she found herself staring. Hurriedly she dipped her chin, eyes fixed on the floor, her own hands, anything but Moira. Dave was watching her and, though she tried not to, she couldn't help glancing round. He grinned at her, his teeth yellow and disgusting and, as their eyes met, he raised an eyebrow. She tried to pretend she hadn't seen, focusing hard on the bubbles of rust on the doorframe and resisting the need to wipe at her mouth. When she turned back, Moira was wearing a bra, and had one arm in the sleeve of a shirt. There was a brief silence as she buttoned it up.

"I wish I could do things like that." Victoria had her gaze fixed on Moira, who was now wriggling her feet into her boots. "It would be so cool." She mimed a throwing action. "I could go for chucking petrol bombs around."

Moira straightened up. "We didn't do it for fun." Her mouth was set in a contemptuous line. "It's an action against imperialism and oppression." She picked up a small bag, embroidered all over with tiny red flowers, and started to rummage inside. She spoke again without looking up. "You two can hop it now."

"Did you know all along that she'd be there?"

"No." Victoria was leading the way up the path between the trees that Moira had pointed them towards. To each side of it, the ground was littered with

144

tins and empty bags. "I knew she was on a boat somewhere along here, but I didn't know where."

"Why didn't you say?" Helen could feel a headache closing in. She wanted to get away before Moira and the man came out of the boat.

"Dunno. Probably because I knew you wouldn't come."

It felt like a long way back. They walked in silence, the path taking them through a stand of trees and over a scrubby no-man's-land. It was well-trodden, and strewn with litter. Helen kept her head down, trying not to step on anything. In the corner of her vision, she could just see the start of the humped-back bridge.

"Typical, we could have come this way in the first place and missed out the jungle." Victoria's voice was jaunty.

"How did she find it? I mean, did she know that guy before?" Helen was beginning to see the sparkling lights of a migraine at the edge of her vision, even though the road here was in the shade.

"What's with the third degree?" Victoria sounded impatient.

"I was only asking."

"It'd be a cool place to stay, though, wouldn't it?" The boat was out of sight behind the trees. "I'd love to live there."

"Hmm." Helen rubbed at her temples. "The floor was sticky."

"Not good enough for you?" Victoria walked a bit faster, then turned with her hands on her hips. "I was watching you, sitting there like you had a lemon in your mouth." Her voice was rising. "I thought you'd like to meet them. They're interesting!"

"But —" Helen didn't get a chance to say anything. Victoria had already spun round and was striding off along the road.

She caught up with her at the highest point of the bridge. Victoria was looking back along the water. As Helen came up to her, she turned.

"You know, the trouble with you is, you can't cope with people making choices that are different." Her voice was conversational and her eyes were fixed on a point somewhere over Helen's shoulder. "You're so worried about getting things dirty or getting them wrong. It's pathetic." She started down the far side of the bridge. "And if you want to know," she carried on over her shoulder, "it's not like you were invited. You followed, like you always do." Her voice drifted back. "You stay at home with your daddy and his stupid boat — I'm going to find one that floats."

Helen couldn't quite grasp how quickly the afternoon had changed. She held on to the rough stone of the bridge until the dizziness subsided. There were voices coming down the road behind her now, Moira and Dave, on their way to hitch a lift into town. As if anyone would stop for them. Helen broke into a run and, keeping her head turned away from the cottages, she headed for home.

CHAPTER
FIFTEEN

She didn't even have to pretend to be ill. The migraine, which had been rolling up since they were on the boat, took over her head. It pinned her to the bed, reacting to the slightest shift by sending a fan of pain across her skull before concentrating itself in one particular spot above her right eye.

She could at least see by the morning, but lifting her head from the pillow set the pain off again. It took Mick until lunchtime to come and see where she was.

"I thought you were round at that cottage again." He didn't come all the way in, but kept the door half-closed across his body with only his head and one shoulder in the room. "Do you need anything? I'm going into town."

As she listened to the car drive away, she shifted her head to a cooler spot, and wished she'd asked her dad to get her some water. And she needed to go to the bathroom and she needed more paracetamol. If they had any. Abruptly, she was weeping. It was so lonely, being ill by yourself. She wanted to have someone feel her forehead and tell her she was OK. Her mum would have got her clean pyjamas to feel more comfortable. She would have settled her on the sofa with pillows and a blanket, and would have brought her tomato soup. The house was indifferent to her tears.

The headache kept her in bed for another day, and she lost track of the time, giving in to the twilight shifting that happened when you slept all day. Her subconscious conspired in not thinking about Victoria, or about Moira. Instead, as she twisted around in her tangled bedsheets, it was Seth that she latched on to. Seth, who never made her feel stupid, who said nice things and had drawn her picture. She replayed every conversation they'd had, every glance, drawing the endings out in new directions, building new scenes where he reached for her hand, her face. He drifted through her half-waking dreams, forever out of contact, but always keeping Victoria at bay. Finally she shot upwards through half-consciousness, her pyjamas drenched, from a nightmare in which she'd ended up with Seth in the narrowboat. He'd been leaning in to kiss her, but his face had transformed into the leer of Dave, and she'd heard two sets of laughter coming from the other end of the boat. It took her a long time to get back to sleep.

The headache dragged on for two days. Even when the pain had receded, getting up felt like too much effort. When Mick brought her a plate of sandwiches and a mug of tea, it was so unbearably touching that she found herself crying again after he'd gone. It was the first time in ages she'd felt hungry, though, which had to be a good sign. She pushed herself up and looked around for a book to read while she ate.

148

She'd swept the books from Victoria's reading list off her desk and into a corner. The cover of *Moby Dick* was bent right back, and the sight of it was strangely satisfying. She wasn't going to read any more of them now, anyway. But the two Piet had given her were perched next to her light. She picked them up. The first had a woman on the front cover, a woman with long blonde hair who had been photographed from behind, her face turned back and her head draped in the loose hood of a cloak. She bore a slight resemblance to Moira, though, which was enough to send it into the corner with the others. The second one was thin, shorter than one of the school stories she'd been reading. *Bonjour Tristesse*. It was one of those annoying books that didn't say what the story was about on the back, only giving a comment from a newspaper. There was a poem on the first page, in French as well. She nearly changed it for something easier, but the effort involved was too much. So she settled back, and began to read.

When she emerged at the end, it was to the same feeling she'd had with *War and Peace*, but this time it was even more intense. She couldn't believe she was back in her room, that only hours had passed. Her hands and feet, sticking out of her pyjamas, the familiar shapes of bed and cupboard and desk: they all belonged to the wrong world. It was as if she'd split in two and one half had been left behind. In her mind, she was on the beach, like Cécile, with white sunlight burning through her eyelids and sand caught beneath her fingernails. She hated Anne, always going on at Cécile

149

and telling her what to do. For a second, Helen came back from the book's world fully, hearing her mother before she'd left, always nagging about homework and exams. And the arguments before she'd left, Helen crouching at the top of the stairs, trying to work out what was happening, watching her dad's face sagging in despair at his failure to understand. Neither of them would have had any place in the villa in Nice, though. Helen pushed the memories away, trying to get back into the book's world, but earlier. On the beach.

She would be lying there, listening to the sound of the sea and feeling the sun's heat. Her eyes closed, she could see the green of the woods leading up to the road and saw him stepping out of the shade. Seth, of course, in her version of Nice. He would come towards her and sit down, letting his fingers trail along her bare arm and then up so that they caught her hair. And he would lean down, like Cyril, and she would feel the press of his lips. Again and again she replayed the scene, using her own fingers to brush against her arm, and along the soft skin of her belly, letting the outside world recede.

It was late in the afternoon before she got around to dressing and leaving her room. She took the stairs with extra care, feeling for each tread. Her head felt too light still, and unused to her height. As she stood in the kitchen, cutting slices of bread to have with butter and jam, she could hear the whine of the jigsaw coming from the garage. The air outside the window was full of the odd fragrance of sawdust. She ate one more slice before slipping out to peer through the open garage

150

door. Her dad was smoothing a hand over the surface of a wide piece of plank, and he gave a grunt as he hefted it up towards the top edge of the hull.

"Try it for size." His voice surprised her, but he was talking to someone inside the boat, not her. Piet's muffled voice rumbled back, the words blurred. She felt a degree of comfort from the normality of the work, and the feeling that perhaps everything would be OK warmed her as she watched her dad cross over to the wood piled against the wall. He spoke again over his shoulder.

"Did I say I found someone giving ballast away?"

It was nice, somehow, to be eavesdropping, as the two of them carried on with their work, oblivious of her presence. Piet's head appeared over the gunnel.

"We'll be ready for it tomorrow." There was a pause in the conversation as Mick began to shape the end of another plank with the jigsaw. When he was done, Piet carried on talking. "And the engine could well be arriving today. I'm reckoning on putting a rope over that beam, there'll be enough of us to pull her in."

Helen backed quietly away.

She was in the dining room rummaging through the sideboard's cupboards when she heard Pippa. For an unsteady moment, she thought the footsteps could be Victoria, but they were too light. Pippa called out, but she didn't respond at first, the weight of it being not-Victoria taking the words away. Pippa's feet went down the hall to the stairs, and she made an effort.

"I'm in here."

The feet ran back, and Pippa's head appeared around the door.

"I haven't got anything to do!" She plumped down on the floor next to where Helen was sitting and backed up her complaint with a sigh. "And you haven't been to see us for ages." She leaned against Helen's arm. "I've missed you."

It was something, however small, and Helen felt a surge of affection for Pippa. She put her arm around her and gave her a squeeze.

"I've missed you too. But it's only been a couple of days." Only a couple of days. She heard Victoria's words again, floating after her as she'd run down the bridge. It felt like weeks.

"Everyone keeps going out, and Uncle Piet keeps coming here to do things on your dad's boat." Pippa sat up again, putting her head to one side and gazing into the middle distance. "And Fred says he doesn't want to make mud bricks any more because it's boring."

Helen smiled. Pippa was tenacious of her plan to have Will called by her chosen name, though even Will himself didn't seem to care. And Pippa's final complaint explained the dried mud streaked through her hair, lodged under her fingernails, and covering her legs with a powdery greyness.

"What are you doing? Can I help?" Pippa gave one shin a vigorous rub and the mud flaked off in a shower. Helen started to say something, but stopped. The air in the room was heavy with disuse, no one would notice.

152

"I'm going through our family treasure." She reached into the cupboard again, bringing out a small, flat box. "It used to be a special treat when I was your age."

Inside the box was a set of tiny spoons, each resting in a velvet-covered, spoon-shaped hollow. Pippa hung over her elbow, her face expectant. Helen picked one out, turning it around so the figure at the top was facing upwards.

"It's got a man on it!" Pippa was delighted. "Who is he? Why is he there?"

The silver was tarnished, whorls of discolour circling round the bowl of the spoon. The figure at the top was enamelled, his robes green and new-looking still.

"He's an apostle. They're called apostle spoons."

"What are they?" Pippa picked another one out. "He's different, look, he's got a different face." She laid it down next to the first and reached for another. "What was that word?"

"Apostle?"

"Upossel, upossel, upossel." The word was making her giggle. "Say it over and over, it'll make your tongue trip up."

Helen obliged, and Pippa joined in the chant, the word getting faster and less coherent as they tried to keep control of their tongues. They both ended up breathless and laughing. Pippa lying on her back in exaggerated exhaustion. She rolled over to reach for a red-robed figure.

"But what are they?" she asked again.

"You know, Jesus had twelve apostles — these are them. On spoons."

"But there's only eleven. Look!" Pippa counted out loud as she arranged them in a line, alternating the colours in strict order. Red, green, blue, then back to red.

"Well, that's because of Judas."

"Who's he?"

"He was the bad one." Helen stopped, wondering how much detail Pippa would demand. "He betrayed Jesus. For thirty pieces of silver."

"Like a pirate?" Pippa pulled her head back to admire her arrangement. "They have pieces of silver and long hair."

"Well, not quite." Helen gave up. "I know, let's see what's in here."

Pippa sat up on her heels, watching as Helen eased the lid from a larger box. Inside was a set of delicate china cups, too small for tea; spoils from a great-aunt, Helen seemed to remember. She took them out, unwrapping the swathes of tissue paper and setting them up in a row. The sides were so thin she could see the shadow of a finger through them. Each one was a different, vibrant colour: purple, jade, sapphire, gold. Next to her, she heard Pippa's indrawn breath.

"They're so pretty! Can we use them for a tea party?"

Helen sat back to look at them.

"Better not. We're a bit big for them."

A door banged outside, breaking through the sleepy heat of the room. Helen felt a change in the atmosphere, her senses picking up something awry without being sure from where or why. She sat up, leaving the cups on the carpet, trying to identify clues. Now she could hear raised voices coming from the back of the house. What was it Piet had said about an engine? She half-stood up, uneasy. Voices rang out, one of them definitely her dad's. Then the kitchen door swung open with a bang, and the noise from the voices resolved into separate words.

". . . come in here and take over!" Her dad barged against the table as he crossed the kitchen and Helen froze. Mick didn't look her way as he crashed down the hall. She heard his footsteps thud up the stairs.

"Helen . . ." Pippa's voice was wavering.

"It's OK, Pippa, it's only my dad." Helen turned back to the small figure kneeling next to the sideboard. Pippa's face was apprehensive, the beginning of tears brimming up in her eyes. One tear tipped over the edge, travelling down through the dirt on her round cheek.

"I didn't mean to, it was when I picked it up . . ." Her voice tailed off in a sob. In her hands she was holding two halves of a delicate, deep-gold cup.

"Oh, Pippa." Helen took the pieces and tried to fit them back together. Would she be able to glue it without the join showing? Her stomach clenched at the trouble she'd be in if her mum saw it. But her mum wasn't here, was she? And a memory clicked into place, her mother's voice, *Why would I want to take anything? Weighing me down — you keep it, that's what you like.* She wrapped the pieces up in the tissue paper and put the whole lot, in their box, right to the back of the cupboard. They'd be there, glowing like a nuclear device, every time she went in the room now, but never mind. She could always pretend she didn't know anything if anyone ever did go in there. Then a vision popped up, of herself in front of the dresser with her own children, making a funny story of the day the cup was broken. She felt a wave of love for Pippa, as if she was one of them.

"Pippa, it's OK." There was no change, Pippa's shoulders were hunched in tightly, her face buried in her knees. Helen thought quickly, keeping one ear out for sounds from upstairs. "Pippa, if I give you one of the spoons, would you feel better?"

There was a nod from the curled-up figure.

"Which colour would you like?" Helen reached for the box of spoons and took out one with a green-robed figure. "What about this one?"

Pippa uncurled, but stayed on her side on the carpet. She took a long, shuddering breath. Without saying anything, she reached out a hand and touched one of the spoons. It was the odd one out, the single white-robed thirteenth figure. Helen eased it out of its slot and put it into Pippa's hand. Her fingers curled around it, and she wiped at her eyes with her other hand. The dried mud and tear stains were the saddest sight Helen had ever seen. She put the box with the remaining spoons back into the cupboard and shut the door.

"Come on." She crouched down and gave one of Pippa's shoulders a squeeze. "Let's go and wash your face."

★　★　★

They went outside afterwards, drawn by the small group standing in front of the garage. Helen could see Piet and a couple of men she didn't know, wearing checked work shirts and heavy boots, oil stains marking the legs of their jeans. With a bump in her chest, she noticed Seth on the far side. A white pickup had been reversed up the drive. As she reached them, her dad came around the side of the house.

"Mick, look . . ." Piet took a step towards him. "Let's talk about it, hey?"

Her dad ignored him, going straight to his car. The engine didn't catch. Everyone was watching him, all at different levels of involvement. Piet was shaking his head, saying something to Seth, who gestured towards the garage with one hand, his face towards her dad's car. The two men in jeans were standing further back, waiting. They were in no hurry: sooner or later the drama would stop and they would get on with their job.

The engine finally turned and her dad wound the window down. With his eyes fixed straight ahead, he spoke. Helen could hear him quite clearly; it was his injured and dignified voice.

"Would you mind shifting your truck? I have something I need to do."

Piet went towards him, bending over and saying something inaudible through the window. Helen had the uncomfortable sense she should go and find out what was going on, but before she could act, Piet stepped back, shaking his head again. One of the men got into the truck and drove into the lane, her dad following. He stopped the car halfway out to wind down the window, and seemed about to speak. Then, with a crunch of gears, he changed his mind and carried on.

They stood in strained silence before the second man stepped out and signalled for the truck to reverse. Nobody else reacted, even after it had come to a halt. The man driving the truck put his elbow on the edge of the window and stuck his head out.

"Right, shall we get on now?"

Seth was standing at the back end of the truck. The tailgate had been let down and the second man was next to him, both of them examining an engine, lashed down in the truck bed with heavy rope. Helen took a deep breath and set out towards them. Seth glanced up and gave her a smile as she approached at the same moment as Piet came round the side and put an arm across her shoulders.

"I'm afraid your dad doesn't like me very much at the moment."

Helen tried not to feel that she was joining the enemy camp. She tilted her head to study Piet's face.

"What was it all about?"

He gave a shake of his head, taking his arm down and reaching into his pocket for his tin of tobacco.

"I had a good opportunity to get this engine. Friend of a friend." He stopped, his head bent in towards the lighter, face concentrating on the first pull as the cigarette glowed red. "It was a bargain, absolute bargain." He stepped towards the truck.

"But why would Dad not like that?" She'd heard him going on about it enough, about how hard it was to find engines, how overpriced the ones he did find worked out to be.

"He was set on having an old engine, a Perkins."

Helen nodded. She had heard a lot about them, and the other ones, Gardners or something.

Piet patted the top of the engine on the back of the truck. "This is a different sort of engine. Better for this boat, in my opinion, and a lot smaller, a lot easier to use. So I've been trying to talk him round."

The taller of the two men came up to Piet, lighting his own cigarette before speaking.

"Ready to get going?"

They both walked away, heads down, Piet keeping his gaze on the engine as the other man demonstrated his idea with sweeping hand gestures. Seth was standing on the other side of the truck, drumming his fingers on the edge. Helen wanted to join him, but she'd built up so many pictures in the last few days, it was disorientating to have the real person there. Had Victoria said anything about the argument? It was possible he thought she was boring and unadventurous as well. She hated herself for being so needy. No wonder they got sick of her. She seemed to hear her mother's voice, coming out with her standard response to upsets with friends: *It's only because they're jealous.* As if anyone would be jealous of her! Even so, the thought, obscurely, cheered her up. And Seth was walking towards her. She was joltingly aware of his every step, but still jumped when she heard his voice.

"You OK? Haven't seen you for a while."

A rush of pleasure rose up in her stomach.

"Oh, well, you know." She turned to look at him. There was a slow pulse beating in his throat; the inside edge of his white T-shirt was dirty. She had an urge to run her fingers along it. She took a deep breath. "Will my dad be OK?"

"Big question. Will any of us, I wonder?" He turned to watch the men and the engine. The shorter of the two was feeding a heavy rope underneath it, with Piet reaching through to pull at the end. "The thing is, this is the best way, and by far the cheapest." He looked at her now, his face amused. "He's gone off in a bit of a huff, that's all. He'll work it out."

She felt the sense of disloyalty return. "The boat's so important to him."

Seth laughed and touched her lightly on the arm. "He'll be fine. He'll think about it and see everything's going to work out, and come back as if nothing had happened."

A pulley had been fixed to the second beam inside the garage. The truck reversed until the back end was positioned as far in as possible. Seth climbed up a ladder and Piet passed him up the free end of the rope, which was now tied in a double loop around the engine. Seth stretched up to poke it through the pulley mechanism, but it was beyond his reach, and he swayed, starting to lose his balance.

"Careful, Seth!" Pippa was herself again, and her voice rang out in clear admonishment. "You know

Uncle Piet says you should never climb unless you can hold on to something."

Seth looked down at her and appeared to lose his footing, both arms flung out for balance. There was a collective gasp, but he gathered himself up and turned to give an ironic bow.

They all put their weight on to the rope to heft it upwards, Pippa catching the very end. Seth stayed on his perch to guide the engine, and there was a cheer as it landed on the frame that had been prepared, Helen realized with a pang, for the solidity of the vintage Perkins. But there was no time to dwell on it. Piet was already waving goodbye to the men, the truck spitting gravel as it turned out of the drive. Seth climbed down the ladder from the boat and stood behind her.

"Are you coming round? I was going to play some music." He must have known something, and seen a giveaway expression on her face. "It's OK, you shouldn't let Victoria get to you. She's always going off on a rant."

Helen smiled at him.

"I'll go and leave a note for my dad."

CHAPTER
SIXTEEN

She followed Seth through the kitchen and up the stairs to his room. The other doors were shut, and there was no sign of Alice or Victoria. Pippa ran ahead of them, scrambling up the staircase to the attic to join Will in some frantic chase. Seth caught Helen's eye and shook his head.

"Menaces, the pair of them." He pushed his door open and led the way in. "One day one of them's going to land in the wrong place and bring the whole house down."

His room was the opposite of Victoria's, with bare floors and unadorned walls. There was a mattress in one corner, covered in an embroidered throw. A wooden box, upended, held neatly folded clothes, and next to that, his guitar leaned against the wall. Along the other side was a line of LPs, matching the length of the bed, and leaning against each other at a slight, exact angle. Below the window a turntable sat on a shelf supported by bricks. On either side, at matching distances and slightly turned towards each other, were two enormous speakers.

Seth gestured to the end of the bed and Helen let herself sit, careful to kick her shoes off before crossing her legs on the cover. She watched as Seth went to the line of records. With quick precision, he flicked them across, going down the line until he found the one he wanted. Then he went to the turntable and slid the disc out of its covering, blowing on the surface and placing it on the spindle with delicate fingers. The needle was lowered gently, the crackle making an unexpectedly loud sound, and he touched at one of the dials on the front.

"Don't want to start by blowing your eardrums out." He came back to the bed, throwing himself down on the mattress and lifting up a pillow to rest behind his head. With his eyes closed, he held an imaginary guitar, making the first simple chord shapes with his fingers. Helen let herself study his eyelids, at the pulse flickering over the delicate skin. The guitar music had been joined by voices, which swelled up in a contained harmony, filling the space in the room and then breaking off for the melody to continue alone. Seth shifted, and she turned her head, not wanting to be caught out.

The wall behind the line of records was stripped of paper and washed with some sort of thick white paint. At the end closest to the door, a figure had been drawn in marker pen, the lines careful and exact. A naked man, bound within the confines of a circle, his face stern and direct.

"What's that from?"

Seth followed the direction of her finger.

"It's da Vinci, the *Proportions of Man*." He smiled at her, surely holding her eyes for longer than was necessary. "I've always thought it would make a great album cover."

That was the thing she liked most about Seth. He didn't make her feel stupid when she didn't know things. The tune faded away to nothing and Seth rolled off the bed to get to the record player, lifting the needle before the next track started.

"I only like that one track," he explained, lifting the record off and sliding it first into its paper sleeve and then into the cardboard case.

"Who was it?" She felt breathless as he came closer to her, but he was only passing her the record. She bent over it, examining the picture, an outline of a branch suffused in golden light.

"Wishbone Ash." He took it back and spun round to the records, pulling another one out. "Now something for Uncle Piet. Early Stones."

She watched him reach over to the windowsill after putting on the next record, lighting a small cone that was sitting in a pile of fine dust. A spiral of smoke began to rise, and the underlying, woody fragrance she'd noticed on her way in wafted across the room with a soft intensity.

The music Seth had put on this time was harsh and unadorned. Helen climbed off the bed and went to pick up the sleeve. Five faces, young, shadowed, smart. She turned it over; down in the corner was a scribble, hard to read.

Seth spoke over her shoulder.

"Signed by the man himself."

Helen held it closer, trying to decipher the swirls. "That must make it worth a lot."

"Well —" Seth gave a short laugh, "less than you think. Although I also have the honour of having been dandled on the great Mick's knee."

"Honestly?" She checked to see he wasn't pulling her leg.

"Before they were famous, of course." He was gathering his hair into a ponytail. "Uncle Piet knew a lot of people. In the middle of everything, he was, counter-culture, all the swings and roundabouts. He's an old hippy at heart."

"And your dad?"

This was met with silence, and Helen bit her lip, wishing she'd not been so stupid.

"And my dad, I guess," Seth said eventually, sitting back on his heels. "A lot of these are his, actually." He gestured towards the records. "My inheritance."

His tone of voice was hard to pin down. She thought of the picture of him and Victoria, hand in hand on the Greek hillside. His hand rested on the floor next to her and she had an urge to touch it. One song came to an end, another started.

"Victoria showed me some photos. You look a lot like him."

"You reckon?" He turned away, sliding a record out, studying it before pushing it back in its sleeve. The sense of closeness she had felt seemed to waver and slide away.

"I'm sorry." Clearly he didn't like the thought of Victoria showing people the old photographs.

"No, it's OK." He pulled another record out, keeping his back turned. "He wasn't the easiest guy to have around, by all accounts. Always wanting to try some big idea."

He didn't say anything more, and they sat there, the music filling the space between them. He must spend all his time trying not to be like that. Helen wondered yet again about the twins, imagined asking him, them having a deep and meaningful conversation, him saying she was the only one who understood.

"Anyway . . ." His voice broke into her thoughts as the record came to an end, the needle sweeping round and giving a jump at the end of each revolution. Seth leaned forwards and lifted the arm. "Enough of ancient history. Let's find something new. What sort of music do you like?"

Again, she was wordless. She couldn't say what she knew, the stuff they danced to at school discos, the top twenty on a Saturday evening. It all sounded so boring.

"Normal stuff." She climbed off the bed and came to sit next to him. With one hand, she started to tip the albums along, hoping to see something she recognized. "I don't have many records. I mostly listen to the radio."

"OK." Seth picked something out, and swivelled round. "Let's see what you think of this." He turned the volume up as an electronic thump came from the speakers. "I was in Berlin in the spring, saw them live."

"Who are they?"

Seth flung himself on to the bed and stretched out, closing his eyes.

"The Neon Judgement. Kind of like Cabaret Voltaire."

Helen made an assenting noise, as if she knew exactly what he meant. She closed her eyes as well, feeling the music vibrate through the floor, up through her spine, around the circumference of her skull. She could, she was almost sure, get to like it.

"Seth —" She stopped. It would be a stupid thing to ask.

"Yes?" He'd lifted his head and was looking at her.

She needed to know. "What did you think about Moira? I mean, what she talks about?"

He gave a laugh. "I think she has a lot to prove."

Helen thought about that, relieved he hadn't asked her why she wanted to know.

"Will she stay around for long?"

"Here, there, it doesn't make much difference in the end. None of us will be here for long." He laughed again. "Wisdom from your very own guru. They'll be lucky to get me."

"Who?"

"University." He lengthened the vowels, almost singing the word.

The music was still playing, its rough anguished edges reflecting her feelings. She was glad of the noise, of the excuse to close her eyes again and pretend she was OK.

"What are you going for?"

"That's a deep question." He repeated it, as if genuinely asking himself. "What am I going for?" He propped himself up on one elbow. "The opportunity came up. I dunno, it seemed a good thing to do. Shame to let all those A levels go to waste."

Such an ordinary set of qualifications was a revelation to her. Victoria had talked about a school, but a different sort of one, where they seemed to be able to do what they liked. It hadn't sounded as if exams featured much. And Pippa and Will couldn't read yet. *Steiner*, Victoria had explained. *It's different, Helen, not wrong.*

"When do you go?"

"September. Feels a long way off yet. Have to help this lot settle somewhere first."

"I wish they were staying."

Seth sounded amused. "Here? There's the damp, no heating. It was only ever going to be for the summer. And they've been lucky with the weather."

They, not we, Helen thought. It was as if he'd already gone.

The thump of footsteps came up the stairs and Victoria's head popped around the door.

"Hey, Helen." She came in and sat down next to Helen on the floor. "What's this shit you're listening to?" She started to work her way along the stack of albums, pulling a handful out and spreading them across the floor. "Let's have this one."

She walked over on her knees, catching the arm of the record player so it squawked across the record that was playing. Over her bent head, Seth caught Helen's eye and grimaced. She grimaced back. She could only hope the relief she was feeling at Victoria's casual return wasn't too obvious.

168

CHAPTER
SEVENTEEN

Everything was nearly back to normal. Helen turned up in the mornings to see what craze had come into Victoria's head overnight: volleyball, with an old sheet for a net and an inflatable world globe for a ball; chalk pictures along the garden wall; taking photographs with an old camera she'd unearthed from Piet's belongings. It felt as though something had shifted, as if a stone had broken the peace of the water's surface and settled on the riverbed, undetectable from above but subtly changing the water's flow, but it was easier to ignore it than otherwise.

Work on the boat picked up again as well. Mick recovered, as Seth had predicted he would, and carried on sawing wood for the deckhouse, though, to Helen's eyes, with less enthusiasm than before. She wanted to ask him about it, but she could never quite work out how to start. Anyway, he was asleep in front of the telly by the evening. And during the day, she'd started to avoid the garage. If she didn't see any trouble, it couldn't be happening.

She heard him in there now as she headed out, hammer strokes echoing from behind the door and following her down the path and out into the lane.

Piet's van bumped towards her and she pressed back into the hedge to let him go by. He didn't stop, but waved a hand out of the window as he passed. The sound of splashing drew her towards the canal bank, and the first thing she saw was Will. On the opposite bank, an oak tree leaned waterwards; someone had tied a rope to the largest of the overhanging branches, and Will was clinging to it as he swung in a wide arc over the canal.

"Jump, moron! That's the whole point!" Victoria was in the dinghy, using her hands to paddle it around. Pippa was holding on to a red-and-white striped life-ring, paddling in circles near to the bank. She let go of the ring with one hand so she could wave.

"Helen, look! We've got a rope swing! And Uncle Piet fixed the dinghy!"

The hand holding the ring slipped, and she disappeared under the surface. When she came up, she abandoned the ring, coming towards Helen with a determined dog-paddle. She clung on to the grass at the side.

"Come on, Helen, you can have the next go!"

Helen sank down to her knees at the edge.

"I don't know, Pippa, the water's a bit horrible. And I haven't got my swimming costume."

Pippa studied her with her head on one side. "Is it because you can't swim? You can have my ring if you like."

"No, but the water . . ."

Pippa was already paddling her way back to the ring. Helen watched her bob along and missed the start of

170

the upset. Then she looked over to see Victoria turn and open her mouth to shout at the same time as Will let go of the rope, flying through the air and landing right on top of her.

The dinghy seemed to fold. Victoria overbalanced with a wild yell and they both toppled into the water. She surfaced first, spitting water out as she looked about, one hand pushing hair out of her eyes, the other grabbing for the rope looped along the dinghy's side.

Helen was stood up, squinting against the reflections from the sun on the disturbed water. She could see Will, but he didn't seem quite right.

"Victoria —" She tried to focus. Had he moved? Surely he was messing; he'd been the one landing on top of Victoria, after all. "Vic!" Her voice started to rise, not quite steadily. Will's body floated, motionless, his face under the surface, his thin arms spread out. Victoria had her back to him as she struggled over the unstable edge of the dinghy, which was between Pippa and her ring and Will's motionless form. Helen started to kick off her sandals, at the same time cupping her hands around her mouth. "There's something wrong with Will!"

She saw Victoria, now in the dinghy, pick up on her tone, and waved her arms. "Over there!"

Her feet finally free, she sat on the edge of the bank, hesitating as she tried to decide if she needed to get in.

She saw Victoria paddle herself around. Pippa, now with a clear view, let out a high-pitched wail as she realized what was happening. She started towards her twin, arms and legs lashing out but not getting her very far. Victoria had jumped back in and already had hold of Will. He seemed to be a dead weight, but they were making a steady pace towards the bank, so Helen turned her attention to Pippa, in time to see her go under and then struggle up again. She was gasping, and couldn't seem to hold her head out properly. There was nothing else for it. Helen held her breath and let herself slide down the side of the bank.

The water was warmer than she had expected, but she felt slime squeeze between her toes. She took a deep breath and kicked off, taking only a couple of strokes to reach Pippa.

"I need to get to Fred!" She was breathless, and her body was slippery and hard to grip. Helen held on, her fingers digging into Pippa's shoulders as she repeated herself until it sank in.

"It's OK, Victoria's got him. Everything's OK."

She was out of her depth now, kicking to stay afloat, hampered by the clinging fabric of her clothes. Pippa started to sob, and clutched at Helen with her arms and legs. The shift in balance was unexpected, and Helen's head went under the surface. The water was cool around her face, but dirty, and full of germs. That disease, something to do with rats. With a huge effort, she fought her way back up, keeping her mouth clamped tightly shut. She could see Victoria struggling to manoeuvre Will's slippery, unresponsive body up to the grass. Pippa chose that moment to kick off, using Helen's stomach as a base, and the force sent Helen under the water again, this time with her mouth open.

By the time she was upright again, coughing and spitting, feeling for the mud at the bottom of the canal, Victoria was on the bank next to Will's prone form. Helen took a step, registering something hard underfoot. She had just staggered within reach of the side when Will leapt up with a triumphant shout, and ran away down the towpath, Victoria in enraged pursuit.

Her arms were shaky, and she wasn't sure if they'd have the strength to pull her out. Everyone else had disappeared. She scrabbled for a foothold in the stonework of the side until, with a final effort, she rolled over and ended flat on her stomach. It was probably a good thing no one was there, she thought, to see her flop about like a whale. She lay there, panting, wondering how much canal water you had to swallow before you died. The sun was warm against her back. Voices were lifted behind the cottage, and a door banged. As she heard the voices coming closer, she rolled over. The sun glinted from the water into her eyes, and a jolt of pain sliced up from her foot.

She was sitting on the bank trying not to feel queasy at the sight of the blood oozing when the others came back. Victoria was behind Will, pushing him forwards in short jerky runs.

"And now you can get back in and fetch the dinghy, you little . . ." Her voice tailed off. "What did you do?"

They gathered in a cluster, Pippa pushing her head through to see what was happening. Seth had come with them, and he took hold of her foot to examine it more closely. His hands were warm, and big enough to surround her foot. She tried not to mind being sopping wet, her hair dripping in tails down her back. Not so much a water nymph as a water goblin. She heard herself make a hiccupping sob. The cut was nasty, slicing right across her instep.

"Ouch." Seth gave her a half-smile. "Glass in the mud probably. Dangerous business, swimming in the canal."

"I didn't want to. I was helping Pippa when . . ." She heard her voice wobble and dug her nails hard into her forearm ". . . when Will pretended he was drowning."

"So you went in for the rescue and ended up the casualty?" His voice was calm. "I wondered why Will was running so fast." He pulled out a handkerchief, and started to wrap it around her foot. "I was a Scout for about three weeks once. I wonder if I can remember what to do?"

He helped her up, and slid an arm around her back.

"Come on. Let's see if you need a doctor." He turned to the others. "Give her some space. And get the dinghy back in."

The kitchen was quiet, the dust on the window filtering the sunlight down to a manageable hue. Seth swept the pile of books stacked up on the chair off on to the floor, and supported her down into it.

"Now let's see what we've got." He picked up her foot again, making her gasp with an indrawn breath as he dabbed at it with a handkerchief.

"Is it bad?" She risked taking a peek. "I don't want to get that thing from the rats."

He placed it down again as gently as if it was made of glass.

"I don't think you need to worry as long as it's bleeding. Pushes all the nasties out." He gave her a grin. "And at least you don't need to worry about sharks."

Her foot was soaking in a bowl of warm, sharp-smelling water by the time Pippa, followed by the other two, sidled in.

"Are you all right?" Victoria spoke first, her hands gripping Will's arm up behind his back. "Will has something to say to you. Don't you?" she hissed at him, giving his arm a further twist.

Will kept his eyes fixed on the floor. "Sorry." He shot a glance towards Helen's foot. "Will you get gangrene? Victoria said your foot would fall off." He gave a yelp as Victoria dug in her fingers. "I only wanted to know — it was you that said it!" His voice was aggrieved.

"That's enough." Seth levered himself off the table edge and herded the twins out through the door. "Off you go and play." On an afterthought, he opened the door again and shouted after them: "And stay out of the water. Get the hosepipe out."

Victoria turned to him, one eyebrow lifted. "We haven't got a hosepipe, have we?"

Seth smiled over at Helen. "Yeah, well, it'll give them something to do, won't it?" Helen smiled back as an involuntary shiver ran down her torso. "You need to get some dry clothes on. Do you want to go home?"

Victoria butted in. "No, she can come up to my room, I'll find her something."

"I'll put a plaster on it."

Helen closed her eyes and let herself feel comforted. It was almost worth the pain.

"Does it hurt a lot?" Victoria was on the floor, leaning on the side of the bed. Helen was lying on it, the jumble of covers pushed down at the end so her foot could rest on them. Seth had said the cut wasn't too bad, but it was throbbing so much she wasn't sure she believed him.

Helen nodded. "A bit."

"It'll feel better once the aspirins get going."

They were silent for a few minutes, then Victoria spoke, this time without turning.

"I was talking to Moira yesterday."

"Oh. Right." Talk of Moira made the emptiness of the past few days sweep back through Helen's chest. She could feel tears coming. It was the shock, she told herself, only to be expected with the scare she'd had, and her foot. She cleared her throat and tried to sound normal. "Is she still on the boat?"

"Yeah, for the time being. She was talking about going to London. There's a big CND rally being planned, and Seth might be going down with her. Me too, if I can get them to say yes. She's got some friends in a squat we could stay with."

"Squat" was a horrible word. Helen closed her eyes and saw it written on the back of her eyelids, the letters swelling in a monstrous dance. She missed the beginning of Victoria's next sentence.

". . . which is weird, don't you think?"

"What? Sorry." She rubbed her eyes and pushed herself up on to one elbow. "Who was what?"

"Dave, you know, the guy on the boat?" Victoria linked her fingers together and stretched up her arms, leaning backwards at the same time. She gave a satisfied grunt. "I reckon he's done some pretty dangerous stuff. Moira started to say something, and he made her shut up." Her arms dropped back down by her sides, and she studied Helen with narrowed eyes. "I wonder what it feels like, knowing you've killed someone?"

"I don't want to know." Helen pictured him, sitting on his stool with that half-smile on his face as he watched her trying not to look at Moira. "Besides, why would he come here?"

"Even terrorists have to live somewhere." Victoria got up and went over to the window, craning her head sideways as if she was trying to see the boat. "And what better place to hide?"

"I bet she's making it up." Helen closed her eyes, the blood in her eyelids throbbing in time with her foot. "You don't get terrorists, anyway. Not in this country."

"What about the IRA?"

Helen felt too tired to argue. She let the silence stretch out.

"Which reminds me —" there was the sound of Victoria crossing the room — "I wanted to show you something."

The door opened and Victoria's feet thumped off down the stairs. Tiredness washed over Helen's body; she buried her face in the pillow and tried not to breathe. When she heard Victoria come back, she pretended to be asleep.

"Helen?" She felt Victoria nudge at her arm, but it was too much effort to respond. "Helen?" The whisper came again, then retreating feet and the closing of the door.

CHAPTER
EIGHTEEN

2013, Manchester: 12.30 p.m.

The shutters go up with their usual rattle and I remember, yet again, that the windows need cleaning. It doesn't matter, though, because the sun only hits this bit of the street for a short burst in the early morning before it disappears behind the shadow of the concrete multistorey opposite. I'm only going through the motions today, and I wouldn't even be doing that if it weren't for the fact I need something to occupy me that doesn't require emotional energy.

Larry bought the place before the Northern Quarter was redeveloped, for a clientele of solitary men who slipped in unnoticed and didn't need shiny window displays. The shop's uninviting position, on a tatty, curving access road, was a bonus then. The sex shops have largely disappeared, but a niche in the market they'd unexpectedly unearthed — selling D. H. Lawrence and Henry Miller — had led Larry into the second-hand book market. By the time I started to work there, it made up most of his trade, and his shop was part of a circuit browsed by wordless bibliophiles, as discreet in their way as the previous clients. They've mostly gone as well now and, with the tramlines and the bus station cutting us off from the bars and vintage shops and no Larry behind the till recounting his stories, there's not much point in making the effort.

There's a customer waiting today. He follows me in, and stands in front of the crime and thriller shelf, pretending that's what he is in here for. He's going to be disappointed. When Larry was alive and in charge, that bookcase was filled with books about walking: Wainwright guides and Ordnance Survey maps, that sort of thing. The men would come in and pause to scan the shelves before strolling around the end and through one of those curtains made of strips of plastic in primary colours. Larry didn't let me go in there, even though it was OK for me to take the money and wrap the magazines into a brown paper roll. One of the reasons he had against me when I first applied for the post of assistant was that I'd remind them of their daughters, put them off buying, but he could see I needed him. So I got to spend my days browsing the shelves out front, learning them by heart.

Some of them drop by occasionally, the old blokes who haven't kept up with the times, and it's always eyes right for the maps, then a step forwards before stopping dead as it hits them: the magazines aren't there any more, the curtain has gone. They tend to buy a couple of thrillers to save face, though some of them like to talk about the old days. I keep a few *Playboys* in Larry's memory. *Never forget*, he would say, tapping his fat forefinger down hard on the counter, *how many writers got their break in* Playboy. *Quality publication*. I often wonder what he'd make of the marketplace today, the online porn, the disappearing second-hand bookshops. He'd have laughed, I think, and set himself up on eBay.

On the wall by the till, there are some framed photographs from his heyday. Larry in his black overcoat, hair combed to the side, hobnobbing with a forgotten comedian. Larry at the dog races, next to a man with a trophy tucked in the crook of his sleeve. There's even one where he has his arm around the shoulder of a very young George Best. They're gritty, grey-toned. I remember the photos Victoria showed me of Alice and Jakob and Piet, the London of the sixties. The same time in history, perhaps, but it might as well have been happening in a different universe.

I close my eyes to let the memories brush through my mind. The runaway Alice, picked up on a street corner by the young artist, who falls in love with her face and her body, painting her into his best work only to lose her to his glamorous brother. I feel Victoria fixing me with a compelling gaze and hear her voice: "You can never talk about it to anyone. I shouldn't be telling you, really." Alice had the most beautiful face I had ever seen, her eyes forever fixed elsewhere. She was the princess in the tower, the lady in the mist. I would have believed anything I was told about her. But was it even Victoria who told me about Alice being a runaway? I press my fingertips against my eyelids, letting the specks of colour swirl and retreat. I don't trust my recollection of the past any more.

At the end of the day, whatever their provenance, these are stories belonging to a summer which existed outside of the bounds of everyday reality. And its abrupt ending, its total, final and underlining cut-off, leaves them floating there, fairy tales from a world so enclosed I am no longer certain what was real and what I had created for myself. The globe clouds over but, before the pictures disappear, I catch sight of Moira, the bad fairy taking the colour away, her mocking face reminding me that I am, will always be, on the outside.

Something falls to the floor and brings me out of the past. I'd forgotten there was anyone else in here. The man who came in behind me has knocked a pile of books over. I pretend I haven't noticed as he bends and stacks them on the floor before crossing to the records. They're on the far side, the big squares of the LPs stacked upright so browsers can flick them forwards one at a time, the seven-inch singles heaped into a box. I keep my eye on him. Not in case he helps himself — I can't work myself up to worry about that, not today. He picks up a record, one from the back of the box, and I send out desperate thought waves. *Not that one,* I ask. *Please, not that one, not today.* He glances round as if he can hear and takes a step away. Then, as he seems about to leave, he walks quickly back, picks up one of the albums and comes up to the desk. It's some obscure prog-rock group. I wave his money away in relief. Take it, it's not worth anything, have a nice day.

When he's gone, I go over to the box and flick through the records myself. There it is, at the back, the cardboard cover foxed at the corners, but the drummer still smiling, the snail serene in his endless slide. It had turned up in a job lot from a house clearance ten years ago. Cumulus. A message from Victoria to me. I wanted

182

to hide it away, to keep it safe, but something stopped me. It's not like I believe in all that stuff, but I left it in the box, with the three-for-fifty-pence Top of the Pops and James Lasts and Funky Aerobics, waiting for the day one of them would come in for it. I didn't need to look at it, didn't need to know when. It was enough that it was there, keeping a tiny crack open for them to come back to me. If some random customer found it and bought it, I would never see the Dovers again. It was my gamble with the universe.

Could that be the other reason I've opened the shop up today? All these years, the record has been there and Victoria has been elsewhere, on another planet. Today, she is in Manchester. Who's to say she hasn't brought the others with her? Piet, Alice. The twins. Seth. My fingers tap on the sides of the box. They could arrive early, take some time to explore. They might well be on the lookout for a dusty-fronted store with a box of old LPs. I go back to my stool, aware of every passing shadow, and I reach for the book I keep under the counter. It's dog-eared and stained, with a cracked spine and only half a cover. *Ulysses*. A relic from another life, almost the only thing I took with me when I left. Altogether, I've probably read it at least three times, but never in the right order. It's become the answer when my mind is unsettled. I don't have to know where I am, and I don't have to remember who is who or what is what. I can open it at any page and let the world retreat.

CHAPTER
NINETEEN

1983

The abandoned glasshouses were majestic in their dereliction. They went on and on, some sheltering the dried and twisted remnants of what might once have been tomato plants. Victoria had been the one to find them, even though they were no more than ten minutes' walk from Helen's house, going across the fields. Once they were inside, they could have been anywhere. It was, Helen thought, a bit creepy. Victoria led Helen through space after space, glass crunching under their feet, fugitive wafts of humid growth dissipating around them. The glass magnified the sun to a vicious level of intensity.

"Didn't I say it was amazing? Wasn't it worth leaving your stupid book?" Victoria spoke in a low voice, as if afraid of being overheard. "I can't believe you've never been here before."

Helen kicked at a stone. "I didn't know they were here. You can't see them from the road or anything. And my foot still hurts."

Victoria giggled. "Why are we whispering? There's no one around." She stuck her fingers into her mouth and let out a long, shrill whistle.

A tremulous shiver ran through the air, as if the glass edges were responding to the sharp wave of sound. Helen held her breath, prepared for glittering shards to rain down on their heads, for the remains of the plants to turn and crawl towards them with grasping tendrils. Nothing happened. The surrounding fields remained quiet; they could have been at the end of the world.

Victoria bent down, grasped a stone and swung her arm around in an arc. From high above their heads came the sound of glass breaking.

Once again, Helen held her breath, but any possible repercussions would have been inaudible in any case, drowned by the triumphant whoops from Victoria, who was already gathering a handful of pebbles for her next throw. She straightened up, saw Helen's face, and stopped.

"What's wrong with you?"

Helen hesitated. "I don't know, I mean, we could get into trouble . . ." Her voice tailed off. How could she explain the level of her discomfort? It was wrong: there would be consequences.

"You honestly believe there's someone out there who's worried about how many panes of glass are left?" Victoria's tone was both incredulous and scathing. "Have you seen the holes? It's like . . . it's like . . ." She screwed up her eyes, grappling for the right metaphor. "It's like poking at a dead dinosaur with a matchstick." She looked up at Helen and grinned. "No one will care! Now come on, throw!" and she lifted her arm and let the stones in her hand trickle over Helen's head.

"Stop it!" Helen turned, more than half-inclined to walk off. There had been dust in with the stones, and she could feel it thickening her hair and sticking to the sweat on her neck. She was too angry to trust herself to say anything, and had a satisfying vision of throwing Victoria herself through the glass walls.

"Come on." Victoria's voice was wheedling now, a hint of a laugh at its tail, and she started to rub at Helen's head.

"Get off." Helen wriggled away, running through the doorway into the next greenhouse. Victoria followed, and Helen dodged behind an abandoned workbench. It was too hot to keep running, though. She tipped her head down and ruffled at her hair to get the grit out.

Victoria scooped up another handful of stones. "There isn't anyone to care, you know." She threw the whole lot, hard, against the end panes. The stones bounced off and scattered, too small and spread out to make an impact. She cast a glance about and took a step towards some bigger stones piled in a corner, then shrugged the canvas rucksack she was wearing off her shoulders and put it down, squatting beside it in the dust as she undid the buckles.

"Have you got a drink in there?" Helen asked, trying to make light of the situation. "I'll do anything you want for something cold and wet."

"No." Victoria was shielding the bag with her body as if on purpose. "Piet let me borrow it. I need to get the settings right."

When she stood up, she was holding an expensive camera with a long lens. She pointed it towards Helen, squinting through the viewfinder, then held it out in front of her, doing something with the dials on the back.

"Does he know you borrowed it?"

Victoria kept her head down as she replied. "You have such a suspicious mind." She positioned the camera in front of her face again but carried on talking. "What I want is an action shot of you breaking the glass."

"No."

"Why?"

"Because I'd be the one who got in trouble. On film." Helen went back to the workbench and leaned against it, her back half-turned. She heard a click from behind.

"OK." Victoria's response was unexpected. Helen swivelled in surprise, but Victoria carried on, as if she was thinking aloud. "I can come back another time. Not the twins, though. I'll have to ask Moira."

There was a half-brick lying a few feet from her. Without letting herself stop to consider, Helen stooped to grab it. The smash was intoxicating, the pleasure of destruction unexpected. She could hear the camera clicking away behind her.

"I hope you got that, I'm not doing it again." She heard her voice shake, felt the remnants of the adrenaline rush burn at her skin.

"This would be a great place to practise for an insurgency." Victoria had let the camera dangle on its strap and was juggling a stone between her hands.

"A what?"

187

"An insurgency, like plotting to overthrow a government."

"I know what an insurgency is, thank you." Helen took a deep breath. She was feeling a bit dizzy. "I meant, why an insurgency?"

"It's so boring sometimes." Victoria threw her stone up in the air, hitting it away with her palm as it came down. "Moira was telling me about all these campaigns she's been in. Barricades and sit-ins. And revolutions."

"How many revolutions has Moira been in? She's making half of it up."

"How would you know?" Victoria headed towards the entrance. "You haven't heard her stories."

Helen followed her; the air outside was almost cool in comparison to the still air of the glasshouses.

"It'd be fun, changing things," Victoria carried on. "And revolutionaries have that cool vibe."

"Not so cool when they're dead. Or locked up."

Victoria reached a patch of semi-shade and flung herself down, setting the camera carefully upright on her stomach. With her eyes closed, she started to feel around in her pockets.

"Nope, not even got any gum." She peered up at the sun. "I need a drink so much!"

The sun was white above their heads, the heat making its edges indistinct, bleaching out the blue of the sky.

Helen perched herself on a fallen tree trunk. "What would get in the way of revolution the most: too much heat or too much cold?" She pulled at a loose piece of bark and tried to fan herself with it.

Victoria remained where she was, eyes closed. "The cold. It freezes your brain and jams up your guns. That's why Che ended up in Bolivia instead of Greenland."

Helen thought about the poster on Victoria's wall, but in her mind's eye, the face was the drummer's. "But would you be able to kill someone just because they didn't agree with you?"

Victoria opened her eyes, screwing them up against the brightness to study Helen's face in apparent perplexity. "Your entire family has been wiped out by an evil dictator and there's someone in front of you who represents the whole rotten system and you have a gun. It's a no-brainer." She closed her eyes again. Clearly no further discussion was necessary.

Helen could feel a wave of stubbornness building up in her brain. "I wouldn't shoot them. It still wouldn't be right."

"OK, I won't call on you when the revolution comes." Victoria blew up into her hair. "But I can tell you one thing, if it's this hot I'm going to demand a siesta."

They stayed where they were for another silent few minutes. Helen slid down until she was sitting on the ground, her back against the trunk. If she tipped her head back, she could see plane tracks crossing each other, turning the sky into a huge web. How many people were up there? Thousands, all reading books or watching films, some of them gazing down at where she was sitting. Were the glasshouses within sight? She imagined someone glancing out, bored with their newspaper or trying to avoid a conversation. They would briefly catch the sunlight reflecting back from all those neglected roofs, but wouldn't have a clue about her and Victoria, down on the ground and discussing insurgency.

"We could do anything we wanted here, and no one would know." She felt it as a great revelation.

"Yeah, well, that's what I've been trying to tell you." Victoria propped herself up slightly and shook her head with the weariness of a long-ignored elder. "You could strip naked and run around with a frog on your head if you wanted." She paused and squinted up at Helen. "I mean, don't. Not while I'm here."

"OK." Helen closed her eyes again and rubbed a shoulder against the trunk behind her to get rid of an itch. "If I feel the urge, I'll find something else. A . . . a . . ." She let her head slump. "No good, can't think of anything else that would sit still."

"And a frog would sit still?"

"A dead frog would."

They lapsed into silence again. Helen stretched her arms out to either side, palms down, feeling the angular edges of the bark against the skin on the inside of her arm. She felt suddenly happy, as if a balloon was being inflated in her chest, the world spread wide out around her.

"What's so funny?" Victoria sounded drowsy. Helen hadn't realized she'd made any noise.

"I dunno, it's —" She broke off. Was somebody there? The rush of adrenaline was back, making her fingertips tingle. It came again, some way into the acres

190

of glass and frame, but surely there. A person-shaped shadow. The owner, come to kick them out? A peeping Tom?

She reached out a foot and gave Victoria a gentle kick. "Look. Over there."

Victoria followed the direction of her nod. The shadow had gone, but they both heard the sound of glass shifting under someone's foot. For a second they held each other's gaze, and then Victoria was up and running, camera in one hand, while Helen scrambled to catch up, one shoe falling off. She paused, trying to tug it back on, but it wouldn't go. She could hear Victoria calling in a loud whisper for her to get a move on. The footsteps were coming closer.

Giving up, shoe in her hand, she started to run again, a half-limp, keeping to the ball of her bare foot, hoping the plaster over her cut would stay in place. When she reached Victoria, they clasped hands and ran on together, laughter starting to force its way out in huge, breathless waves, until they stumbled back into the lane.

"Let's go to your house." Victoria came to a halt outside the gate. "I need a drink."

CHAPTER
TWENTY

They found a bottle of lemonade at the back of a kitchen cupboard, and Helen chipped at the icebox until she could force out the ice-cube tray. She filled a couple of glasses with what she dug out, and carried them through, the bottle wedged under her arm. Victoria was already in the sitting room, sprawled across the sofa.

"Have you got anything we could add to it?" she asked as Helen began to loosen the cap, her hand curved over in case the bubbles came out too fast.

"Yes, but we can't —" Helen paused, glancing at the drinks cupboard. It wasn't as if anyone ever checked it. "I suppose we should celebrate our escape." She screwed the lid back on again. "Hang on a sec."

The car was gone and, when she stuck her head around the garage door, there were no signs of life. The boat was starting to change, a framework sketching out the shape of a cabin, some of the gaps already filled with pale sheets of ply. The smell of fresh sawdust hung in the air. Helen climbed the ladder to be sure, but the boat was empty, the new engine marooned on its base, the old office chair fallen on to its side.

When she got back to the house, Victoria greeted her with a wave of a bottle.

"Martini! The perfect afternoon cocktail!" She handed Helen a glass of lemonade and poured some in.

"You could have waited 'til I was back." Helen took a sip. "My dad might have been right behind me."

"S'OK, we'd have given him some." Victoria sat back and gestured to the television. "Now, entertainment!" She already had hold of the remote, and she cycled through the channels: a quiz show, someone in a garden, horse racing. She paused on a black-and-white film, then carried on round before ending back on the film.

"But it's in French," Helen groaned. "I'm too tired to read subtitles."

"Then you'll have to guess at what's going on, won't you." And Victoria dropped the remote down beside her and settled back with her drink.

The film had finished and Mick still wasn't back. Had he said where he was going? Helen didn't think so, and she felt a buzz of annoyance. It was fine for him to shout when he didn't know where *she* was. Victoria had wandered into the kitchen and was eating a slice of bread from the packet. Helen followed her and started to hunt for butter, but a thought struck her as she opened the fridge door.

"You know what?"

"No I don't. What?" Victoria pushed her to one side and helped herself to a pot of jam.

"The actress in the film, the one with the short hair?" She picked the butter up and turned back to the table. "She's on the cover of the book Piet gave me, the French one."

Victoria looked blank.

"You know, the one I was telling you about? Where they're on the beach, the father and daughter?" She didn't want to say the name again — Victoria had been scathing about her accent — but she wasn't even trying to remember. "*Bonjour Tristesse*."

"Better, much better." She'd known all along. Helen decided to ignore the jibe.

"She was beautiful, wasn't she, the actress? With her hair and everything?"

"Well, short hair isn't hard. Take a pair of scissors, *voilà*!" Victoria leaned over the sink and filled her glass with water.

Helen sighed, and took another bite. "Piet said that you would suit short hair, but I should keep mine long."

"You've been doing a lot of talking with my uncle lately." Victoria poked her head forwards, one eyebrow raised and the other scrunched down. "Are you sure there's nothing going on there? I mean, he does find long hair veeeery sexy . . ."

"No!" Helen felt her cheeks redden. "I mean, he's your *uncle*."

Victoria gave her an assessing look. "I don't see why you can't be a French girlie, if that's what you want. Let's swap, I'll cut yours off, and you do mine."

"I don't know." Helen drank the remainder of her glass and reached for a knife. She was starting to feel a bit sick. "Tomorrow, perhaps."

"Although," Victoria continued, giving Helen a poke. "Seth is quite into long hair as well, if you ask me."

They'd no sooner drifted back into the sitting room than Mick arrived. He didn't say anything, but sat down, a four-pack of beer to hand, and reached for the remote, turning over to some documentary. Helen managed to edge the empty bottle of Martini round the side of the sofa, and, as the voices on the TV droned on, closed her eyes to avoid the jerky procession of images that were making her head swim. It was soothing, lying there without having to talk. She didn't realize she'd slept until she came to. The credits were rolling up the screen and her dad was speaking, but she missed it. Victoria, though, was jumping straight in.

"But they were fighting for what they believed in! That's got to be better than sitting back and pretending everything's OK."

Mick reached for another can of beer, shaking his head. "They were half-arsed, self-indulgent and irresponsible. They killed innocent people and destroyed property for no good reason." He tipped his head back for a swallow. "And for what? Not a lot, as far as I can see."

Victoria took a deep breath and leaned forwards to reply.

Helen stood up, too quickly, to create a diversion. "Shall we go upstairs?" She walked across to the door, trying to appear casual, but Victoria ignored her.

"It's better than sticking your head in the sand. Look what happened to the Germans when they tried doing that."

"Well, I'm going to put the kettle on." Helen said it to no one. As she let the door swing to, the voices continued. She filled the kettle, then sat down at the table, vaguely surprised to see it was nearly dark outside, and rested her head on her folded arms. When the kettle boiled, it took her several minutes to be bothered to stand up. She noticed her book, jammed down the side of the bread bin from when she'd been reading it this morning. She took it back to the table, but the words swam around and she let it drop.

She'd drunk most of her tea by the time Victoria clattered through.

"What are you reading?" She tipped the book sideways to see the cover, knocking over Helen's almost empty mug. A small puddle of cold tea ran out on to the table. "Sorry."

Helen wiped at it with her sleeve. "Not reading, more giving up. It's *Moby Dick*. Did you read it?"

"What, the book? No, skipped to the end. Everybody dies." Victoria was over by the window now, gazing out into the dark. "Can I have a cup of tea?"

"There's the kettle." Helen rested her chin on her hands. "So did you come to any conclusions in there?"

Victoria picked a mug up from beside the sink, peered inside and rinsed it briefly under the tap. "Not exactly. East is east, and all that." She opened a cupboard, shut it, opened the next one. "But it was fun. And he'll be swept away in the new order, anyhow."

"Second on the right, the thin one." Helen got up. It was easier to get it herself. "And you call that fun?"

"Well, you're out here reading *Moby Dick*. Wild."

"It's from your list."

"Oh yeah." Victoria picked the book up again. "We'll have to finish that one day." She fell back in a chair. "Sugar. I want lots of sugar."

Helen made herself some more tea while she was up. The garden was impenetrable beyond the window, a blank darkness where anything could be happening. She drew the blind.

"Can I stay over?" Victoria was leaning on the table in mock exhaustion. "I can't face the walk home."

"I guess. We'll have to get some cushions from the sofa."

"Oh, your bed's wide enough. We can go top to tail, then we won't disturb your dad. He's having a sleep to recover." Victoria spent a minute stirring her tea. She lifted the spoon out, watching the swirl of the tea as it carried on with its momentum before dipping the spoon down again to make the circling stop. "Did you stay because you felt sorry for him?"

It took Helen a minute to catch up. "What? Oh . . ." Sorry wasn't the word. She had stood there on that awkward, hideous day with her mother's explanations still hanging in the air, and she had looked into her father's face and seen the defeat and she'd made her decision.

"A bit." She shook her head to rid herself of the memory. "Anyway, who'd want to live with my mum? She's a nightmare."

CHAPTER
TWENTY-ONE

Helen slept on the floor in the end, on the spare winter quilt she'd remembered was kept on top of the wardrobe. It took a long time to get to sleep and then she dreamed of breaking glass and bombs. When she woke up in the morning, there was no sign of Victoria. She got dressed and went downstairs, checking the rooms before going out to stick her head around the garage door. Piet was sitting astride the gunwale holding up a piece of ply, and she recalled what Victoria had said about him liking long hair. How would she feel if he did, well, think of her in that way? A wave of disconcerting warmth tingled through her stomach as he glanced up. She was glad she was in the shadows.

"After your dad?" He had seen her, then.

She was about to shake her head when Mick's voice came from inside the boat.

"Too busy. If there's no milk, she'll have to go to the shop by herself." Piet caught her eye and winked. "Teach her to get up earlier," the voice carried on.

"Have you seen Victoria?" Her voice came out in a croak, and Piet cupped a hand around his ear. "Victoria?" she said, more loudly.

He shook his head. "Try the cottage."

The back door was open but there was nobody about.
Helen called out, her voice absorbed into the empty
space with no reply. She had been there before when
the cottage was empty and it had felt friendly, ready for
her. Today it seemed to be waiting for something. She
hovered outside, wondering what to do. A flapping of
something behind made her jump, but when she
turned, it was only a T-shirt hanging on the washing
line. She put a foot inside, straining for a sense of life. A
box of cereal lay on its side on the table, cornflakes
spilling out in a scatter of orange. It didn't necessarily
signify that anyone had been there, eating breakfast.
The Dovers all grabbed handfuls in passing at any time.
She stepped back out again. Had she missed Victoria?
She was probably back at the house, wondering where
Helen was. But the house had been empty . . . There'd
be no harm in running up the stairs to check Victoria's
bedroom.

She was halfway across the sitting room when she
sensed something was wrong. She paused, waiting for
her eyes to adjust to the dim light. The room smelled of
stale cigarette smoke. Nothing so very unusual. One
of the curtains hung off its rail, the fabric falling in a
bunched-up pile at the end of the sofa. The bundle
twitched, and Helen had to stifle a cry. Then the outline
took on a shape. It was Alice, rocking herself in tiny
jerks, her hands crossed over and gripping her
shoulders. Above her was the oil painting, the whiteness
of the painted skin glowing out in the half-dark. Helen
took a step back, trying again to locate sounds to tell

her where someone, anyone, was. But the house was quiet and still, other than a relentless low humming, which seemed to be coming from Alice.

Without warning, Alice's head came up, her face barely visible under the curtain of hair. It made Helen gasp again, the reflex moment of shock leading into an equally automatic giggle. The high-pitched sound lingered in the air, but Alice didn't appear to have heard. She had stopped rocking and her gaze was fixed on a point not quite in line with Helen's own eyes. As Helen waited, her voice picked up again, this time in a rapid garble. Helen resisted the urge to glance over her shoulder. Was there someone there, a shadow, a weight in the air? She couldn't check, though; she was hypnotized by the force of Alice's focus. She was going to have to do something. Should she aim for minimal disturbance and slide out of the frame without saying anything? Or should she at least try to help, hold out a hand to connect, even comfort? The thought made her squirm.

Before she could decide, Alice's tone of voice changed and her eyes began to focus.

"Was it you?" She sounded puzzled.

Helen managed to shake her head. Alice seemed normal, as if the past few minutes hadn't happened. But the question, what did it mean? She took a step back as Alice floated to her feet and came closer, one hand extended until it was cupping Helen's face. She put her own head to one side.

"You're not the sort." Her hand fell. "Where did he go?"

Helen sensed the air behind her change again, but this time in a way she could recognize. A second later there were footsteps, but she didn't turn. She was pinned by Alice's gaze: blue, intent, demanding something of her she wasn't able to give.

"Help me find him." Alice's voice was urgent, and her hand gripped at Helen's wrist. "My Jakob. You can help me."

Her pulse quickened under the pressure of Alice's fingernails. Again, she felt the urge to say something. The presence behind her intensified and Seth was there, prising Alice's fingers away and wrapping them around his own hand instead. He stepped in front of her, repeating a barely audible sequence of words. Eventually his eyes met Helen's, and he gave a nod. She slid out of the room but hesitated when she reached the back door, trying to decide what to do. There was Victoria to track down, but the decision of where to look for her felt overwhelming. Besides, Victoria would want to talk, and Helen was struggling to make sense of what had taken place. She found herself looking at the apple tree. It seemed as good a place as any to go and think.

She was still up there when Seth came out. Helen watched him come out of the door and stop, looking around. She gave a half-call, but he didn't seem to hear, so she stayed in her perch and watched him. The sunlight glowed through the white fabric of his shirt as he linked his fingers together and pushed his arms above his head. A slice of belly bisected with a thread of dark hair showed above the waist of his jeans. He leaned to one side and then the other, and then stretched up again to the centre before letting his torso flop down. His hair brushed the grass and his shirt fell over his shoulders. His back was golden and the skin seemed delicate, the bump of his spine leading down to the flat triangles of his shoulder blades. Helen felt her chest swell, a wave of goosebumps run over her skin. A narrative reeled through her head so fast that she only saw the end picture: Seth standing behind her on a sunny beach, running his hand through her perfectly cropped hair.

Footsteps came from the side of the house. A voice sounded, and she came out of her daydream to see Piet approaching. He walked up to Seth, laid a hand on his shoulder and leaned in to say something, a concerned expression on his face.

". . . talking about Jakob again." Seth was speaking now as he and Piet walked up the garden. Helen gripped the branch more tightly. She couldn't let them know she was here. A second earlier she could have called down, made it casual, but the moment had gone. She felt a tickle in her throat, needed to cough. They'd come to a halt right below her.

"I've put her to bed." Seth was talking. "She was asleep when I left her."

"What set it off this time?" Piet struck a match, lit a cigarette, and Helen felt the smoke blow past her face.

"It's possible she's not been taking her medication. There were too many pills left over." There was a pause, and she heard the faint rasp of Seth's hands in his hair. "Would it not be best to tell her?"

Piet had put an arm around Seth's shoulders. Helen could almost feel the weight of it on her own neck. On the top of his head, the hair was thin, the glimpse of sun-reddened scalp on show only to her.

"Seth, I know it's hard. But you're going to have to trust me." She saw Piet's arm lift and give Seth a gentle shake. Her heart felt as if it was never going to beat again. Piet's next few words made no sense to begin with.

"Jakob was bad news from the start."

Seth had his head down and was picking at the bark of the trunk. He didn't appear to be listening. Piet carried on talking: "But Alice wouldn't see it like that, she never did."

Seth gave his shoulders a jerk, dislodging Piet's hand, and punched a fist into the tree. Helen, gripping on to her branch, felt the tree shudder. Seth pulled back for another strike, but this time Piet caught his hand before it connected.

"Why did he have to die, though?" Seth sounded on the edge of tears. Helen held her breath. Victoria thought her father was alive, Helen was sure about that. So what was Seth talking about? She bent her head, torn between catching Seth's low voice and staying hidden.

"I know, buddy, I know. But he wouldn't have stayed away. It's better like this." Piet rubbed his hand on the nape of Seth's neck. It looked huge, a weathered knot against Seth's smooth skin. His voice changed. "Did you say Helen was there?"

Helen froze, panic flooding down her arms and up her spine.

"Yeah." Seth sounded flat. Helen dared a glance down — he was examining the skin of his knuckles. "But Alice wasn't making much sense. I got her out of the way as soon as I could."

Out of the way. She felt the words hit her, one at a time. She hadn't shared a special moment with him after all. She was nothing but a nuisance, intruding on their family.

"OK. I don't want her involved. Victoria's been spinning her tales, let's leave it there." Piet held both of Seth's shoulders now, forcing him to engage. "Are you all right?" He waited for a response, which to Helen's watching eyes didn't happen. He seemed satisfied, though, and pulled Seth into a hug. "It's the best way." He sounded as if he was trying to convince himself as much as Seth.

At last they left. Helen kept her grip on the trunk until she was sure they were out of earshot. One leg had gone to sleep and, as she slid down, she caught her T-shirt on the stubby leftover of a branch and scraped a long red trail down her ribs. The tree felt solid in front of her, and she gripped at its roughness, willing the sick giddiness to go. Victoria, she had to find Victoria. But she couldn't tell her. Opposing arguments ran through her mind, catching up with each other and tangling around. A faint sense of importance played an underlying beat, one she tried to ignore. She'd been trusted with a secret, and it was her task not to let Seth down, Piet down. Victoria mustn't know. She ignored the internal voice telling her that she wasn't supposed to know either.

She stood up. The warm air seemed to her to be humming, but whether it was with excitement or indifference, she couldn't tell. She needed to go, though, before Seth or Piet came and found her there. As she went along by the hedge, Mrs Tyler's voice made her jump.

"She sorted out, is she?" The old woman didn't wait for an answer. "Screaming round the garden like that. Enough to scare the crows." She turned away, muttering to herself as she went. With a twist of her head, she spoke again: "I've got the young 'uns here. You tell 'em now. They'll be all right with me."

CHAPTER
TWENTY-TWO

"Where've you been?" Victoria was rooting through the drawer of odd bits under the sink, only lifting her head for a second before going back to her search.

"Trying to find you." Helen stood for a second, the Helen who knew hovering sideways of the Helen who mustn't say. Even as her mouth opened, she wasn't sure which one would win out. "I saw. Mrs Tyler. She's got the twins."

"What does she want, a reward? She's welcome to them."

Beyond the sound of Victoria's rummaging, Helen could hear small, distinct sounds from outside. A bird sang, then stopped. There was a distant whine of engine noise. Victoria's voice punctured the space.

"What have we here?"

She was holding a pair of scissors, proper hairdressing scissors with the extra hooked bit on the lower finger hole. Helen couldn't recall them ever being used, wasn't sure she'd even seen them before. She doubted they would be very sharp; picking them up from the table, she tried an experimental snip across the ends of her own hair, and the blades dragged, pulling at the strands instead of slicing through them.

Her mother's six-weekly visits to the hairdresser and her and her father's less frequent "trims" were still on the calendar, planned in advance for the whole year. Funny, now, with no mother to read them. Had she known when she pencilled them in that the information would be obsolete? Presumably she still had her hair done somewhere in town. Mick, on the other hand, had stopped combing over his balding patch, and his hair now touched the edge of his collar. She should have offered to trim it for him.

Victoria grabbed the scissors back and tried them on the end of her own plait. With a bit of effort, she got through. She turned and gave Helen an assessing look.

"Have you cut anyone's hair before?"

"No. And I'm not starting with yours, so don't even ask."

"Come on, everyone has to start somewhere. I'm sick of having it long." With a challenging stare, Victoria started to hack away right at the top of one of her plaits, working the blades backwards and forwards across the fat strands until she was left with it dangling from one hand.

"Victoria . . ." Helen couldn't hold it in, she had to say something. "You know your mum?"

"Yes, she's bonkers. And what's that got to do with anything?" Victoria dropped the severed hair and held up the other plait. "Now you can balance them up. And if you don't, I'll sneak in one night and cut one sleeve off every item of clothing in your wardrobe." She waved the scissors as if they were a sword, ending the pass with blades pointing at the middle of Helen's forehead.

She leaned in, widening her eyes in mock hypnosis. "And when you've cut my hair, I'm going to cut yours."

Helen reached up and wrapped her fingers around the metal, pulling Victoria's hand away. She pitched her voice at the same singsong tone.

"Oh no, you're not. I don't want any of my hair cut off. And if I did, I wouldn't let you do it."

The plait lay on the table in a limp spiral, the twist starting to unravel where it had been sawn off. She rummaged in the drawer herself and found an elastic band.

"What's that for?" Victoria was watching her, her chair tilted on to its back legs.

"I was going to tie up the top of the plait. You're not going to throw it away, are you?" Victoria's hair was soft in her hands. It looked different to the one hanging over its owner's shoulder, as if it had lost some degree of spirit. She registered a feeling of desolation under her ribcage. Hair is always dead, she thought to herself, don't be so stupid. She wound it round her fist like a bandage, then let the length unravel and fall on to the table.

"Would your mum like to have it?"

Victoria let her chair down with a bang, and picked the plait up herself.

"What for? Not much she could do with it." She held it at arm's length to consider. "Use it for a *Sound of Music* revival?"

Victoria wrapped the plait across her head and tilted the chair sideways so she could see her reflection in the oven door.

"Ah, such a pretty *mädchen!*" The chair wobbled as she tried to keep one hand on the table, one on the plait and stay at the right angle. "*Ach, nein, wie nicht die blumen haben!*"

The chair slipped further and, with a shriek, she slid down on to the floor. Helen bent double and peered down at her.

"Are you OK?"

Victoria was lying on her back.

"Yes, but something's happened to my hair." She waved the plait with one hand and beckoned to Helen with the other. "Come here, I want to tell you something."

Helen crouched down until her head was under the table. Victoria reached to pull at her arm, and she fell sideways, landing with her face next to the amputated hair. She felt it twitch against her skin and pushed it away with a squeal.

"Get it off me! I'll be having dreams about it as it is."

"Yeah, it'll be crawling up the bed." Victoria wiggled it. "And up your pillow . . ." A snort of laughter stopped her from saying what it would do next.

Helen grabbed for Victoria's remaining plait and tried to say something, but already she was giggling too much to get the words out. She waved it, struggling to breathe, feeling Victoria's shoulders shake beside her. She'd never felt this happy before, never.

The second plait also came off in one piece. Helen stood and examined what was left, scissors held at a professional angle. She was beginning to enjoy herself.

"And what would madam like me to do with what we have left?"

Victoria was holding a hand mirror, tilting her head from side to side with a thoughtful expression.

"I think," and now she sounded quite serious, "you're going to cut it all off up here," she ran a hand along her head from her left temple and down to the nape of her neck, "and carry on round the back, and then make what's left hang over the other side and be kind of shaggy."

"You're sure about this?" Helen couldn't quite believe that they wouldn't get into massive trouble at some stage. But then, she reasoned, who was there to care? Piet and Seth had other things to worry about, and Alice — well, would she even notice? Victoria obviously didn't think so. *And*, her mind was whispering, *there's no one to stop you cutting yours off either*.

"Yes, I'm sure." Victoria looked up. "Do it."

The hair kept slithering out from between the blades without warning, leaving an erratic line across the back of Victoria's head, and there were patches of scalp showing through in the odd place. But Helen worked out a bit of a strategy along the way, so it wasn't exactly disastrous. More . . . asymmetric.

Victoria held up the mirror to inspect. "A bit more here." She pointed to the area above her left ear.

Helen had the feel of it now, sliding the scissors back at the moment the blades started biting into the hair. She made a circuit of Victoria's head once more, nicking off the bits that stuck out the most.

"That's enough. I can't stand the tickling any more!" Victoria wrenched the tea towel away from her shoulders, and tipped her head over, rubbing at her scalp with her fingertips.

"Go outside! You're getting it everywhere!"

Victoria stood back up.

"No, it's all right now." She ducked down to see herself again in the front of the oven, and pulled at the hair to spike it out. "How is it?"

"Hmm. Interesting."

Victoria crossed to the sink and ran some water into her hand, wetting the hair over her ears and pulling more strands forwards over her eyes. She looked, thought Helen, like a wild thing, a feral child pulled from the jungle. And, no doubt about it, it suited her.

"Sure you don't want yours done?"

Helen felt herself wobble. The hair massed against her neck was so hot. And Victoria looked amazing.

"You could look like that French film star." Victoria waved the scissors in front of her, using her most coaxing tone. "Come on! Be free!"

"I don't know . . ." Helen could hear herself giving in. "OK . . ."

But as Victoria began to saw at the first chunk of hair, Helen pulled away.

"No, I don't know!" She grabbed at her head with both hands. "I can't do it!"

Victoria chucked the scissors on the table.

"If you say so."

Helen crossed over to the door and reached for the broom.

"Let me think about it —"

But Victoria shrugged and slid off the edge of the chair, placing it carefully back under the table.

"It's up to you, Helen. It's your hair." She pushed past her towards the door. "You never do anything, anyway."

And she was gone.

Helen stood, frozen, holding the broom in front of her. Victoria was so . . . But no, she wasn't going to let her walk away from it this time. She let the handle fall, and slammed out of the door.

"Yes, it is my hair!" She yelled down the path, only to find Victoria in the other direction, towards the garden, watching her with an amused expression.

"All right, all right, no one's saying anything else."

"You . . . you . . ." It was no good. Helen let out a laugh. "Well, you got one bit." She put up a hand to find the place with the chunk missing.

"Go on, let me balance it out. I'll make a good job of it, honest!" Victoria was smiling as well now. "You can do it with a ponytail, it works every time." She drove in on her advantage. "You want to, I can tell. And it's not true you never do anything. Feel the fear. Remember the greenhouses!"

Helen put a hand up level with her chin.

"No further than this."

It worked quite well in the end. Victoria had her gather a bunch of hair together and hold it over her head as she attacked it with the scissors. She did look sort of French, Helen thought to herself, checking in the hand

212

mirror and seeing the short, shaggy layers fall down around her face. She turned, making her lips pout. Victoria pushed her on the shoulder.

"All you need's a beret." She cocked her head to one side. "Is that what I think it is?"

Through the open door came the sound of an ice-cream van. Helen held a finger up. One came by on its regular route around the villages, occasionally pulling in at the end of the lane for a rest before carrying on. The chimes came to a halt.

"Have you got any money?" Victoria was already feeling in her pocket. She pulled out some coins and counted them up.

"Dad's usually got a bit in here." Helen checked in the cup on the fridge top. "Yep. Quick! Let's run!"

It felt good to be running in the toasted air of the afternoon, the ends of her hair just tickling her neck.

Victoria gave her a grin as they reached the van. "Good feeling?"

Helen grinned back and turned to the window, where the man was standing with a resigned expression.

"Icepops. Give us icepops."

They walked back down the lane, holding the frozen tubes by the ends so the top bit would start to melt. Helen held the coolness against her cheek.

"What we need . . ." Victoria paused to suck up the mouthful of the cold liquid pooling at the bottom of her tube ". . . what we need now is a lot of black eyeliner." She stuck her tongue out as far as it would go, squinting down to see the colour. The violent blue of the icepop had already left a streak down the centre. "I've got some in my room, come on."

"In a minute." Helen's tongue was green, the colour draining at every suck from the remaining ice.

A car came up behind them and beeped for them to get out of the way. As it drew level, it slowed down, and the window rolled down. A woman with careful make-up and a padded neckbrace leaned out.

"Helen." Her voice was treacly. "How are you? Mr Weaver and I only came back from Spain this week." She indicated her neck. "I've been having terrible trouble with my cervicalgia." She paused to smooth her already immaculate hair. "How are you and your father doing? I bumped into your mother when we were over in Southport, she said she hasn't seen much of you this summer."

The Weavers' house had been built facing the main road, but the entrance and sweep of gravel drive was some way down the lane. Helen could make out the fancy arches which ran all the way along the house front, as if it was a toy ranch. She could hear her father's voice, *Paid a nice sweetener to the planning to get that through*, and she had a vision of the Weavers as plastic dolls being positioned in their world by a cosmic child playing a game of pretend. That would explain Mrs Weaver's stiff neck. A cough made her realize everyone was waiting for her to reply. What had the question been? She forced herself to concentrate. Something about her dad.

"He's fine." Helen kept her eyes fixed on the corner of the windscreen. A dribble of cool liquid came up and over the side of the icepop, and she darted at it with her tongue. At the same time, she glanced round at Victoria, who, lightning fast, stuck a vivid blue tongue out at her. A huge giggle began to force its way up into her chest.

"And this must be your friend from the cottages." Mrs Weaver turned herself round. "Now, then, is it your father who's driving that van around the place?"

Victoria copied her tone, managing to give her voice an even more patronizing edge but with such a straight face that the older woman looked unsure of herself.

"No, it isn't."

Mrs Weaver waited for more, and then carried on: "Well, whoever it is, Mr Weaver's Rover was almost scratched very badly yesterday, from having to drive so near to the hedge."

"That is terrible," Victoria agreed. "I've never heard of anything so awful in my whole life."

Helen had to start walking away, her shoulders heaving. She heard Victoria finish.

"Perhaps if Mr Weaver would like to pass on his driving schedule to us, we can make sure the road is kept quite clear for him in the future?"

"There is no need to be cheeky, young lady!" The window buzzed up and the car completed the short journey to the Weavers' driveway.

They laughed all the way to the canal, leaning against each other helplessly, repeating fragments of the conversation. Finally, breathless, they sat on the bank with their feet dangling above the water and sucked up the last of the melted ice.

"You know the funniest thing?"

Victoria leaned out to rinse her fingers in the canal. "No, what?"

"Remember the day I met you, when Pippa came round to my garden?"

Victoria nodded. "Yes."

"I thought you were her grandchildren."

"No! Can you imagine?" Victoria imitated Mrs Weaver's voice again. "Now, children, in bed by nine o'clock, or Mr Weaver and I won't have time for our after-dinner games. Chop chop."

She blew up into the hair hanging over her forehead. "It feels funny with it all gone. It's so . . . short." She blew again, her eyes on the canal. When she next spoke, it was a complete non sequitur: "You know when Piet was talking about a party for the boat?"

Helen turned to look at her, wondering where she was going with that. "Yes?"

Victoria sat up, and hugged her knees in. "And we're going to have a bonfire?"

"Yes."

"I've had the best idea."

"What?"

"Can't tell you yet. But if it works, it'll be ace."

216

CHAPTER
TWENTY-THREE

The boat wasn't quite ready on the day it was launched, not in Mick's eyes anyway. But Piet had a friend with a flatbed trailer, and this was the only day he could bring it over. The boat was on the trailer and endless time had been spent pushing it into the right place for Piet to get his van through ready to reverse it down the lane, and still Mick was trying to delay things. Helen could hear him arguing about it as she stood in the lane. The sun was almost too hot to bear. She was supposed to be watching out for cars or people coming down the lane, though it seemed unlikely that anything would be out and about by choice. She fanned herself with a hand that barely disturbed the weight of warm air around her, letting their voices drift by.

"If we can have a couple more days in here . . ." Her dad sounded stubborn.

"We can finish up once she's in the water." Piet's voice was soothing. "It's not as if we're going to have issues with rain."

Helen let herself drop back into the meagre shade of the hedge. *Come on,* she thought. *Make your minds up.*

Right on cue, there was the sound of shoulders being slapped and, a few seconds later, Piet's engine turning over. The boat began to edge out, Piet seeming to have some trouble getting the angle right as he reversed. The shouts of instruction had nothing to do with her, though, and she let them wash around in a meaningless buzz. She was so deep in her abstraction that the boat caught her by surprise as it reared above her. It was taller than ever; oblivious to the raised voices and mayhem below, it inched backwards, its sides crushing into the hedge. To anyone watching from across the fields, Helen thought, the boat would appear to be sailing smoothly down the lane. She heaved herself upright. They were on their way.

It was a tedious process. Piet reversed slowly, with Mick shouting for adjustments in his angle. Seth was walking to one side, watching for any shift in the boat's balance, and the twins were leaping ahead, their yodelling voices getting in the way of Mick's directions. Helen saw him glance at them with annoyance. *Don't say anything*, she begged silently. *Make this a good day*. There had been no sign of Victoria. Helen wondered again what her plan for the launch celebration was.

As the boat reached the water's edge, the wheels of the van slipped, pulled backwards by the weight of the boat. The van's engine roared, keeping her steady. They were all cheering her in, everyone except Mick, whose eyes were fixed on the boat's progress towards the bank. Then a small figure ran out from behind the truck: Will, whooping as he danced down to the point where the

218

wheels of the trailer balanced on the bank's edge. Seth reacted first, keeping his voice level.

"Will, you need to get out of the way." Will took no notice, and Seth raised his voice. "Will, get away, now!"

Will ignored him again, leaning into the trailer, his thin figure braced against the end, his face scarlet with effort. Voices crashed together:

"Brake! Brake!"

"Will, stop!"

The boat was pulling at the restraining presence of the van's engine again, the trailer's wheels slipping with an awful finality. And Will was there, right in their tracks, about to go under as the boat and trailer crashed over the edge and down into the water. Helen couldn't look.

Then the engine cut out, and Will's voice floated up:

"I stopped it! Did you see, Uncle Piet? I stopped it going in the canal!"

Helen opened her eyes. Piet had stopped in time, with the boat balanced, somehow, right on the edge. She caught sight of her father's expression. He was pale, his mouth open in mid-yell, sweat pouring down his cheeks. She held her breath for the explosion, but it didn't come. Instead, he squatted down by the boy and put a hand on his arm.

"Do you know how much that boat weighs, sonny?" His voice was calm, gentle even.

Will shook his head.

"Enough to flatten someone twice your size." Mick pushed himself back to his feet with a groan. "So you need to think twice about putting yourself in front of it,

219

because the boat can't do it for you, all right?" He was studying Will's face. "All right?" he asked again, this time getting a small nod in return. "OK." Mick gave him a push. "You get up on the towpath with your sister."

It was as if everyone else drew breath at the same moment. Will ran to join Pippa, and Piet started his engine again. Only Helen saw how her dad's hand was trembling as he rested it against the side of the boat.

She was graceful, despite her bulk, as she slid down towards the water in slow motion, barely needing the restraining hands on the ropes. She hit the water with a gentle bounce. Helen felt emotion rise up in her throat, for the boat being in the right place, for her dad, for Piet making it happen. She focused on the water. The disturbed surface bobbed around the hull, fussing, checking, approving and, finally, subsiding. Then Piet was behind her, resting a hand on her shoulder.

"We'd best get some ballast into her." He gave her shoulder a friendly shake. "All turned out OK in the end, eh?"

In the evening, Helen had a long bath, reading until it was almost too chilly to be sitting in the water. Downstairs, Mick was sitting in the dark. She hesitated by the door to the sitting room, picking out her dad's shape on the sofa, not certain if he was awake or sleeping.

"Dad?" There was no immediate response, and she trod carefully backwards, heading for the stairs. His voice came as if from a far distance.

"We did it," he began. There was a pause, and he tried again. "She's on her way, isn't she?" His voice was sodden.

"Yes." Helen held the door frame, feeling the edges press into her palms. "Yes, she's afloat."

His face was wet, gleaming in the light coming through the door.

"He could have died."

Helen gripped harder.

"I know." She pictured again the moment, Will straining to hold the boat in place. One moment longer and —

"He's all right, though." She felt strange to be the one doing the reassuring. "He was all right."

"I just . . ." Mick's voice slurred. "I didn't . . ."

She waited a long time for him to finish, even after the rasping of his breath told her he was asleep.

CHAPTER
TWENTY-FOUR

2013, Manchester: 7.30 p.m.

The café is full of people milling around. Nobody seems to be going in to the exhibition. Have I got the time wrong? There is no sign of Victoria, none of the buzz that must surround the centre of the evening's attention. I stand inside the door for a bit, sweaty and awkward, then go to the counter and order a coffee. I don't really want one, but it might make me feel legitimate. As the girl grinds beans and fusses with milk, I use the time to gather information. There is a framed cutting by the till, a glowing review from the culture section of a national newspaper. I imagine a life where this would be exciting, where I would be tugging on someone's sleeve to point it out, *Look, there, that's someone I know.*

I take my cup, careful not to spill any coffee on the tiny macaroon balanced on the saucer's edge, and search for an empty chair. The couple already sitting at the table give those false smiles and then ignore me. There are leaflets propped in a transparent plastic holder and I turn them around to face me. They have the same image as the poster, the one of calm water. I wonder if it was chosen because it truly reflects her memories of the time. I may be wrong, I remind myself. For a blissful second, I wonder if my memories have grown out of proportion, if that summer should be remembered as a time of tranquillity. Or the exhibition may have nothing to do with the canal, with me, at all. I am, I tell myself, going to be disappointed. It's hardly the right word. Disappointment conjures mildness, a small measure of regret. It is a flimsy word, a shallow dip easily escaped. I go to drink my coffee but, before I even take a sip, sharp nausea burns up in my throat. I can't wait any longer. My hand shakes as I put the cup back down in its saucer. A spill snakes across the table and pools under the plastic leaflet holder. I ignore the sideways glance of the woman across the table and go over to the stairs. Nobody stops me.

The sign on the first floor announces a permanent exhibition. I want to skip it and follow the arrows up towards the next level, but a gallery assistant is coming down from there. I wait for her to go past but she stops, and holds an arm out towards the doorway.

"Upstairs is for the Dover launch only," she says. "It will be starting very soon." She smiles an air-hostess smile. "In the meantime, please feel free to experience our permanent collection."

She watches until I am safely out of the way.

I am in a narrow, long space, the opposite of the tall whiteness I was expecting. The walls and ceiling are hung with patterned fabric, but the light level is too low for me to make out the colour. Darkly glowing oils of still-life flowers are surrounded by an aura of light. They alternate with large glass backlit cases in which big, daisy-like flowers have been mounted and left to decay. Even though my consciousness is elsewhere, my mind fogged with apprehension, I am drawn to them. Are the oil paintings as old as they seem? I don't trust my judgement. Is it an elaborate joke? They are labelled as being "in the style of . . ." and the accompanying blurbs talk of statis and change, of what we keep and what we lose over time.

In the final oil painting, a worm emerges from a perfect apple. The apple is balanced against an open book, which in turn is half-covered with a white cloth. The portion of the page that can be seen has writing on it, lightly scribbled, as if the owner jotted the phrase down to remember it for later: *media vita in morte sumus*. I know enough Latin to recognize life and death when I see it, but have to check the label for the translation. *In the midst of life we are in death*. I stand there for a long time, looking at the shine of the apple's skin. It is only when voices tell me that other visitors are on their way that I cany on to the next room.

I pass straight through this time. I don't want to stop again: I need to find the photographs, I need to find them now. There is another room, an unexpected corridor. I hear voices, but can't tell where they are coming from. There is a door, but it won't open. Finally, a right turn brings me back to the staircase.

The hostess is nowhere to be seen.

My legs drag, each foot an inert weight, and when I reach the top I am once again finding it hard to breathe. A tape has been stretched across the entrance, and a sign tells me the exhibition is not yet open. I duck under the frail barrier and take a step inside.

The corridor stretches ahead, lined with small frames. Each frame contains the image of a child, and each child is going somewhere. Some look back over their shoulders, some remain focused on their goal. They are going somewhere I know. With each step they take, I see myself disappearing around a corner. In among these captured moments, I know for certain that I do exist.

The corridor is as long as an optical illusion, and I imagine being trapped here for ever, forever hearing the voices of children calling, always out of reach. I have to feel my way as the lighting dims, and as I grope along, there is the sound of a counting down, the ticking loud and clockless. It takes me a long time to arrive at the closed door. My first push is tentative, and I wonder if it is locked. I try again, and it whispers its way over a thick, bristling mat.

I am alone in near darkness. My eyes adjust and I see there is a seat, an armchair with winged sides, upholstered in fabric covered with tiny rubber spikes. Something is painted on the wooden arm-end, and I bend to read it. *Accept comfort, but stay alert.* Another sign hovers in mid-air, directing me to "Sit Here". I can feel the spikes push into me as I lower myself down. A light flickers on, illuminating the wall in front of me. The wall is tiled with shining blocks of a uniform size. Each contains a black-and-white photograph. They show city and field; air, water; indoor scenes, skyscapes. Each one captures, in amid the setting, a fragmentary piece of body. A toe. The lobe of an ear. The space behind a knee.

I am held in the chair. I feel a thousand fingers pushing into my body as I try to make sense of the display. Do the pictures show some kind of exploded configuration of the body? I try to map them, but there is no immediate sense that the hands make up the right and left, or that curves which must come from the buttock, the waist, the spine are distributed with more frequency in the centre of the space. So I allow them to remain separate, each disappearing flick of skin staying out of reach. Finally, I notice the inside edge of a foot. The skin is dirty and the camera angle is pointing towards the heel; right in the instep, there is a deeply angled, partly healed cut. It's my foot, from the afternoon Will fell in. But who took the photograph? I press my hands to my eyes, trying to remember when the camera turned up. Victoria didn't start carrying it around until later. And wouldn't I remember her taking this picture? I seem to catch a fugitive coil of antiseptic in the air but it's gone too fast to be real. I let my hands drop and concentrate on the photographs again. Where are you? Where am I?

Someone is shaking my shoulder. It's the gallery assistant from the stairs. As I turn my head she steps back, as if wary of what I might do. Perhaps she thinks I might bite.

"I'm sorry, madam, but this part of the gallery is closed to the public."

Madam is a funny word. A term of respect: Madam Speaker, Madam Justice. It signals anonymity, *Dear Sir/Madam, I am writing to complain*. I hear a voice telling me off: *You little madam, wait until your father gets home*. Except he never did.

"If you'd like to —" The assistant is only young. She is holding an arm out towards the doorway. She knows I have seen the tape keeping this floor closed off. She must also have seen the tear that now rolls down my cheek. She glances over her shoulder, hoping for backup. I wonder what she would do if I told her — if I said, *I am in these pictures. Look carefully and see if you can spot me*. Instead, I stand and go in the direction she indicates. I duck back under the tape.

As I go towards the stairs, I hear her voice again. "It won't be long now. The artist should be here any minute."

CHAPTER
TWENTY-FIVE

1983

The canal was undisturbed in the dawn light, with a fine mist lingering on the surface of the water. Helen didn't know what had woken her, but she hadn't been able to go back to sleep, and the desire had grown to be out by herself, to sit in the boat and sense the water beneath her. Under her feet, the ground was damp with dew and even though she kept to the trodden part of the towpath, the hems of her jeans soon became wet and uncomfortable against her bare ankles.

The cottages seemed closed in on themselves, huddled in their compact row. It was odd to be standing on the outside, awake and looking in. The empty pair in the middle were desolate, the uncurtained windows revealing the peeling wallpaper, with lighter squares where pictures and cupboards once rested. Mrs Tyler's cottage had a coldness to it, the front door there to keep you out, the rooms netted and unknown.

The Dovers' house was different; she could see into it with her mind's eye as if it were a doll's house, the front taken off, leaving the interior open to view. There are the twins, curled into foetal balls on the bunk beds, covers pushed to the bottom of their mattresses. There is Alice, beautiful enough, even in sleep, to alter the clothes-strewn room from slovenly to picturesque. Seth's room is bare: bed tidy, chair positioned in one corner, committing to nothing. Seth is lying straight under the covers, his face turned steadily to the ceiling. But where to place Piet? He had no definite space, no sense that he had imprinted himself on any one room. He could be sitting on the edge of Alice's bed, watching the twitching of her eyelids, the slow rise and fall of her chest, or sprawled on the couch, or out in the back garden with the first coffee of the day. Or not there at all, an absence, a negative image. But surely he would be there for the evening, for the party?

As she reached the boat it started to rock, and she stopped where she was, heart in mouth, while a figure hauled its way on to the back deck.

"You're down early." Her smile was cautious. She hadn't expected to find her dad here. He was rough, his shirt rumpled and his eyes bleary.

"I couldn't sleep, so I decided to come down and see how things were."

"You were pretty fast asleep when I went to bed." She couldn't help the edge in her tone. She didn't exactly mind him going out, leaving her to sleep in an empty house. It was more that she hadn't noticed he wasn't there. Surely she should have had a sense of emptiness, a subconscious knowledge of the lack of another person breathing, turning over in bed. Was that why she had woken early? And the back door had been unlocked; anyone could have come in.

"Dad, you could have told me."

He rubbed both hands up and down his face, rasping against stubble more grey than it should have been, a symptom of decay rather than growth.

"You were asleep, I thought it was better not to disturb you." He blinked up at the sky, as if surprised it was still there. "I'll put the kettle on."

In the end it felt right to be sitting there together, the two of them, her dad in his old office chair and her on an upturned box.

"Is it how you thought it would be?" Helen held the tea out to him.

He took the mug and sat back, putting one foot out to stop the chair rotating.

"Well, you know." His chin sank down to his chest. "It's funny."

He lapsed into silence. Helen drank some of her tea. The cabin reminded her of a child's toy, the plywood pieces cut to make walls and window spaces. The ply was pale, still marked with outlines and dirty fingerprints. There was a bench to one side, topped with a raw-edged piece of foam, in front of it a folding table. The kettle sat on the table next to a jam jar full of teabags and a camping gas burner.

Her dad cleared his throat.

"I always thought I'd have teak panelling, a proper galley. You know, fitted, with a nice finish." They sat again in silence. Then he raised himself a bit, shifted his backside further into the seat. "I mean, this ply . . ." He waved his hand around at the walls.

Helen picked up a curl of wood shaving and twisted it around one finger, staring at the floor. She wanted him to be cheerful, to be planning things.

"But it's good, though, being on the water? It's like the boat's in the right place at last." She struggled to find what she wanted to say. "And there's time to do it better, isn't there, now you're waterborne?"

Her dad gave her a smile.

"Waterborne." It was as if his gaze was travelling through her, that she wasn't there. "I always thought we'd be having adventures together, you and your mum and me."

She felt the boat rock, heard tiny slaps of water hitting the side. Her dad's eyes came back into focus, and he stared at her as though for the first time.

"Funny how things work out."

She thought of all the years he'd spent sitting in the empty hull, all those afternoons and evenings, sitting in his chair with his beer on the floor, imagining his perfect boat. Her vocal cords were tight, almost painful.

"I wish I'd helped you before."

He reached across to pat her knee, his gaze once more lost in a private world. She wanted to ask him why: why the boat? How did he feel about his wife leaving, what was it that made him so sad? Words crowded to the front of her head, swirling, as she tried to think how to start. The moment hovered, opening into a sense of infinite possibility before, without warning, collapsing as if it had never been. She coughed to hide her mangled thoughts and her next words came out in such a cheerful tone that she felt herself blush.

"There's the party tomorrow, and we'll christen it properly."

He gave a shake of his head. "She." He turned his face towards her and smiled. "They're always she."

CHAPTER
TWENTY-SIX

Helen left him there, in the end, his eyes closed and his chin resting on his chest. It was as if he'd forgotten about her. As she climbed down on to the bank, Victoria's head came out of her bedroom window.

"Come round the back, I want to show you something!"

There was no sign of her, though, when Helen reached the garden. The cottage had a sleepiness about it, so she sat on the back step to wait, running her fingers against the cropped ends of her hair. The grass was yellow and defeated, and a scuffed bareness was creeping across the area nearest to the cottage. Helen thought about the Weavers and their perfectly smooth lawn, and the sprinklers circling in their choreographed patterns. If the world came to an end, the Weavers would be there, worrying about the effect it was having on their borders. The door opening came as a surprise, and she fell backwards. Victoria was wearing a beret, pulled down over one eye, and baggy black trousers with a faintly military appearance. She stepped over Helen's supine form.

"Come on."

"What are we doing?" Helen got slowly to her feet and followed her. "Planning an insurrection?"

"Not yet." Victoria carried on walking. "Though I do have a plan."

The bottles were in the shed at the bottom of the garden, standing in a row on the shelf. Old beer bottles with hanks of flowered fabric stuffed into the tops. The glass was brown so Helen couldn't see what was inside, but there was no missing the smell of petrol.

"What are they?" The fumes were making her feel dizzy, as if they were soaking into her hair, her clothes.

"Molotov cocktails." Victoria regarded them with a pleased expression. She glanced round. "Petrol bombs?"

"I know what it means." Helen turned her head to check on the door, knowing it was stupid but unable to stop herself. "But why? And how did you find out how?"

"I went to the library to find a book about it but they didn't have one." Victoria was straightening the bottles, making minute changes to their positions. "That's what I was doing yesterday."

"You don't say." Helen put the heaviest sarcasm she could into her voice. "Nothing there under P for petrol, or T for Terrorism?"

Victoria's voice got louder. "So I was wandering down the road, wondering what to do next, and there were some boys sitting on a bench and they sounded Irish, so I went and asked them."

Helen stuck her head outside, breathing in a head-calming lungful of air.

"Oh right. Yes, of course." She glanced back in. "Can we carry on outside? I'm going to be sick if I breathe in any more of that stink."

Victoria seemed surprised. "Don't you like the smell? I think it's lovely." She carried on talking as she pushed herself upright. "If you must know, I found something in this book of Moira's."

Helen let herself fall out of the door, collapsing on the grass and taking in an exaggerated breath. Victoria wasn't paying any attention, though, which made it all a bit stupid. She shifted back so she could lean against the wall. Moira. Of course.

"What book of Moira's?"

Victoria stepped over her legs and carried on towards the corner beyond the blackcurrants, where a patch of old concrete was all that remained of another old shed. Helen pushed herself up with a sigh. Victoria had settled into a spot warm from the first of the sun and as Helen followed, she couldn't help wondering how hot the shed would have to get before the bottles spontaneously exploded. Victoria's eyes were closed, her face tilted towards the sky.

"A book. It was in a bag of stuff she left."

"What bag of stuff?"

"Just stuff. Do you want to hear my idea or not?"

"What idea?"

Victoria gave a long sigh. "My idea for the party?" She rolled her head from side to side, letting it come to a rest facing Helen. "Forget the champagne and ladies with nice gloves. Let's launch the boat with a Molotov!"

235

She apparently expected applause, but what the hell was she on about? Helen's brain fumbled with her meaning for a split second before turning up a mental image of the Queen standing by an ocean-going liner, swinging a bottle, flames exploding on impact: "*I name this ship . . . boom!*"

"Why would you want to throw a petrol bomb at the boat?"

"Not at the boat, stupid." Victoria was enunciating clearly as if Helen was very stupid. "It's *symbolic.* We've got the bonfire ready to go, but instead of lighting it with a boring old match, we use the idea of breaking a bottle to launch a ship and throw a petrol bomb in."

That was the trouble with Victoria. She made it all sound so clever and plausible, and any objections sounded so . . . *boring.*

"I don't see why you have to bring petrol bombs into it." Then she remembered the afternoon in Moira's boat, listening to her going on about resisting the power of the state, of violence being a necessity in the struggle. Bombs, she had said, were symbols of action, of standing up and saying change was going to happen. "So whose state are you protesting against?"

Victoria sat up, locking a fist across her chest and staring over to one side.

"Oppression in all its many forms." She kept her head fixed, but swivelled her eyes so they were turned towards Helen. "You know you want to."

"I don't, actually." Helen scraped a thumbnail across the lichen on a lump of concrete. "Is this because of Moira?"

"No, it's because of me." Victoria's voice took on an edge of annoyance, but her next words were matter-of-fact. "I want to see what happens, that's all. And it won't be any fun unless you do it too."

It was her weak spot, as Victoria well knew.

"OK, one. Though I don't think you'll be able to light a fire that way."

"We'd better try it, then, hadn't we?" Victoria grew businesslike. "The greenhouses would be the best place. No worrying about broken glass and there won't be anyone watching."

So the details were already worked out. As if it was a picnic or something. Helen's attention slipped. Victoria suited the beret, the longer ends of her hair sticking out beneath the slanted edge and her eyes darkened by the shadow it cast. Helen leaned over and made a grab for it.

"And if the peeping Tom turns up, we can ask him to join in." She pulled the beret on to her own head and tried to see her reflection in the glass of an old window frame propped against the hedge. It was too dirty to show her much, but she thought it suited her.

Victoria frowned.

"Look, if you're not going to take this seriously . . ." She made a long arm and took the beret back, giving one edge a sharp pull as she settled it in place. When she was satisfied, she pointed at Helen. "If you're good, we'll get you an Arafat scarf."

They took a bottle each, and scrambled through the hole in the fence. The field beyond had been harvested

237

and stacks of bales dotted its expanse. Helen had an urge to run from one to the next like secret agents, but Victoria had already set off, and was far enough ahead that Helen had to jog, holding her bottle at arm's length and hoping she wouldn't spill any. She was beginning to feel light-headed, her limbs working independently of her brain. She pictured herself emptying the petrol on to a haystack and dropping a match on to it, and a flutter of panic jiggled under her ribcage and made her stop. What if she actually did it? It seemed possible, as if her hands were about to start the action.

"Come on!" Victoria's shout jerked her back to the early heat, the intact bottle in her hand. She took a deep breath and set off again.

The glasshouses were silent. Helen hovered by the entrance, straining to hear any sound that would suggest another presence. Victoria didn't even stop. The way she had the lighter out of her pocket and lit was almost choreographed.

"Here we go!"

Her voice sounded thin, disappearing up and out of the broken roof. She swung her arm back and then forwards and let go of the missile with a whoop. It wasn't a very good shot, though, and it landed on a patch of ground where earth had built up on the concrete. Instead of exploding, it rolled and the flame went out. Victoria stood with her arms held out as if she was playing statues, not letting them drop until the tiny spiral of black smoke from the smouldering material burned itself out.

238

"Well, that was exciting." She tossed the lighter towards Helen with no notice, and Helen fumbled it to the ground. "I hope you can throw better than you can catch."

Helen bent down, sudden fury driving her against her better judgement. Trust Victoria to blame her for everything, when it was her stupid throwing that had been pathetic. She felt a need to do it better. It was someone else's hand holding the lighter, turning the stiff wheel, watching the fluid inside rock backwards and forwards inside the purple plastic shell. The stuffy air was wrapping her up and she was watching from a distance as the bottle arced upwards in slow motion. And at the moment she let go, there was Victoria, stepping forwards into the line of flight. Helen's mouth opened to shout, but at the same time she felt her eyes close in denial. There was the sound of glass breaking, a thump of explosion. She didn't want to see. She had to look.

"Vic!" her voice wobbled. "Vic, are you OK?"

She wasn't sure her legs were steady enough to make it over to where Victoria lay huddled on the ground. The flare of flame died down, leaving the giddy after-scent of fuel. A scrubby clump of dried grass smouldered, sending out a thin plume of smoke. She gave Victoria a shake.

"Vic!"

Victoria was shuddering. Helen touched her rounded back again, and the touch sent her rolling over, until she was lying with her arms and legs outstretched on the ground. She was laughing, her breath coming in short gasps.

"Did you see me? Commando roll or what?" She pulled herself up to sitting and wiped her eyes. "Helen, you're a maniac. But did you see it go?"

"It wasn't my fault! How did I know you were going to get in the way?" Helen rubbed her hands down the side of her legs, but it was as if petrol had soaked into her skin.

"What was that?" Victoria scrambled up to her feet, and came over to where Helen was standing.

"What?"

"I heard something." She held on to Helen's arm, turning her head like a scenting dog. "Look, over there."

Helen followed the line of her finger across the hedge and over to the first of the haystacks. She couldn't see anything. Victoria bent over and ran across, playing up to her quasi-military persona. Her foot kicked at the bottle she'd misthrown, and it clattered across the concrete. Like disturbed pheasants, the twins broke cover and made a run for the house, whoops of laughter drifting behind them.

"They must have been following us all the time." Victoria spotted a tiny strand of smoke some distance from the point of Helen's explosion and went over to step down on it. "That's all the world needs, Will as a revolutionary."

"You don't think they'd . . ." Helen was looking over the field to where the twins had vanished into the garden.

"Try to blow up the Houses of Parliament?" Victoria sounded amused. "I wouldn't put it past them." She kicked at the patch of ground again, then came over to where Helen was standing.

A shiver ran up Helen's spine, and she gave an involuntary shudder.

"What?" Victoria turned to look at her.

"Nothing. Goose walked over my grave."

"No geese here." Victoria started to run across the field, turning back to shout over her shoulder. "Come on, I'm starving. No breakfast!"

With a last glance back at the glasshouses, Helen followed.

CHAPTER
TWENTY-SEVEN

The bonfire had been built on the scrubby lawn at the back of the cottage, as far away from the building as possible without being close enough to the apple tree to scorch the leaves. Helen came around from the side path and stopped in surprise when she saw how big it had become. She hadn't left until teatime the previous day, when the pile of wood had been reasonable, but nothing like this. Layers of pallets had appeared, and lengths of planking peeling with old paint. The scratched framework of an old sofa perched on the top, a layer of rusted springs supporting a loose-limbed effigy. It wasn't much more than a pair of trousers and a jumper fleshed out with newspaper, but someone had painted a leering face on to what appeared to be an upended pudding basin, and it wore a battered captain's cap at a rakish angle.

"Pretty good, huh?"

Victoria was leaning in the open doorway of the kitchen, scraping out the contents of a mixing bowl.

"It's amazing! Where did it all come from?" Helen pushed away the knowledge that it had happened without her.

"Friend of Piet's." Victoria put the bowl down on the doorstep and gave her fingers a final lick before strolling over to where Helen was standing. "He turned up with all this stuff on a trailer at about eleven. We had to have the headlights on the van lighting it all up."

"And when did you make it?" Helen pointed at the guy.

"This morning." The guy's arm was hanging down the back of the sofa frame, and Victoria reached up to lay it along the top edge. She seemed to be avoiding Helen's eyes. "I was going to come and get you, but I thought you must be busy, you know, otherwise you'd have already been here."

Helen opened her mouth, but Victoria's last words blistered on her consciousness. She forced herself to smile.

"He's fab. Who thought of the cap?"

"Oh, Moira." Victoria swung round and headed for the apple tree. "And this is where I've hidden you-know-what."

Helen stayed where she was, staring at the guy without seeing him. She wanted to kick the whole stack of wood over, to tell Victoria to use someone else's boat as an excuse for a party. Her fingernails dug into the soft flesh of her forearm and she concentrated on the sharp pressure until the wave of anger rolled back. She still didn't trust herself to turn around.

"Here." Victoria was behind her.

"What?" She glanced round to see Victoria holding a bottle in each hand.

"We need to work out exactly what we're going to do." Victoria was oblivious to her mood. "I think we should come up here," she waved towards the side of the cottage, "and sort of burst in on everyone."

"And what if the bonfire's already lit? Or if people are too close and it blows up in their faces?"

Victoria groaned. "Are you back on all that again? I thought we'd finished with the worrying."

"How would you even get them to explode?" Helen pushed it a bit further. "You know how hard they needed to hit the ground. They'd bounce off the wood and who knows where they'd end up?"

Victoria had one of the bottles with its neck between finger and thumb, watching the liquid rock from side to side. Her mouth was clamped in a tight line.

"And if we buried them in the middle, the glass could hurt someone. I say we forget it . . ."

"Is this all because of Moira?"

The abruptness of Victoria's question made Helen stop. Said out loud like that, it made her feel stupid.

"Well —"

Victoria didn't wait for her to finish.

"Because we didn't invite her to come and do the guy, she just turned up. And if I wanted to do the petrol bombs with her, I'd do it." She bumped Helen's shoulder with her own. "I want to do it with you. Moira would only take over."

From inside the house, Pippa's voice sounded in a squeak of indignation, followed by a laugh and a rumble of words from Piet. Seth came out of the kitchen with his amplifier under one arm, ignoring

244

them and paying out a line of cable as he went. Helen watched as he set it on an upturned tea chest and checked something at the back before returning to the house. A few moments later, a needle crackled on the edge of a record before a billow of sound swept through the air. Helen recognized it straight away, the music Seth had said he would come on stage to when he was famous, surrounded by billowing clouds of dry ice. The layers of sound built up in a crescendo of grandeur, heading towards the final, triumphant crashing blast, and then the needle stuck. Two notes hiccupped on, dah dah, dah dah.

"It's going to be a rubbish party otherwise." Victoria glared at the waiting bonfire, swiping an arm across her eyes. "Sparklers if we're lucky." She sat down on the grass, balancing the bottle on the ground in front of her. The end bit of the fabric flopped sideways, releasing a scent of leaking fuel.

"It looks like a weird table decoration." Helen sat down next to her, and reached for the other bottle to line it up with the first.

"Yeah. Perfect for a revolutionary restaurant. Light it before you leave."

"They'd have violin players bringing them round . . ."

". . . specially for when you're breaking up with someone."

"Comrade, there comes a time in every relationship . . ." The lifting of tension was making Helen want to laugh. "Comes a time . . ."

"What are you two up to?"

It was her dad, heading towards them, beer in hand. He had changed his shirt and smoothed his hair down with water.

"All ready for the big moment?"

"Oh yes." Victoria's face was bland, but she shot Helen an amused glance, making her dip her head and cough into her shoulder. "It's going to be a blast."

Helen shifted across so she was hiding the bottles, but the attempt backfired.

"What's in those bottles?" Her dad's attention had shifted. He sniffed, and took a step towards them.

Victoria stood up, trying to block him off. She pointed towards the cottage.

"Isn't that Piet? I think he's looking for you. It must be time to get the fire started."

He pushed her aside, bending down with a grunt of effort to reach for one of the bottles. He straightened with difficulty, holding it up to his nose and again inhaling.

"What's going on?" He looked at Helen.

She tried not to catch Victoria's eye, clamping her lips together to stop herself from giggling, even though it wasn't funny any more. Sweat prickled her back as she thrashed about for a convincing explanation. She felt caught out and guilty, and angry with him for making her feel small. Like being ticked off by a teacher in public.

"A . . . a game. Nothing." She felt stupid, sitting down on the ground with her dad towering above her, and scrambled to her feet. Without thinking, she found

246

herself right up against Victoria. *Shoulder to shoulder into the fray*, she thought.

"It's not nothing. These are petrol bombs. They're extremely dangerous." Mick drew himself up, cleared his throat, and fixed them both with his serious look. The edge of pomposity made Helen want to giggle again. She stared down at the ground, telling herself to keep quiet, let him get it out.

"What you two don't realize is that people get killed . . ."

Victoria's voice interrupted him.

"We do realize, actually. We know quite a lot . . ."

"Now you listen to me . . ."

". . . about it. And the reason it was . . ."

". . . now just you . . ."

". . . was a secret," Victoria's voice rose to finish her sentence, "was because we knew you'd make such a big deal out of it."

Their voices faded into silence. Then, "You, young lady, have too big a mouth for your own good."

He bent down again, reaching for the other bottle and manoeuvring his beer under one arm in order to manage them both.

"One day you'll understand why I had to do this." He fixed them both with a look of sorrow. "I'll dispose of them somewhere safe, and I expect you to be more sensible in future." After a few steps, he stopped and seemed to come to a decision before turning and walking towards them holding the bottles out in front. "On the other hand, perhaps you should take responsibility for your actions. I want them somewhere safe, understand?"

247

Helen reached out automatically to take them. He looked straight at her. "I'm trusting you here. Don't let this one talk you into anything. And I'll be checking on you later."

They watched as he turned and walked away down the garden. Helen caught a waft of fuel in her throat and tried not to gag. She felt like throwing them after him, smack against his head. Or against the boat. She pictured it, the boat drifting away in flames, the orange glow reflected up from the water, remote, unsalvageable, then the fire reaching the fuel tank and exploding outwards in a raging fireball. Victoria's voice broke in.

"Well, your dad really is a bit of a wanker, isn't he?"

And she too was gone. Helen could feel her legs shaking. Stupid, she told herself, when nothing had happened. The bottles felt like ton weights. She should go and put them in the shed, she thought, but it seemed such a long way away. A crackle from the amp broke the quiet. Everyone would be coming out and she couldn't face explaining what she was doing. She shoved the bottles behind Seth's tea chest and broke into a shuffling run to get around the corner before whoever it was saw her.

CHAPTER
TWENTY-EIGHT

She went home to wash the petrol off her skin and change her clothes. As she came out on to the bank from the lane, she paused. The boat was tied up on the far side of the cottages, nearly at the bridge, and the canal stretched out beyond the grey stone arch. The sun was beginning to set, grazing the top edge of the treetops. The air felt full, the moment holding itself in readiness, warmed through from the day and not yet at the point where it would slide into evening. Everything was touched with a golden light, the leaves and the grass and the figures around the boat taking on the permanence of an oil painting, and the water swallowing the colours before giving back its own dappled version. Pippa broke through the frame, jumping down from the side of the boat to run along and take her hand.

"It's all ready!" She was practically hopping, brimming over with excitement. "I made a garland and Fred has got a bottle with some fizzy wine and Uncle Piet says he can bang it on the side." She slowed almost to a halt, pulling Helen's head down to whisper. "I wanted to do the fizzy stuff, but Fred said first." She sighed. "Uncle Piet said I could do it next time. But he

249

gave me this to use instead." She held up a black object slung around her neck on a strap. "It's called a Polaroid, and I have ten pictures to take." She pressed a button, and the bottom part of the camera slid open. "Come next to me and I'll take our picture."

They stood with their heads together, the boat behind them. Pippa tried to hold the camera steady, but it was too big.

"You do it, Helen." She unhooked the strap from around her neck. "I'm all right when I'm pointing it forwards, but I can't do it this way round."

Helen held it at arm's length and they both smiled. There was a whirring sound, and a square of white slid from the camera's base. They stood with their heads touching, waiting for the picture to come. When it did they saw that their heads had ended up in the bottom corner, and Pippa was slightly blurred, as if she'd been turning her head.

"You can look after it." Pippa held it out like an award of merit, then grabbed her hand. "Come on, let's get ready for the launch."

Victoria had appeared at the far end, keeping herself at a slight distance from everyone. Helen tried to catch her eye, but there was no response, so she stopped next to Seth, who was bending down to untie the rope from a stake buried in the grass. Pippa ran across to pick up a chain of coloured paper flowers, and tried to make Will hold one end, but he was jumping about with a bottle in his hand, swinging it around by a piece of string tied about the neck; if it was the fizzy wine, there wasn't going to be much fizz left at the rate he was going.

"Are we all here?" The flap of plastic that served as a door was rolled up out of the way, and Piet was there, looking out of the gap, a bottle of beer held up in one hand.

Helen stood on tiptoe to whisper in Seth's ear.

"Shouldn't we wait for Alice?"

Seth scanned the front of the house and Helen followed his line of sight to Alice's window.

"She won't mind," he said. "Though I might —"

He was interrupted by Piet's voice. "Come on, Mick, we need you to set us off."

Seth bent sideways, his mouth almost touching her ear. "I think we'll leave it."

Piet stepped on to the bank with a flourish as her dad appeared, struggling to keep his balance as the boat rocked from Piet's departure. Piet took a grip of his arm as he followed, and handed him a beer from a box down by his feet.

Helen held her breath as her dad turned around, holding the beer out as if he was proposing a toast. She remembered at the same moment that she'd not done anything about the bottles of petrol. It wouldn't matter for a bit. She'd get them afterwards.

"I'd like to start by saying," Mick began, leaning over to hold on to the cabin roof, "that today is the end of a very long road."

Piet's head came into view over Mick's shoulder, and he clinked his bottle against the one in Mick's uplifted hand. The boat rocked, and her dad nearly lost his balance. Seth stepped across to pick up one of the ropes which held the boat in. Helen watched him as he leaned back to keep the tension as the boat steadied and, beyond him, noticed a figure standing next to Victoria. It was Moira, wearing a white vest and cut-off denim shorts, her army boots unlaced on her feet. She had a bulging plastic bag in one hand, and was watching the activity on the boat with a dismissive interest.

Helen swung her eyes back to her dad, who was getting into the swing of it now. "We have waited for this moment for some years." He gave the nearest piece of timber a slap, and drew himself up. "She doesn't need a christening . . ."

Moira detached herself from the group and set off down the towpath. Helen couldn't help noticing that Seth, too, watched Moira leave.

"If we're all ready?" Mick nodded to Piet, and a plume of smoke drifted up from the far side of the boat as the engine roared into life. Mick's voice shouted above it.

"May God bless her and all . . ."

Before he could finish, Will darted forwards and swung his bottle on to the edge of the deck. Glass and liquid sprayed out over Mick's legs, who hovered on the brink of a bellow of anger before visibly changing his mind and lifting his own beer bottle in a salute. Helen felt her throat swell with emotion as a cheer spread along the bank. She wished she was close enough to give her dad a hug, to tell him how pleased she was the moment had come. She even took a step towards him, but the engine shuddered to a halt and

Piet was there, slinging an arm around Mick's shoulders and leaning in to say something in his ear. The two of them stepped over to the bank and, still talking, headed for the path around the side of the cottage. Mick didn't even see her.

She turned to see Pippa, tears running down her cheeks.

"They trod all over my flowers." Pippa held them up, wet from the wine, and torn out of shape.

"Never mind." Helen gave her a hug, glad of the distraction. "Shall we go and see what's happening with the food?"

Pippa nodded. They set off towards the gate in time to see a swirl of colour appear around the side of the cottage. It was Alice, wrapped in a glittering, embroidered kaftan. She ran down the path, stopping halfway to spin in slow motion. It didn't seem to be for admiration. She was absorbed in her dance, her eyes following the swoop of the robe. Helen and Pippa stopped to watch her as she paused, both hands lifted up, and then gathered her hair up from her face, shaking it down behind her shoulders. She took no notice of them. Her attention was directed only at Piet as she drifted down towards the boat.

"Am I too late? Have I missed all the fun?"

Helen sat with her back against the garden wall, watching the spiral of smoke from the bonfire as it coiled up into the air. The moment of the bottle breaking and the cheers and excitement felt distant, far longer than a couple of hours. The sky wasn't quite

253

dark, but lemon yellow was spreading up into a pale blue which, by the time it reached the eastern half, became a clear sapphire. There was one star, a faint, steady glimmer at the top of the treeline. She fixed her eyes on it, letting the figures grouped around the fire blur away into her peripheral vision. The canal felt distant as well, kept away by the bulk of the cottages. She thought of the boat, bobbing in solitary abandonment as they celebrated back here. Though celebrating wasn't really the right word. The party, so long anticipated and promising so much, had turned into a flat anticlimax. Victoria had vanished straight after the launch, presumably with Moira, and Helen was pretty sure nobody cared whether she herself was there or not. The star wavered, and she dug the heels of her hands into the ground, concentrating on the sharpness of the stones as they pressed into her skin. She heard the sound of the back door opening, then approaching footsteps, but she kept her eyes fixed on the point of light in the sky until the very last minute.

"You're very contemplative." Seth was standing over her, holding a glass in each hand. "I thought you might like one of these."

He held one of the glasses out to her, then lowered himself down as well.

"Cheers." He held his glass out to her. "Here's to the rest of time."

Helen touched her glass to his, and took a sip.

"Mmm, that's lovely." The first taste was sour, but it left a trail of burning sweetness down through her throat and chest. "What is it?"

254

"That would be telling." He leaned closer. "I call it the Jazz." His voice lowered and he started to sing, "Take a spot, cool and hot . . ." He drank from his glass, leaned his head back, and half-closed his eyes. Helen realized he was not quite sober. She took a swallow of her own drink. Their arms were almost touching.

"So, Helen, with the face full of secrets, what are you thinking about?" He gazed into her eyes for a second, before letting his head roll back to centre again. "Hey, hey, Helen, what's the matter with you?" He crooned the snatch of song in a low voice, playing the tune on an imaginary guitar. "Hey, hey, Helen, don't you know what to do?"

His face was so beautiful. She wanted to lean closer and kiss him. Maybe she should tell him that. She took another mouthful of her drink.

"I was thinking about the stars." She waved upwards. "They might all have exploded already. We think we can see them when it's nothing but the light they left behind."

"Better wish on one, then, before it's gone. More than one." She felt Seth's hair touching her face. "What would you wish for? Where do you want to go?"

The stars seemed to be pulsing and, for a second, it felt as if her blood was pulsing in time. The world felt as big as the sky, and she saw herself flying through it.

"Everywhere!" She laughed, her hand brushing the side of his leg. "As long as it isn't here."

"Getting away, huh?" He was silent for a long moment, as if that was all he had to say. "Getting away." He hummed a couple of bars, a tune she recognized but couldn't place. "However far you travel, it's only ever you that goes along."

And then he was leaning down, his breath stirring the hairs by her ear, his mouth brushing against her cheek as she turned in response. It was more awkward than she expected, the roughness of his skin catching her, their noses bumping, his teeth hard against her tongue. And it was over so fast.

At the edge of her vision, the bonfire caught a fresh piece of wood, and a flame shot up, its brightness making the rest of the garden seem dark. Seth lifted his head.

"We seem to have empty glasses."

She couldn't collect herself enough to say anything back. He smiled at her, one hand resting on her arm. She was still gazing at him with her mouth half-open when he stood up. "I'll be right back," he said.

She lost track of the time as she waited, listening as the low acoustic swell drifted across from the speaker, sending her into a dream. Flames from the fire leapt out, forked ribbons detaching themselves in glorious, momentary separation from the glowing centre, before they were sucked back into the heat. She held her glass by the rim between finger and thumb, letting it swing beneath her hand. There was a change, something missing, but it was a while before she realized that the music had stopped and the only sound was the hiss of the needle at the end of the disc. Seth had been gone for a long time. A dark shape came around the edge of the fire, and her heartbeat accelerated, but it was only Piet. He disappeared around the corner of the house, and a second later another record started to play.

"Helen, what are you doing all by yourself?" Piet was back on the path, one hand up against the wall, a mazy smile on his face. "Come and join us."

He held out his hand to pull her up, and the movement made her head spin. Piet was laughing, and she joined in: it was funny to be standing up, why hadn't she noticed before? Piet's hand was large, folding itself right around her fingers. She could feel his calloused skin rubbing the underside of her fingers. For a second she was leaning against him, feeling his chest rise and fall, then he led her across to the fire.

Her dad was there, sitting on a chair with a bottle of beer resting between his knees. He seemed to be asleep. Alice reclined on a pile of cushions, the embroidery on her kaftan shimmering in the firelight.

"Sit down, sit down." Piet pushed her down towards the cushions; it was further than she thought and she fell against Alice as she landed.

"Oh, I'm so sorry!" The fire was brighter on this side, and the cushions were soft. She closed her eyes, but it made her head spin. When she opened them, Alice was replying.

"S'all right, don't you worry." Alice didn't seem to be talking to her; her head was tipped back, and she was staring at the flames. She made a noise in her throat as if her voice was stuck. She coughed and tried again, and Helen realized she was humming along with the music, her voice hoarse and slightly off-key. She stopped, and turned to Helen, holding out her cigarette. With one eye on her dad, Helen took it. It was like the one she'd had by the canal with Victoria, except now she knew that the sweet, thick smell was marijuana, and it felt like a coming of age to be sitting here as a member of the group. She drew in, and the smoke coiled up through her head and down her spine, and the flames jumping up from the fire seemed to swell and then contract. The guitar sound rose up, as if it was taking off with the line of orange sparks, and voices pushed together in aching harmony, reaching their climax and spreading out with the heat before running down in a cascade of notes. She had heard Seth practising that very sequence, over and over, never quite managing it.

Where was Seth, anyway? With an effort, she lifted her head to look around. Piet was standing by the fire, his long legs outlined by the glow. Further round, the twins were squatting with their heads together, whispering some top-secret plan. Then Will grabbed a stick from the edge of the fire and waved it over his head, leaving a trail like a Bonfire Night sparkler. Pippa squealed and ran as he swooped it towards her, and they both disappeared into the darkness. Her father gave a snort and lifted his head as if wondering where he was, before lifting his beer to his mouth.

Alice reached across and took the cigarette from Helen's fingers. A voice was saying something, but Helen couldn't place where it was coming from so she swatted it away.

"Come here." Victoria was right behind her, holding a bottle in one hand and beckoning with the other. "Come and see."

It was complicated, trying to stand up; the cushions seemed to be under her feet whichever way she tried to go. Victoria grabbed at her arm, and Helen felt her head start to balance. She blinked, trying to focus on Victoria's face.

"Where have you been?" The afternoon felt like another lifetime, and that was so sad, so incredibly sad. "You've been gone for ages."

"I've been talking to Moira." Victoria held the bottle in her hand towards Helen. "Do you want some?" She didn't seem steady on her feet, either.

Helen took a swallow, the alcohol hitting the back of her throat and doubling her over in a fit of coughing.

"No, no, quiet!" Victoria was making exaggerated shushing gestures with her hands and trying not to laugh. "You've got to be quiet," she added, in a loud whisper.

She took hold of Helen's arm again, pulling her down towards the bottom of the garden.

"I was talking to Moira, and we ran out of vodka." She was still whispering, the words interspersed with giggles. "So I went and got this," she waved the bottle, "and when I got back . . ." She stopped, pushing Helen forwards. They were at the clump of overgrown blackcurrant bushes that straggled across the corner, hiding the concrete footings of the old shed. It seemed like years since she'd been there with Victoria, talking about petrol bombs. The idea of the petrol bombs reminded her of something, something she was supposed to do. But Victoria was shaking her arm, distracting her. There was something on the ground. She put a hand out to hold on to Victoria, because her head was feeling light and she needed to balance before she could focus. The moon was flat and dead after the flickering red of the fire, but it gave enough light to see by. It was what she was trying to see that didn't make any sense.

The first thing she recognized for certain was a leg. She gazed at it. Why was it there? A joke, of course. Victoria had set it up to freak her out. Helen slumped in relief. Then the leg slid away, and she felt her mouth open in shock. Something clamped itself over her mouth, blocking off the sound. She fought it, trying to get away. It was going to drag her down there, pull off her legs, her arms, and throw them on the ground. Victoria's voice wavered by her ear, but it was competing with the thump of blood as she struggled to breathe.

"Sshh! Don't let them know we're here. Where's a camera when you need one?"

What did she mean? Helen felt reaction shiver down her spine at the very same moment that the scene in front of her swam into order. There was the leg, yes, but also arms and hair and a spine curving up as the bodies tumbled over and one half detached itself in a triumphant arch. It was Seth and Moira, entwined and grappling, their clothes scattered all around.

CHAPTER
TWENTY-NINE

2013, Manchester: 8.15 p.m.

The café is crowded now, complimentary wine on offer at the counter. The smell of something spicy reminds me I haven't had anything to eat today, but at the same time my stomach tells me it wants no food. I don't think I can do this. I make for the door, but as I get close there's a coordinated surge towards the stairs. It's easier to go along than fight.

Those of us on the upwards path squeeze to one side and come to a halt as a chattering group make their way down. The man in front of me lets his hand rest on his companion's tightly skirted behind. They are discussing Derrida and his influence on modern art, and are in no hurry. There's a wound-up spring in my abdomen, and coloured lights are playing at the edge of my vision. The smell of the clashing fragrances from so many warm bodies is making me feel nauseous. I pinch hard at the skin on my thigh and the feeling retreats as I step on to the landing and walk past the vanishing children and the door which leads in to the chair.

The next room has a series of photographs arranged along one wall. They are mounted in identical frames. There is a shot of a head in each, manipulated to be of an identical size, but the prints themselves vary wildly in colour and tone and age. There's no way Victoria could have taken them all, because the first two at least must be from a time well before Victoria was behind a camera. The card at the side confirms this.

Not many photographs of my mother remained from my childhood. Of the ones that did, I was struck by those taken from recurring angles, and I began to consciously replicate those poses.

They are all of Alice, and frame her head and shoulders. In the first, we can see her face. She is young and ecstatically gorgeous, with perfect skin, her hair curving around the fingers that are cupping the back of her head. She is looking over her shoulder, laughing, alive in a way that I never saw. I think of Alice the muse, captivating her artist, the Alice from the oil painting above the sofa. I try to remember Victoria taking photographs of Alice, anyone taking photos of her, but the only thing that springs to mind is an old black-and-white snap from Victoria's collection.

The next four shots show the back of her head. In each, the head is captured at the same angle. I walk along, trying to spot the moment that Victoria became the person behind the camera. The hair loses its glowing young shine, the length goes up and down, becoming coarser, changing colour. I realize with a jolt that the second one is of the Alice I knew. The recognition is deep and immediate. She's wearing her embroidered kaftan and looking out across a landscape

I would surely know if the edges of the frame extended a fraction further. It gives me a sense of dislocation, standing here and seeing this image as a random spectator, knowing I might have been there when it was taken, may even be there, in the unseen edges of the subject's view.

The final photograph has her turning again, face towards the lens, this one set up as a conscious reconstruction of the first laughing shot. Except she isn't laughing here. Her hair is white, the fine soft lengths resting gently on the bones of her shoulders, and there is a definition to her face that wasn't there before. It is a study in the underpinning structure of beauty revealed. I am rooted to the spot, struck dumb by the speed of the passing of time.

The assistant from earlier comes along, welcoming people. She knows the couple in front of me, and they stop to chat. I ease my way past. Behind me, I imagine the three of them standing with their heads together, following me with their eyes as she tells them of our earlier meeting.

I stoop to go through a low doorway, and find myself in front of a screen. There is no sound; the jerky reel shows black-and-white footage of a little girl skipping. A distant part of my brain tries to figure out if it is original cinefilm or digital with effects added. It has a crackly, out-of-time look to it. The girl's back is turned, and a plait bounces on each shoulder as she skips. She turns, but before I see her face the quality disintegrates into white fuzz, out of which emerge split-second flashes of other images. I think I see a boat among them. The child is there again, this time running in a field. There is a close-up of her feet, wearing sandals which I know are made of red leather. I need to sit down. The child starts to dance, a formless spinning joyful dance, with her arms outspread and her braids flying out. Then the film melts, holes forming from the heat, followed by flames. The screen is black for a second, and then numbers appear, white on grey, counting down from ten, a line like the second hand of a watch, sweeping around each one in a circle. A pause, and the sequence begins again.

My brain is running ahead of me. I don't want to accept what it is telling me. My fingers are cold, and my legs are starting to feel insubstantial.

The reason I know the sandals are red is because Pippa got them the week before the party. I can picture her jumping out of Piet's van to run into the garden, and pirouette in front of us all.

I need to leave.

I see the skipping rope twirl again.

Across the room, somebody pauses in the doorway. It is a small, delicate woman with dark hair. She takes up hardly any physical space: her outfit of subtly coloured layers of creased cotton adds to her insubstantiality. The crowd parts as if to give space to a delicate moth. For a second her head is turned towards me, and I am looking into Victoria's eyes. They register nothing, and the next moment she is gone. It's happened to me before, thinking I've seen her until she dissolves into a stranger's body. This time I know it's her. Those other forms were never more than a pale echo. She's no bigger than I remember her and her hair, though silvered through the darkness, is cropped in a way I remember. But it's more. It's Victoria herself I feel, the coiled energy and the sense of her knowing exactly who she is, and where she is going. Her imprint stays behind in the shifting air.

I stumble out of the room and on to the street, my foot coming out of my shoe as I stagger into the wall of the next building. I leave the shoe behind. I don't want to stop and run the risk of catching the eye of anyone who saw my exit. I can't, however, escape the feeling of her eyes as they brushed over me and carried on. I keep replaying the moment it happened, trying to decipher the message they left. I feel an accusation, but I don't know what for. She was the one who left, after all. When I reach home I don't consciously look for the scissors, but somehow I am standing there with a handful of my hair wrapped around my fist, wanting to tug each strand out by the roots, and with the fingers of my other hand curled around the steel of the scissors. Better the scissors than a razor.

It hurts as I pull at the hair, forcing the blades to close around the resisting mass. I pull my head sideways, panting as I grind my way through. A lament makes its way into the darkness above my head, a keening for everything that is falling with the discarded hair and piling up around my feet.

By the feeble light from the door, I look in the mirror of the window and see a floating head, shorn and pathetic; I am like *les femmes tondues* shamed in a hundred grainy post-war photographs. I finally identify the scent of cowardice. I have been running away from the knowledge for more than half of my life. It is time to find out what happened.

I have to talk to my mother.

CHAPTER
THIRTY

1983

She wasn't sure who was laughing. Not her, because it wasn't funny. Victoria leaned over. She said something Helen couldn't quite catch.

"What?" The tree she was sitting against was handy, because it stopped her from falling down. She liked the way you could get your fingertips caught in the bark. She missed what Victoria said again.

"Have some more." Victoria was holding out a bottle. "More hurt —" She stopped and giggled. "I mean more heart medicine."

Helen held it out in front of her, trying to get the label into focus. The letters jiggled about. The glass was clear, though, and so was the liquid inside. She tilted it up. "There's not much left." Vodka. She remembered the name as it burned down her throat. Talking and drinking at the same time made her choke, and the words came out in jolts. "There isn't any left."

She let the bottle drop to the ground and closed her eyes to try and remember who it was who was sitting under a tree. But when she closed her eyes, the world began to spin too fast, so she opened them again and she was the one sitting under a tree, which was the funniest thing she'd ever heard of. Where was Victoria? She had to tell her, she'd love it. She stood up with care, grabbing at the trunk.

"Boo!"

The sound made Helen lose her grip and she stepped back and leaned over to hold on to her knees. She must have told Victoria about the tree already, because Victoria was laughing. She was laughing so much that she fell over, so Helen let her knees bend and fell over as well and they lay there staring up into the tree, which was in front of something orange.

"Why is it orange?" She heard herself say it, but she didn't know why, so it was OK that Victoria didn't answer. And, anyway, there was something wrong with Victoria's head, only she couldn't put her finger on it. "Where has your hair gone?"

She needn't have worried, though, because Victoria was laughing so much. Helen tried to get up, but it was so very difficult to balance. On the third go she managed, and reached across with great care to touch the spiky bits sticking up over Victoria's face. Her finger slid down, though, because they were so high up, and then she had her hand on Victoria's cheek and underneath the skin she could feel the line of bone, and underneath that her jaw, and then she was touching her ear and the back of her head.

It was all so very, very sad. It was the saddest thing she had ever thought.

"You're going, you see." She took hold of Victoria's shoulder and shook it to make her understand. "I love you all so much and now you're going to go away." She had real, actual tears in her eyes now. "Because it's only good when you're here."

They fell down to the ground at the same time and lay there, quite still. Helen heard the sound of their breath floating on the subdued crackle of background noise. She could feel each tiny vibration feeding through her brain, being allocated sense and dropping off into her subconscious being. Her hand was resting on Victoria's cheek again. She let her fingers drift downwards and over to Victoria's mouth. Her hand was moving by itself but she didn't do anything to stop its journey. The skin of Victoria's lips felt different, smoother than the skin of her cheek. There were tiny muscles flexing under her fingertips, and her body was nothing but a carrier for a thousand nerve endings. Even if she'd wanted to, she wouldn't have been able to stop. She would be here for the rest of her life.

"Helen." Victoria was trying to sit up. Helen sympathized. It was a difficult thing to do when the world went round so much. She let her hand fall down, watched it lie motionless on the grass. The grass should be green, she thought. Victoria was leaning over, resting her forehead against the side of her head. Her voice was a breathy whisper right in Helen's ear. "Helen —"

"Yes?"

"Helen, I don't fancy you." Victoria paused for a second before letting a giggle escape. That didn't make sense, because what she was saying wasn't funny. "So that's two of us who don't." She pulled herself up to a wobbly balance and held up a hand, the fingers curled down. Using her other hand, she unpeeled the first two fingers and held them up straight. "One, two." She pointed them both at Helen. "I saw you snogging Seth before, Who are you going to try next?"

Helen wasn't rooted to the spot, she was turned to stone.

She knew she was somewhere different, but she couldn't remember how she'd got there. The ground felt damp, and was pressing into her cheek. The pounding in her head got worse when she lifted it up, so she let it stay where it was. The fire was getting bigger, with flames that shredded off and jumped into the sky. But as she lay there, the flames began to take over the sky. Alice came into her field of vision, and she must have liked the flames as well, because she was dancing with them, holding out her arms to catch them as they flew around. She was so beautiful. Helen wanted to get up and dance with her, but it was hard, because the ground was so sticky.

Seth. There was something about Seth she needed to remember. She'd done something, she was sure, something that was bad and would make Seth run away, but she couldn't think what it was. Then the air was full of smoke. Someone must have put the wrong wood on the bonfire. The smoke bowed down, reaching out to her and wrapping her up. It was nice to be noticed, but it made her cough, and she was sure there were eyes peering out, and she'd see them if only she could turn her head. Before she could spot them, the smoke had retreated, back behind the mountain of crackling fire.

She tried her head again, and this time she managed to lift it up. Where was Victoria? Helen couldn't see her anywhere. It wasn't fair. Helen felt a wail rising up in her throat, expanding and growing until she couldn't breathe. Victoria was always going off somewhere, leaving her behind. There were people running past now, but none of them had faces. They were all leaving her behind.

Screaming. Helen put her hands over her ears because she didn't like screaming. But if her hands were over her ears, what were the hands that were pulling her up? Why was her mother here? She wasn't supposed to be here. She didn't live here any more. Her mother wouldn't let her sit back down. It was because of the lights. They were blue, too blue, and they kept flashing on, and flashing off. Flashing on, flashing off. She wanted to stop and count them, but the hands kept pulling, pulling.

They were in the lane, and Mrs Weaver's face was there too. Why was she there? She hadn't been invited. Helen tried to tell her, to point out that it was rude, turning up at other people's parties, but it was difficult because she couldn't walk and talk at the same time. "Drugs, I shouldn't wonder . . ." Mrs Weaver's mouth was talking by itself. "Disgraceful. A total lack of supervision." One minute she was there, and the next she'd turned into Helen's mother. "Thank you, Officer . . . yes . . . home with me . . ." And she was going to be sick, nausea sending her head into a spin, sweat enveloping every bit of her. Hands were turning her about, holding her down, and she heaved and heaved until all she wanted to do was lie down and die. Her feet were a very long way away and she tried to tell someone, but they couldn't hear her. The hands forced her along, with her stranger's feet, and then she was lying in a car and her mother was there, saying something she couldn't hear.

And then she was gone.

CHAPTER
THIRTY-ONE

Rain was pounding in a steady stream against the window. Helen made her eyes focus on the spot beyond the rain but before the houses opposite, so it all merged into a grey blur. She couldn't hold it for long. Out in the street, an old lady pushed her way along behind a walking frame, and the cat from the house opposite bounded up on to the wall and made a slinking run over to the other side, hiding under a parked car. Behind her, she could hear her mother rummaging through her handbag for the car keys. She swung the curtain cord with a final vicious force, wishing she could break the glass.

"I don't see why I can't go."

"Because there's nobody there and there's nothing you can do." The impatient tone was back in her mother's voice. "You've been ill and you need to rest." Her bag closed with a snap. "I have to go to work today, and you need to make a start on the book list from the sixth form."

"I'm not going to the sixth form."

"Helen." Her mum made her turn round. "We've been through this, and I don't want to argue." She came up to Helen and put a hand on her forehead. "How is your head feeling today?"

"It's all right." Helen shrugged her hand away. She heard her mother sigh as she reached for her coat and crossed the room. Then came the sound of the door opening and Helen willed her mother to leave quickly to leave her alone. But the door didn't close.

"Why don't you give one of your friends a call? Find out what results they got?"

Helen clamped her mouth tight and leaned against the window. Once again, she struggled to pin down how she'd ended up here. The days she'd spent in bed, blinded by headache and nausea, were impossible to fit into the time she could see had passed on the calendar. She didn't trust herself, was scared of the shaky episodes of unreality that swept over her when she tried to put things together in a proper chronology. The cat reappeared from underneath the car and ran across the road. Helen held her breath as a car drove past, but the cat was disappearing through its flap, one leg left outside as it eased its way in.

The flat was silent. Helen went into "her" room and lay down on the bed, trying to calm the throbbing over her right eye. It was nothing like it had been, when she couldn't get away from the pain. Those days had been awful, the walls breathing themselves in and out with the whooshing sound of a huge set of bellows and the air as dense as water, swirling faces passed too fast for her to recognize them, shooting words in rapids and whirls before sucking them away and leaving her stranded.

274

The worst was the not remembering. All her mother would say was that she'd be better off forgetting about it. It was bad enough knowing she'd been sick in the car, and she couldn't bring herself to press for more. So she kept it inside, the knowledge that she was crazy, or that she was going to die. One or the other seemed a certainty. The pain had made every day seem the same, the aureole of light on the edges of her vision and the rocking instability forcing her to lie still, but not letting her sleep. Was it four days? Five?

One thing she couldn't believe was that the Dovers had gone. Was her mother making it up? She said the house had been damaged by the fire, but the bonfire hadn't been that big. She closed her eyes and tried to remember something, anything, of what had happened after she'd seen Seth and Moira. The vision played out in her head endlessly, sometimes as though she stood there hidden, and sometimes with Moira laughing up at her face. Anything later, however hard she tried to summon it up, slid away. Sometimes she was sure she'd seen the bonfire dying away, but then the certainty would dissolve and she'd be back at the start. Hidden away in a corner of her mind was the feeling she'd done something. Why else would Victoria leave without saying anything? She'd mentioned leaving at the end of the summer more than once, but they were going to stay in touch, visit each other.

Helen went through to the kitchen and lifted the telephone receiver, listening to the dial tone making its indifferent sound. Her finger went to the first digit of her dad's number before she put the receiver down.

She hadn't seen him since the fire, either. Sometimes her mother made excuses about him being busy, and sometimes she let slip a comment that showed she was angry with him, but would never explain why. She hadn't exactly said that Helen couldn't talk to him, but she hadn't suggested it either. Helen picked the receiver up again but stopped with it halfway. Was it that he didn't want to talk to her? Slowly, she carried it on up until it rested against her ear. It was worse not knowing.

There was no answer.

Propped against the row of new and shiny cookbooks was the envelope with her exam results. She had refused to open it, had left the room when her mother read the list aloud. Now it sat there, containing within its square brown corners everything that was wrong: the flat, the town. The dreary and endless clouds, the grey line of sand that went on and on towards a sea that knew better than to come any closer. Grabbing it, she tore at the edges, ripping again and again. Her breath came in sobs and the envelope wasn't enough. She wanted — no *needed* — more. But the kitchen offered nothing. The edges of the worktops were too smooth, the drawers too efficient. She sank to the floor, her fingers writhing into her hair, catching, pulling, dragging her forehead down against her knees and making it bang into them over and over.

Afterwards, nothing had changed. The apples sat in the bowl on the table, the clock on the cooker made its click as the numbers turned over.

But Helen knew what she could do.

She searched for coins in pockets, drawers, and the jar on the kitchen shelf. There was enough for the bus. She couldn't find a key, but it didn't matter. She wasn't coming back. The door slammed behind her, and she picked up speed as she went down the stairs and out into the road.

CHAPTER
THIRTY-TWO

The rain was plastering her hair against her cheeks and her neck. She didn't care. It didn't seem to be enough, in fact. The cottage was nothing but an empty shell, a black and broken tooth at the end of the row. The roof was gone, the rafters crossing the gap, but themselves eaten away, ready to crumble. And the smell: it had been there even as she got off the bus, a trail of scent that hadn't seemed real. Coming down the lane, it became stronger, building into a heavy and acrid weight that settled in her throat and scoured the lining of her nose.

The furniture was piled out in the rain: armchairs, a broken-fronted cupboard from the sitting room, all of them blackened and wet. She picked up a couple of books, scorched from the fire and pulped by the rain. One had half a cover remaining: *War and* . . . Through the rain and the mud and the smell of the ash, she recalled the sound of the flames and realized she was standing in the blackened circle where the bonfire had been. It was so small, so contained. Something was sticking out of the ground and she crouched down to pick it up. A spout of white china, the inside edges stained with brown, and half of a pink flower visible on the broken end. She could picture the teapot, standing on the top shelf of the sideboard in the kitchen. Her fingers curled around it, and she felt the sharp edge digging into the heel of her hand. This was why they'd had to go, she could understand now. A ball of anger squeezed at her stomach, displacing the suppressed sense of unease. How could her mother not have told her? And obviously Victoria hadn't been in contact; she'd have so much to do with settling in to a new place. There would be so much to replace as well. She heard Victoria's voice: *You should learn to travel light, Helen. Who knows when you'll need to get somewhere fast?* It was only a matter of time. She'd hear from her.

The doors were boarded up, but one side of the back door was loose. Helen squeezed through, hearing nothing but the flapping of the plastic, which covered the holes where the windows had been.

There was nothing left of the kitchen. The sink was hanging from the wall and a trellis of lath was visible where the plaster had fallen off. She stepped across to the sitting-room door. There was a pattern of smoke on the walls, but the devastation was less than in the kitchen, although everything was sodden, mould already spreading up the walls. On the wall behind the couch, a pale rectangle marked the position of the painting of Alice. Helen stood and stared at the space, imagining the paint blistering, Alice's beautiful skin bubbling away from the canvas, running over the frame and sliding away down the wall, and she turned to run, clawing at the plastic sheeting.

How had it happened? Again, she felt certain she'd watched the bonfire dying away. None of it made any sense. The trembling started to rock at the pit of her stomach. If she imagined it hard enough, Victoria would stick her head out of an upstairs window, asking her where she'd been. Pippa would come running around the corner of the house, full of a scheme to turn the garden into a swimming pool or something. She tried harder. It couldn't have been more than a week since they'd all been sitting around the bonfire, with music pouring out and Seth's hand on her arm?

The trembling carried on up the left side of her body and spread over her chest until she couldn't breathe. She was going to die here, with the cold, dead smell of spent ash swamping her senses. It was everywhere, layered on the walls and the grass, swallowing up the smell of the canal, mocking the pathetic ring of blackened grass where they had sat and watched the docile flames of the party. Why couldn't she remember? Everything was turning grey. And she was crying, but she didn't know who for, and the shadow of it all blew up like a mushroom cloud and was going to bury her. With an effort, she forced her feet to lift and fall, and soon she was staggering down the side of the house and back to the canal.

The boat was there, tied to its mooring pins and shifting very gently under the onslaught of the rain. Had it been there when she arrived? She couldn't remember seeing it, and now it seemed too normal. She peered in through the window, holding her breath for something, she didn't know what, but there was no one onboard. A couple of mugs stood on the upturned box, a crate of empty beer bottles sat against the edge. Everyone had gone. She stepped back, keeping one hand against the side of the cabin.

"Won't find nobody there, my dear."

The voice came from behind, making her jump. The boat rocked and she almost lost her balance on the edge of the bank. It was Mrs Tyler, under an umbrella, her head bobbing.

"Where have they —" Helen wiped her face with her sleeve, and tried to take a deeper breath. "Do you know where they are?"

But Mrs Tyler was already turning away. "No good asking me. What do I know?"

She came to a halt and turned again, pointing at Helen with a gnarled, unsteady finger. "It was a bad night's work, a bad night. And now they say I've to go as well, not safe, some such rubbish." She went back to her shuffle, heading towards her cottage. "Fifty years I've been here, and they say I have to get out. Terrible business." She stopped again, shaking her head but not seeming to know that Helen was there any more. "Poor little maid."

She was being left behind by the last person on the earth. The bus had dropped her by the bridge, but she didn't need to go back there. She was never going back. Now that she'd seen the cottage, she was going to find her dad. Surely, whatever she had done, he would want to see her. But nobody answered her knocking. There were no lights on in the house, and the curtains were open, everything was quiet. The car was in the drive, though. Was he in the garage? She would open the door and he would be there, and everything would be all right. Sort of all right.

But the garage door was locked. She banged for a bit before giving up. There was nothing she could do. She slid down the door until she hit the ground. Her legs hurt and she felt lost and she didn't have any money for a bus. She didn't even have any tears. She had come to the end.

Somehow it was dark. Headlights appeared. For a moment, she thought it was her dad coming back. When the car stopped, though, it was her mother who stepped out, pulling her up, wrapping her in the blanket from the back seat, rocking her backwards and forwards.

Nothing was said the following morning, or the morning after. But it was only a matter of time.

"You have to understand, I'm only doing what's best for you."

Helen wriggled up the bed to the furthest corner. She refused to meet her mother's gaze.

"But I want to go back to Dad's." Nervous tension was making her shake; she pushed her spine up against the headboard to steady herself. "I don't know why you keep saying I have to stay here, but it doesn't matter, I'm going back."

The silence in the room continued for longer than felt right. She was shaking again, staring out of the window so she wouldn't have to see her mother's face.

"I don't need to unpack those boxes, because I'm taking everything back."

She stole a glance sideways. Her mother had her hands folded on her lap. She didn't seem to be listening to her statements of intent.

"I hate it here, I want to go home." Her voice went up like a child. She hated herself for sounding so pathetic.

Her mother's voice, when it came, was matter-of-fact, with a hint of sadness.

"I can understand how you feel, but your father and I have talked about it, and, for the time being, I'm afraid you'll have to get used to being here."

"No." Helen rubbed her sleeve quickly across her eyes; she was not going to cry. Her fingernails dug themselves deep into her forearm, and she felt the sting of tears subside. "I'm not going to."

"Helen, you're going to have to be grown up about this." Helen pulled her legs away so that her mother couldn't pat them. "Your father is not coping well at the moment. If you were there, he would find things too difficult."

"Why? What's the matter?" She hated it when her mother used that voice. "Are you stopping him from coming here? Why isn't he telling me this?"

"Of course I'm not. And he will come and see you when he's feeling better, then he can explain properly."

They both waited for more, but in the end her mother got up and left the room, and Helen lay there and stared at the wall. The deep emptiness of everything expanded around her until she was nothing but a grain of sand hidden in the corner of a cavern so vast that the sound of her voice would go unnoticed for the whole of eternity. The balloon inside her chest was growing until her lungs could no longer draw breath, and her skin was pulsing with the effort of holding herself together. She pinched at her forearm with her thumb and forefinger, digging in hard with her nails. She wanted to pierce the skin, because once it was breached she could peel herself out, leaving her old self lying on the bed like an empty carapace.

But it wasn't enough. With painstaking slowness, she pushed herself over and reached under the bed for the wooden box with the hinged lid. The shard of broken china felt cool against her skin, and she let her eyes drop their focus. The soft surface of her arm pillowed against the sharp, delicate edge; she could almost hear the exquisite moment when it gave in to the pressure. With the blood came a clear line of pain that sucked at the morass that was her being. She felt herself grow distant, watching from far away as the space inside pulled at the darkness until it had all of the hurt contained.

The following morning, she woke to find the boxes unpacked. It didn't matter. Nothing mattered. Under the concealing length of her sleeve, she felt for the throbbing surface of the cut.

CHAPTER
THIRTY-THREE

Helen used what felt like her last bit of energy to stand out against going to the sixth form of her old school and, towards the end of September, began her A levels at the town's technical college. Each day she turned up and went through the motions, her main aim to stay anonymous. She had given up on hearing from Victoria and, most of the time at least, managed not to think about the fire. It wasn't that it had gone away, more that she was in some sort of soundproofed space where not much was allowed in. The college was all right. She did enough work to stave off attention, and soon got a reputation for surliness that kept the other students at arm's length. At least no one she knew from her old life went there. Much of the time, she didn't feel that she existed at all.

The year was drawing close to Halloween, with the dark coming early and damp piles of leaves underfoot. Sometimes, she caught the smell of smoke in the air, perhaps from a chimney or the occasional bonfire, and the reminder made her heart race and her palms sweat. One day, as she was leaving college, she saw her dad waiting at the gates. She slowed to a halt, letting a chattering crowd surge past. Beyond his head she could see the lights of the nursery school across the road. Its windows were covered in paper pumpkins, their wobbly cut-out teeth grinning in anticipation. She counted them all, first one way and then the other, before she went forwards to meet him.

"Hi." Her hands were deep in her pockets to stop them from shaking. Under the orange light of the streetlamp, he was old, as if the elasticity in his skin had given up. She didn't know what to say. He reached an arm out as if to touch her shoulder, but let it fall back down by his side.

"I thought I could drive you home." His voice sounded rough, as though it wasn't being used much.

"To the house? Do you mean I can come back?"

He seemed confused, and the realization that he thought of the flat as her home left a hollow space before he even spoke.

"I mean your mum's."

She couldn't meet his eyes. "No. It's OK. The bus stop's right here."

He fell into step beside her, and they reached the shelter in silence. The bench inside was full.

"So, how are things at college?" He was wearing his old anorak, the one he'd never throw out, with pockets that hung down with the weight of everything in them. Helen took a sideways glance at the hair straggling over the back of his collar and the pouches under his eyes. She dropped her gaze, and had to wait for her voice to steady.

"OK."

They stood for a bit longer. A bus came along, stopped. She was aware of the door as it hissed open,

286

the flurry of bodies shifting forwards, waiting to flash their passes and sway along to find a seat. The doors closed, and the lights from the windows drew away.

"Is there anywhere we can sit down?"

She made a gesture towards the bus shelter.

"No." His smile was sad. "Where we can talk."

The air in the pub smelled of old cigarettes and bleach spray. Her dad paused as they went through the door, and she wondered if he, too, was wondering how they had arrived at this place. The table had uneven legs, and the faux leather seat of the chair was sticky. She watched as he went up to the bar and waited for someone to appear. He had changed, his shoulders were smaller, all his bulk sitting at a lower point, dragging his whole body down. Under the table, she pinched the skin on the inside of her leg, the soft bit above her knee, and felt the pain in her chest subside.

Coke was the wrong drink, too cold, the chinking ice cubes setting off a shiver that travelled up her arm and over her whole upper body. Her dad had beer, the frothy head slopping over the side before coming to rest in a diminishing mass on the table.

"These were your favourite, weren't they?" he said, holding out a packet of prawn cocktail crisps.

She let him put them on the table in front of her. She didn't want to eat anything.

"I want to say sorry." His attention was too much now. All she could see were his eyes, burning out of the greyness of his face.

"Dad —"

"No, listen." He turned back to his beer, and a tremor passed over his face. "I can't explain why, but . . . well, things have been difficult lately." He cleared his throat, and her fingers closed back on the skin of her leg. "I know it's been difficult for you too, and I'm sorry."

"Dad . . ." Her voice came out louder than she had expected. It wasn't fair. He'd had time to think, to prepare for this. She closed her eyes for a second and then tried again. "Dad, when can I come home?"

He gave a sort of a laugh, drawn from the back of his throat. "Love, it's not that easy."

"But it is." She could feel tears starting, deep in her chest. "I know Mum doesn't want me to go, but I hate being in her flat. I thought you'd understand." Her voice wobbled, and the last words came out in a rush. "I'll make tea every night. I'll wash the dishes. I'll tidy up. I won't complain about anything. Let me come back."

But he didn't touch her or come around or say comforting words. He sat in his seat and she sat in her seat and she let the tears run down her cheeks and felt them drip round the edge of her chin and run under her scarf.

"The trouble is . . ." He stopped for a long time, long enough for her to start to feel scared.

"Dad?"

"If I'd made sure, if I'd been more careful." His head came up but it wasn't her he saw. "It was negligence, they said. That's a terrible thing to live with."

She waited for more but nothing followed. The woman behind the bar went out through a door at the back, leaving it swinging to and fro. From some dim corner Helen could hear the slow ticking of a clock. Her father lifted his glass as if he was going to drink, but his hand stopped halfway. He stared at the glass as if wondering what it was, and then placed it back on the beer mat.

"I'd better get you home."

He meant it. Her home, the flat. With her mother. Helen pushed her drink from the table. The glass shattered, the ice skidded and the liquid hit the floor and bounced up and crashed against the edge of her world like a wave. She dragged her coat sleeve over her eyes, the rough material scraping at her skin.

"I'll get the bus."

Her dad stared at the glass on the floor and the widening pool of Coke. He didn't seem to be able to understand what had happened.

"I've got the car, I can take you home."

"Don't you understand?" A whiteness flared in front of her eyes. "I don't want you to take me back to that place. I don't want to see you ever again!"

And as she grabbed for her bag and stumbled against the chair, he was saying something, but she wouldn't listen.

Somehow she was in the bright box of the bus watching him getting smaller and further away. In her pocket was the bag of prawn cocktail crisps.

CHAPTER
THIRTY-FOUR

In the end, she couldn't keep the silence going, not everywhere, not with everyone.

November turned out to be a month of unseasonable warmth, a delayed Indian summer, the days beginning with the lightest touch of winter's bite that was gone by the middle of the morning. On the news, statistics were bandied about: it was the warmest November since records began, they'd found the earliest duckling, photographed the most unseasonal blossom.

Other, gloomy, voices warned that the cold would come and these unseasonal portents of the new year would die, and nature would withdraw, wrong-footed and bruised. In the meantime, Helen felt herself uncoil, allowing approaches towards friendship to extend their roots and conversation to draw her in. Sometimes, she found herself laughing. It was only at home, now, that she kept the blanket of silence pulled down close and heavy, and even this began to show some fraying edges. Until the day in December when her mother called her from her room and asked her to sit down, as she had something she had to tell her.

Her mother was spitting out waves of energy. Her eyes glittered and a restless force kept her pacing over to the window, back to the door, across to the fireplace where she fidgeted with the china figures.

Helen kept her eyes fixed on the carpet, at the spot where some of the nylon pile had snagged and a curly tuft sprang out, no matter how many times her mother poked it back under with the point of a knitting needle.

She didn't understand: in what sense was her dad gone?

"Is . . ." Her voice was croaky, as if the remembered smoke had come back to steal it. She coughed, swallowed. "Is he going to come back?"

"That's what we don't know." Her mother took a deep breath. Helen wanted to shut her eyes, to block her ears. She wanted her mother to stop, but the tension rising up in her chest, the sort of feeling she had when she was going to be sick, told her that it was coming, whether she liked it or not. Her mother came to sit down, tried to take hold of Helen's hand. "The house has been left as if he's gone out for a walk. The car is in the driveway." She stood up again, smoothed her skirt over her hips. "There are no reports of anything, the hospitals, the police . . ."

With a remote part of her brain, Helen could see there was worry there, but as ever, none free from the taint of anger. She watched as her mother forced a smile. "We thought you should know, that you needed to be . . . prepared. He may turn up. They do, sometimes."

"Who's 'we'?" Helen asked, finally able to grab hold of something recognizable. "Who decided I should know?"

"There's a very nice policewoman, she supports people like us."

People like us? What did that mean?

"How long has he been gone?" Rage was starting to build in her stomach now, but it was cold and heavy, weighing her down in the chair. "When did he go?"

"They've given me some leaflets, and you can go and talk to them as well."

"How long has he been gone?"

Her mother had been standing by the fireplace, one hand on the mantelpiece, looking at her with an expression that must have been aiming for understanding compassion. Had that policewoman been teaching her how? Her eyes met with Helen's, and she faltered, turned, and seemed to be studying the painting on the wall.

"The milk in the fridge was dated from the beginning of November." She swung back round. "It's been a terrific strain, you know, trying to find out what was going on, not letting you worry."

From somewhere, the impulse came to get up, cross the room, escape. But as she reached the door, she stopped.

"What about the boat?" She knew what had happened. He'd taken the boat and sailed away. And she didn't blame him, not one bit. A tiny bubble of relief detached itself from the weight in her midriff and forced its way up towards her brain. A whole month they'd waited to tell her, and she was the only one who knew what he'd done. "Has anyone tried to find his boat? Why don't you ask your police friend about that, Barbara?"

Her mother stepped forwards and put her hands on Helen's shoulders. Helen was not going to fall for the pretence of understanding; she was not going to listen.

"Helen, the boat was tracked as far as the sea."

Helen pulled away, took a step backwards. So they knew? Why was everyone so sombre, then?

"So he sailed away. Don't you see? He made it! He went out to sea like he always wanted to!"

"I'm so sorry."

Her mother's voice was relentless. "He had no navigational equipment, no radio. And his boat hasn't been seen since it left the estuary . . ."

CHAPTER
THIRTY-FIVE

2013

I have been angry for such a long time. In the journal I kept over the winter that followed my father's disappearance, it spilled out in automatic writing, the words scraped into the page and spilling dark thoughts in long and furious sentences. I kept the notebooks hidden, but not well. I wanted my mother to find them, read them, see what she was doing to me. It was anger that propelled me from my mother's flat, from my mother's life. It got me to Manchester, has been sustaining me for my entire adult life.

I can hear Larry's voice, coming across the counter, followed up by his rattling cough. *You should call your mother, get it all out in the open.* He made me tell her where I was, that was his condition for me staying. Other than that, he largely left it alone. Not one for emotions, Larry. Even so, he would occasionally let something drop. *Young girl like you, should be out having fun. You need to leave it behind, whatever it is. Face it or leave it.* I couldn't do either, and he was generous enough not to force the issue.

He saved me, Larry did. He gave me first a job, then a home, and finally, by leaving me the shop, he gave me the option to stay hidden. I think of him as I sit on the train, watching the flat Lancashire land roll past. I have my back to my destination, even though travelling backwards makes me feel sick. I can't bear to look at where I'm going.

The station has that jarring sense of being the same but different. I'm not even sure of what I should be remembering. There are so many things I'm not sure about. Will my mother even be in the same flat? Can I remember how to get there? What exactly am I going to say?

Southport. The end of the line. When the train pulls in, I am submerged with the memory of unhappiness. The word feels inadequate, what I felt was misery, despair. The air is so heavy around me that the thought of getting off the train is too much, and I'm there in my seat when the conductor gets back on. He asks me if I'm all right, but he wants me out of his way. I can see it in his eyes. I'm another loony tune, sitting in his carriage wearing a knitted hat in spite of the sun. It was the best I could find, I want to tell him. You should see my hair. But he's already moving away and there are people climbing into the carriage for the return trip, so I force myself to stand and, before I'm ready, I'm down there on the platform.

Things are familiar but wrong. There's a brown china jug with a highly glazed swirl of green and yellow running around its belly; a pair of brass ducks, one larger than the other; an owl made out of shells. They belong in a different house, in my childhood world. If I were to reach out, I feel as if I could touch the wallpaper from that time, step back into myself and be back there, Dad in front of the TV, the boat in the garage, the world intact.

I sit on a hard chair and anchor my hands beneath my thighs. There is a smell, a subtle combination of minutiae of life: cleaning products and food, breathed air, soap, the Welsh wool blanket on the back of the sofa, a particular type of hand cream. I've not smelled it for more than half of my life but my brain recognizes it immediately.

We haven't said anything yet. Quite literally, we haven't said a word. I found the flat by not thinking about it. I kept my head down and put one foot in front of the other until there I was, ringing a bell, and there she was, peering out at me. I followed her into the room I'm in now, and she silently left me to make a pot of tea. At least, that's what I assume.

The woman who finally comes back, carrying a tray, is too small. She has the hands of an old lady, and I can see scalp through the thinning waves of her hair. I feel too big here, as if I have been pumped full of air. The lightness in my head is tugging me towards the ceiling, and I hold on to my seat with both hands.

The mugs are new, white and slightly tapered towards the base, but I recognize the teapot: stainless steel, the inside darkened to the mahogany tint of many hundreds of spoonfuls of tea.

"I went to a gallery opening last night." The words come out with no preamble. "It was Victoria." I take a breath. "Do you remember her?"

What am I expecting? Guilty silence? Denial? Tears?

She sits down in the wing-sided armchair facing the fire and leans forwards as if she wants to poke the flames. But it's gas, not wood, and she sits back, her hands folded in her lap, her body angled towards me.

"I need to know what happened." The words hang in the air, and I am confused about my meaning.

My mother clears her throat and speaks for the first time. "When, exactly?" Her voice sounds hoarse. I wonder if I am imagining that her grip has tightened.

"Well, the fire, for a start."

"You knew about the fire. You were there."

I find muscles clenching in familiar patterns of frustration.

"I only remember the bonfire." I swallow, trying not to let the images in my mind take over my consciousness. "But afterwards. I went to the cottage and it was burned. I didn't see that happen. And you told me they were all OK, that they'd gone away." My voice is shaking, and I have to find something to wipe my eyes on. I can't find a tissue anywhere, and use my sleeve.

Her hand plucks at the arm of the chair.

"Why didn't you tell me about the fire, that the cottage was burned?" Despite myself, I hear my voice rise into something very close to a whine.

Her fingers are tracing the raised pattern of the upholstery now, her eyes fixed on the picture above the fire. The stag stands in his glen, looking right back at her. I hope so much that she will tell me I am overreacting, that I am imagining the whole thing. But I am not going to be that lucky.

"It seemed the best thing at the time." She glances at my face, then back at the stag. He must be easier to face. "I . . ." She pauses. "We thought you had enough to deal with."

My throat is tight, not wanting to let the words out. It's like a safety mechanism, because if the words came out, so would all the anger, and I'm scared of the depths I might yet discover. "I thought I'd done something wrong, and that was why they didn't find me." Despite my best efforts, tears are forcing their way out again, and the wet cloth of my sleeve is rough as it sweeps them away. "Pippa . . ." My throat locks shut this time, finally getting to the question that's been pushing itself up at me ever since last night. I try again. "Did something happen to Pippa?"

Her hand reaches across towards me, even though I am too far away for contact. I realize that I have drawn my legs further back at the same moment as her hand drops.

"Your father never forgave himself," she says.

I wait for her to elaborate, but her face is lost somewhere distant. I am about to ask her what she means when the quiet is broken by the sound of the front door opening. There are voices in the hallway, and a child comes running through and launches herself on to my mother's lap.

"Nanny Babs, I've got a new doll!"

My mother's face breaks into a smile. She leans towards the child, reaching a hand out to smooth her hair.

"You'll have to show me." Her voice has lifted in pitch, and I am taken aback by the tenderness in her eyes. "Why don't you go and find a biscuit?"

A young woman is standing in the doorway. She is much younger than me, probably not thirty yet, and she watches her daughter charge into the kitchen before running her eyes over me and turning to my mother.

"Everything OK, Babs?"

She's beautiful, with glowing black skin, a bundle of curls tied up in a red scarf, a gap between her front teeth. As she stands there, she slips off her jacket and throws it down on to the end of the sofa.

"Yes, yes." My mother stands up now, and waits for the woman to come and give her a hug. Then, keeping her hold on the woman's arm, she turns to me, but talks to her. "This is my daughter."

The woman's head goes up, a tiny gesture that shows she knows exactly who I am. Her expression suggests that her thoughts are not positive. I feel myself shrink, and I put up a hand to push hair behind my ear, and only remember it's not there when my fingers touch the rough wool of my beret.

"I'm Olivia." She holds out a hand and I give it a tentative shake. "I come and help your mum out."

The silence is broken by the girl, who runs back in holding a biscuit in each hand. She stops, the atmosphere bringing her to a halt as effectively as a brick wall. Her gaze is uncertain as she turns to her mother, peeking at me from the corner of her eye.

"And this —" My mother holds out an arm, and puts on a cheery voice — "is Lola."

Lola smiles again, and carries on towards the chair, leaning on the arm as she takes a bite out of first the right-hand biscuit, then the left.

"Lola comes every week to tell me about everything she's been up to, don't you, poppet?"

My fingernails have found their way under my sleeves, and I dig in hard. I sense Olivia's glance, but cannot risk making eye contact with anyone. My gaze is fixed on the carpet. Any minute now, someone is going to tell me to mind my manners. Instead, Olivia steps forwards and holds a hand out to her daughter.

"Lola, baby, we forgot to get the milk!" The words rise in mock horror, and Lola reacts to what is clearly a familiar game. Her hands go up and she opens her eyes wide.

"Oh no! Nanny Babs won't be able to have any tea!"

"That's right." Olivia squats, and holds the palm of her hand for a brief instant against Lola's round cheek. "Let's go to the corner shop and see if they have any." She checks my mother again, and receives an imperceptible nod. These two know each other well.

When they have gone, silence falls again. I have cracked open my anger, and found nothing but an empty husk. They have left so my mother and I can say what we need to say, but I don't know what that is any more. When I tell her I am going, my mother doesn't argue. She pushes herself upright and disappears into her bedroom. I stand with one hand on the front door, wondering if she has gone in there for good, whether she is making a significant gesture; shutting out the past, leaving me standing there in uncertainty. The

300

wallpaper in front of me has a raised pattern of circular bumps, in the same inoffensive cream as in all my mother's homes. I scrape my fingernails down the wall, catching them on those smug bumps. One of them lifts away from the wall. I feel the urge to sink my nails right in, to grip the plaster and tear it out in chunks. I want to rip at the paper, pulling it off in long, ragged strips. I imagine it coming away from the wall, widening outwards to become a mighty triangular flag. Instead, I push the tiny bump of texture back into place. Nobody would know it had ever been torn.

The door from the bedroom opens, and my mother comes out carrying a brown cardboard box. She comes towards me and, although it's hard to tell in the dim hall light, it seems her eyes are red.

"I've had this saved for you." Her voice is normal. "I never knew whether to send it or not." She passes the box across and I stand there holding it, wondering what to do next.

"Does Olivia come every day?" It's a stupid question, and it is not enough to take the place of all of the questions I thought I wanted to ask, but it's all I can come up with.

"No." In spite of myself, I have an empty feeling as I see the happiness that briefly lights my mother's face. "Once or twice a week." She holds my gaze. "All I ever wanted was a daughter, you know." The words are so quiet, I'm not even sure that I've heard them.

In the end, she makes the first move.

"Shall I get the door for you?" she asks.

I step out on to the landing.

"Helen."

I stop and turn back, barely able to see around the edge of the box. It's the first time she has used my name. She is talking to me as a person, not a daughter.

"Yes?"

"I wanted to protect you."

She hesitates, then carries on.

"I didn't hate your father. But he didn't leave an explanation. He left you with nothing." She is holding the side of the door as if she needs its support. "I found that hard to forgive."

CHAPTER
THIRTY-SIX

There's a tall stand of leylandii along the front now, their feathery green branches obscuring the view. I pay off the taxi, and step closer to the gate, so that I can see through to the house. New windows and smooth, cream paint; a white plastic porch with a lockable door and fake stained glass; heavy drapes at the windows with matching pelmets. It reminds me of the Weavers' house further up the lane, as it used to be. I draw closer, and more of the garden comes into view. It's smaller than I remember. The grass seems greener, and there are tidy flowerbeds in front of the house. Then I see an empty space. Our garage is gone, our ugly garage with the breeze-block walls, the corrugated roof and double doors. There's a new garage further across, built closer to the house with a brick walkway connecting the two. It's much bigger, and there are windows in the roof: a workroom? Office? There are no cars in the drive, no sign of life beyond the half-drawn curtains of the house, so I push at the gate to get closer.

My memory is unreliable. I'm not sure if the drive is in the same place, and the new garage blocks off the side of the house, making it hard to calculate angles and distances. I think I can see a line under the grass where a wall might have been. Standing back, with my eyes half-closed, I try to overlay the sense of what I remember with what is in front of me. As the details slip into place, a voice comes from behind.

"Excuse me, but can I help you?"

Standing by the gate, wearing Wellington boots and holding the lead of a heavy, black Labrador, is a white-haired lady with an expression ready to tip into suspicion. What I should do is shift the box on to my left hip and walk towards her with my right hand outstretched and apologize for my intrusion. I should explain why I'm here before apologizing again, complimenting her on her display of Michaelmas daisies, and taking my leave. But the image of the boat, resting in the dim light of the garage, Dad sitting in his chair staring at who knows what visions and working his way through his crate of beer, is filling my mind, and I stumble on the words.

"I . . ." My throat is bunched tight. "I'm so sorry." Not for being here. For being here like this. For not asking more questions and for ignoring the gaps in other people's stories. For the house and the garage and the boat. And for Dad. The lady stands there with her gardener's hands and her well-behaved dog and regards me with a frown. Perhaps she is wondering what I have in the box, and what I am intending to do with it.

I try again. "I used to live here, you see." My emotions are settling to a manageable level, and I even squeeze out a deprecating smile. "I was passing, and I wanted to . . . revisit."

Her face relaxes.

"That must have been quite some time ago," she says, her voice less icy now she is able to place me in a category. She unclips the dog's lead and he slumps on to the ground, resting his muzzle on his paws. "The folk before us had no children, I believe."

"Oh, goodness, yes." I hear myself laugh and wonder where this is coming from. Who on earth am I pretending to be? "It's all very different."

"I should imagine so." She bends her head, as if accepting praise.

"In fact, I was trying to decide where my dad's garage used to be."

"Ah, yes." She smiles, giving a small shake of the head at the same time, and I follow her as she walks over to where the garage used to be, where the boat spent so many years. The Labrador heaves himself up. When we come to a halt, he ambles across to sniff at my feet.

We both stand and regard the grass.

"Absolute deathtrap," she says.

"Sorry?"

"The garage. No foundations, and the wrong cement had been used, so none of the blocks were stable." She turns to give me a stern look. "And the roof was made of asbestos. Terrible!"

I make some noise of shocked agreement. From where we are standing, I can see into the back garden. The tree has been cut down.

There is nothing more to be said.

Her eyes follow me as I walk down to the gate and out on to the lane.

I expected the house to be different, but I'm totally unprepared for the sight of the canal. There's a whole line of boats, for a start, shiny doll's houses with names like *At Last!* and *Dream On*, moored in a neat line against the opposite bank. The canal I remember was thick with weeds. The few boats that came by were dilapidated, and their roofs were stacked with bags of coal and ramshackle trolleys, cats curled onboard in the sun.

I slip back to the summer that was ours. I don't remember anyone else being there for all of those long, hot weeks. Only us and the water. The boat.

One of the fields on the far side is now a marina, with thirty or so boats packed in rows along wooden pontoons. There is a footbridge, a sign for a coffee shop. The landscaping around the basin still looks raw, with grass growing in thin patches and bare saplings strapped to supporting posts at regular intervals. To the left are apartments, some sporting flat Juliet balconies. The water is the same, though, a thick grey-green, flowing at a sluggish pace in the breeze.

I turn away from the edge and push through an unfamiliar black-and-white kissing gate. And here are the cottages. The hedge has gone and rose bushes, heavy with big, pink blossoms, edge the gardens instead. The basic proportions of the buildings are the same, but they hold no sense of the place I remember. The first cottage has a white cruiser tied to the canal bank, and a trampoline on a patch of grass. A dog barks in the front window of the second. I see the old lady's face peering out at us, complaining about the racket we were making, always grumbling about how young people behaved. How everyone behaved. Except Pippa. More than once we'd found her sitting on a high stool in Mrs . . . Mrs . . . Tyler's kitchen, eating bread and jam and chattering away. A pain twists in my stomach.

The last time I saw Mrs Tyler was the day I found the empty shell of the cottage, the burned and ashy remains. Very clearly, I recall what she said. *Poor little maid*. I'd thought she was saying it about me, but I realize there's something wrong with the memory. If I had been the one to feel sorry for, she'd have done something, surely. Asked if I was all right, taken me inside for sweet tea. She was crusty and abrupt, but not unkind. If it wasn't me, though, who did she mean? The third cottage is paved right up to the door, a large motorbike propped in the middle, like a decorative feature. I stop and study the final cottage, and feel nothing. I have no emotion left. The walls are straight and the windows are clean. The roof is weathered. There is nothing to suggest it has ever been any different. I rest my cardboard box on the wall. A spot of rain lands, leaving a polka dot on the brown surface. And another.

As the droplets increase I cross over the road. The bridge on my left is the same, at least. The path on the other side lapses into gravel, and soon there are fields again. The breeze is more demanding now, and more rain dots the top of the cardboard box. I keep walking even when the gravel peters out. This time, there are no brambles stopping my progress. My feet step on and on. They go over the tussocks, round the molehills and past the dog mess. The canal stays in my peripheral vision and it seems as if it's the towpath that's rolling along in step with the water and I'm walking to stay in the same place. It comes as a surprise when I reach the lock.

The lock gates are straight now, and freshly painted. The black arms end with a section of white, the line between dark and light ruler-straight. A laminated board shows the route of the canal in either direction, but I'm not ready to see that yet. The lock itself is in its empty phase, green slime coating the walls and a steady trickle of water running over from the higher side of the canal and splashing into the water at the bottom of the pound. An elderly couple, wearing full walking gear and swinging fancy aluminium sticks in pace with their stride, come up the short slope where the towpath climbs to keep up with the rise of the water. The man tips his cap at me and they both smile. A swallow darts past and makes a tight turn. Where the canal stretches away, I can make out a pair of swans. Life has carried on.

When my dad took his boat out on what I don't want to think of as his final voyage, he wouldn't have come this way because of the state of the lock at the time. If I want to find him, I'm going to have to follow the water on the far side of the cottages. I stop in front of the board now, and see where the canal loops around the alluvial plain. I can put my finger on the big lock which lets canal boats through to the river, and therefore the sea. He went this way. There are witnesses who remember his passage. I set off, this time keeping my head up. As I approach the cottages and the new marina, I see a figure standing at the bottom of the new footbridge. I don't immediately process what my eyes are telling me. It is Victoria.

CHAPTER
THIRTY-SEVEN

Her face is turned in the opposite direction, but I recognize the way she stands, the tilt of her head. Even if I'd not seen her at the gallery, I would know.

"How did you know I'd be here?" My hand reaches out by itself to touch her sleeve, as if it wants to check, independent of me, on her reality. My fingers stop short, though: she might as well have a glass wall around her.

"I'm sorry?" She steps away from me, one hand grasping the handrail as she casts a glance down the towpath.

"I've not been back here since —" I turn my head towards the cottage. "I thought, you know, at the gallery . . ." She still isn't getting it. "After I saw you at the gallery. That's why I'm here."

"I'm sorry —" she repeats, and then it's as if a curtain opens. "Helen?"

Rain starts to come down in earnest, huge drops bouncing up from the canal's surface as they hit, spreading the water out into urgent, overlapping circles. Victoria turns and half-runs across the bridge. I follow her.

My arm is pressing against her now, as we squeeze into the doorway of the café. Rain catches me on my left side, the fabric of my blouse sticking with cold heaviness to my arm. A girl in jeans with a white apron folded down and tied around her waist opens the door behind us. It catches Victoria by surprise, and I'm aware that the girl is making apologies, taking us to a table.

The air is warm and slightly humid. We sit by a window, and I forget about my hair until I pull off my hat. Victoria gapes at me.

"Helen — that was you yesterday?" She might as well have seen a ghost. "At the gallery. But you had long hair."

The elderly couple sitting a row or so away are staring at me, but I don't care any more, and the hat falls to the ground. I'm trying to put myself back in the gallery, to reclassify the expression I saw in Victoria's eyes. She didn't know who I was. How much else have I got wrong?

The waitress comes over and puts a menu on the table in front of me, as if this is a normal day. I pick it up as a reflex action, but the print moves around as if it's underwater. The waitress comes back. I shake my head. Victoria asks for coffee.

"You didn't recognize me, did you?" I say. It's all I can focus on.

Victoria weaves her fingers together. If I didn't know her, I'd say she was embarrassed. Her face wavers, a pale shape beneath her short, dark hair. *I did a good job with that haircut.* As if in response to my thought, my hand reaches up and touches the prickly ends covering my scalp. Victoria's hair has grown out many times since I cut it for her. I think of replenished skin cells, nails clipped away in millimetre increments. We are not the people we were.

"I thought you'd come because you saw me at the gallery." My voice is small.

She's fiddling with a napkin now, folding it and ripping tiny crescents of paper with her thumbnail. She glances up, giving a short laugh and shakes her head. "It's not all about you, Helen."

She has gone all blurry, so I close my eyes as she carries on talking. "I come here every year. To remember. This time it happened to be today."

Under the edge of the table, I push at the wet fabric of my sleeve so that I can drag my nails along my arm, from the crease of my elbow down to my wrist. It's an emergency action, the best I can do in the situation. I don't want to draw attention to myself.

The waitress brings Victoria's coffee. She waits for the waitress to leave, picks up the spoon and stirs.

"I owe you an apology, actually."

My voice doesn't come out at first, and I clear my throat and try again. "About what?"

"The fire, after the fire." She finally meets my eyes. "You do remember the fire?"

I swallow and try and tuck hair behind my ear. There is no hair there, of course, but the gesture is an instinctive way of gaining time. Already the silence has gone on too long.

"Yes. Well, sort of." I catch the waitress's eye and ask for a glass of water. "But it was —" I pause. I don't know how to put it. "I lost some days. Afterwards." My mouth is dry. I want to know, but I'm afraid. "I saw the house. Later on. I went back to see it. But no one would ever say what happened."

Victoria lifts her mug, but doesn't drink.

"I can't believe nobody told you, I mean, what about your dad?"

"My dad . . ." I can't manage it. I can't say that he walked out, left, that he didn't say anything about that, either.

"You genuinely don't know anything about it?"

I shake my head.

There is another silence, and this time Victoria takes a mouthful of her coffee. When she starts to talk again, she's changed tack.

"We all come, most years." She puts the mug down, fidgets with a sachet of sugar. "Piet. You remember Piet?"

How can she think I have forgotten him?

I nod.

"He's had some health issues. I knew he couldn't make it this time." She puts the sugar down. "But the boys were here. If you'd been ten minutes earlier." She looks at her watch. "They'll be on the train by now."

I close my eyes. Ten minutes.

"Seth," I say, the sound barely squeezing past the lump in my throat. "And Will. What about Pippa?"

"Pippa died, Helen. In the fire."

There's part of me that's known this ever since the film installation at the exhibition, perhaps on some level for the last thirty years, but hearing the words out loud is too much. The world contracts to enclose us in a bright square, and then expands out with nauseating speed. The force of it should knock the tables and chairs and the blackboard sign with the specials written on it out through the window and scatter everything, ourselves included, down howling streets that have no end. I hear the sound of flames bursting out. The girl in red shoes skips away from me, her plaits swinging in the heated breeze.

Victoria reaches forwards with a napkin. Her mouth is opening and closing but I can't hear any words.

"Helen!" Victoria's voice is sharp. I catch my breath in a gasp. A hand grabs on to my shoulder. "Helen, look at me."

I look. Victoria is half-standing. She keeps hold of me for a second longer, then backs into her chair. I see her turn to catch the waitress's attention. A mug of coffee appears on the table in front of me, and Victoria spoons sugar in, puts my hand around the hot china.

"Will was OK. He had minor burns and smoke inhalation." Victoria's voice is matter-of-fact now. She tilts her mug as if she is trying to read the leaves. Coffee doesn't have leaves. But she is not gazing into the future, of course; she is staring back into the past. "Alice went crazy." She looks up at me. "Sectioned. In the loony bin for months." She gives a sort of a smile, but not the kind with humour. "Seth and Piet were both in hospital for a while, too."

She pauses, takes a deep, shaking breath, and reaches for another napkin.

"Helen, what *do* you remember about that night?"

CHAPTER
THIRTY-EIGHT

"There's nothing. I don't remember anything." *Don't, or won't?* I press my knuckles into my eyes. Bright speckles invade the dark space behind my eyelids, then join and turn in patterns like a child's kaleidoscope.

"I drank so much —" I remember what she said earlier. I have to know. "What did you mean, you had something to apologize for?"

It has stopped raining now. A bright beam of sunlight slants on to the table, making Victoria hold up a hand to shade her eyes. I can't tell where she is looking.

"After the fire," she begins, "everyone blamed Piet, for not, I don't know, taking enough care. But I saw you with the petrol bomb."

I'm shaking. I see my arm go back, smell heat and petrol. But I'm in a field, and the sky above me is full of sunshine. I hear the echo of a laugh. The coldness in my stomach grows heavy. *It was me.* I struggle to follow what she says next.

". . . and Piet were in hospital, I went a bit mental. I was so sure you'd done it, but I couldn't tell anyone."

I catch the most important words. Was sure. Isn't any more.

". . . screaming at your mum." The pile of shredded paper in front of her is growing. "She was pretty cool, actually. She talked me down, got me in her car." Is she talking about my mother? Did I ever hear about this? "I was in an emergency foster home, she took me back, talked to the woman."

The point she is making finally hits me.

"You came to my house?"

"Well, you know, where you lived with your mum."

I strain to remember, to recall any hint from my mother. She must have believed it was me. I hear her voice, *anything I did, I was protecting you.*

Victoria picks up the thought, as if she is reading my mind.

"They were around for ages, these men, investigators."

I feel even more sick, as if the top of my head is coming off with the pressure.

"I picked things up, bits and pieces. First that petrol was involved." She rubs a hand around the back of her neck. "I was sure it was you, then. I knew I'd made you angry."

I don't remember.

"But you threw the bottle down the side path, the one that went along by the road." I remember the path. But I don't remember throwing anything there. I don't. "And the fire started in the kitchen."

I squeeze my eyelids together again. I try so hard to see it.

Victoria's voice carries on. It is heavy, the words burdens to be laid down. "I've gone over it so many times. I mean." Her voice wavers. "Alice didn't even know about the stupid bloody petrol bombs." She grabs at one of the napkins and drags it across her eyes. "I've always wondered . . . Alice didn't ever *say*." She bangs at the table with the palm of her hand. "She wasn't ever that coherent. They had to write it off as a probability." I feel her frustration, her desperation. "Can you imagine what it's like? Not knowing?"

We sit in silence again.

"I used to search for you, you know." My words come out of nowhere, taking me by surprise. "When the Internet came along, every so often I'd search for you." I pick up a napkin of my own and blow my nose. "There's a Victoria Dover who lives in Oregon and practises crystal therapy. I sent her a message once, in case." I laugh, and the sound is too loud.

"Did you get anything back?"

"I was on her mailing list for a while." I smile. "I kept being offered exclusive opportunities to be healed with amethysts."

The conversation is building a temporary skin, as if by sharing this trivia, the worst of the pain will subside.

"It could have been worse, I suppose." Victoria gives a tiny laugh of her own. "I could have been confused with Victoria Dover, Kipper Importer."

"Never came across her."

We pause. I have a picture of us in a parallel universe, one where we sit and swap stories and make ourselves sick with laughter.

"I never found anything about you being a photographer."

Victoria rubs at a spot on the cloth. She almost seems embarrassed.

"You know how it is, nothing for years and then you get to be talk of the month." She shakes her head. "And I had this thing about being underground and noncommercial. It's more difficult than you'd think."

"I've never thought about it much." I've never thought about it at all.

"And I wasn't Victoria Dover for years." She gives a sort of laugh with her mouth closed, a sound like a reverse sniff. "I was so pissed off with the world by the time I was, what, seventeen? Eighteen? I changed my name by deed poll, became somebody else."

"What did you change it to?"

"Something pretentious." She shakes her head. "I had a serious Indo-mystic thing going on."

"Dreadlocks?" I had given these to my imaginary Victoria, twisted with rags and ribbons, and I feel an obscure pleasure in getting something right.

"Yep. And vegan."

"How long for?"

"The hair or the diet?" She leans back in her chair, her eyes fixed on the ceiling while she calculates. "I spent a couple of years living in a sort of commune." She flicks me a glance. "Kind of inevitable. We made paper and ground our own wheat. I planned on spending the rest of my life there."

"So what happened?"

"This guy offered us a house and some land up in Scotland, and we had this huge conflict about whether to go." She gives that shake of her head. "And most of us did, but he turned out to have a hidden agenda."

She pauses, her face far away.

"And?" I want her back.

"And, well, Piet came up one day and kidnapped me. It would be called an intervention these days. And then he gave me enough money to go and travel around India. He said if I was going to do mystic, I ought to try out the real thing."

The sides of the bubble begin to thin.

"So when did you change your name back?"

"Well, you know how it is." She gives her hair a rub with the flat of her hand. "When I got married, I had to think about names again. I wasn't, you know, going to take *his* name. Once a feminist . . . So I decided to take my own name back."

"You got married?"

"No need to sound so surprised. People do, you know." She smiles as she leans sideways to get her hand into her coat pocket before holding out her phone to me. "Three kids as well."

Two boys and a girl. They are beautiful.

She turns the phone to examine the screen herself and then puts it down on the table.

I want to stay in this place, this neutral space where we can talk about normal things, but it's like when you have a scab and it makes you go back. I have to pick. The normality is only a temporary plaster.

"You said a foster home. When everyone was in hospital, I mean?"

320

Victoria's face makes a visible shift as she goes back through the intervening years.

"We went to a foster home. Will and me." She puts her head between her hands and laces her fingers into her hair. "Those poor people. We hated them so much." She sighs, sits up, and rubs her eyes. "Can you imagine, Will without Pippa, me being sent off to school in uniform, rules, deadlines?"

"But surely they understood? I mean, what you were going through?"

"Not so you'd notice." Her mouth twists in a reluctant smile. "I have to say, I'm not sure that I'd have liked us much. We were . . . resistant to being helped."

"It shouldn't be a question of liking."

"We ran away once, back to the cottage." Her voice is so calm. "I'm not sure what we thought we'd find."

I think about my own visit to the burned cottage. What should have happened is that we should have arrived at the same time, joined forces, gone to the house and insisted Dad let us all stay.

"It was awful, just so . . . empty." She is looking through me, back to a wet afternoon filled with the stench of abandoned ash, and I know what she is seeing. "Will was screaming and trying to get in, I was holding him back. We didn't have a plan. If your dad hadn't turned up, I don't know what we'd have done."

"Dad?" The word hits me in the pit of my stomach. "What —" My voice wavers. I clear my throat before I can carry on. "What did he do?"

"He was amazing. He took us back to your house and made us sandwiches. Total lifesaver." She shakes her head. "He was so good to us."

I concentrate on the chronology. "What —"

Victoria has picked up a spoon and is sliding her fingers down it, turning it over, sliding them down again, turning it over. "We stayed with him for a few days, I don't know, couple of weeks. Then Piet came and got us."

I am overtaken by involuntary spasm, a deep, inner shaking which rattles my body from its central core. All that time, when he didn't come to see me, while I was being kept away, he was there. They were there.

Victoria has a hand on my arm, and from a distance, I am aware that her mouth is forming words. It takes a time for the meaning to surface.

"Helen, what is it? What's wrong?"

I cannot speak.

"Helen?"

I don't want to open my mouth because, as soon as I do, I'm going to start crying. And then I start crying anyway, so it doesn't matter. With a tiny, lucid part of my brain, I watch a lady at another table with absolute clarity. She is sitting there with a scone on the plate in front of her, giving up all pretence of eating. I can't blame her: I would be doing the same.

The walls are too close. I stand, sending my chair down on its back. I have to get outside.

CHAPTER
THIRTY-NINE

I don't stop until I am by the water's edge, where I crouch down, holding on to my stomach. I am retching as if I'm going to be sick, but what comes up is a howl with roots in the base of my being, torn out by forces beyond my control. I am the person curled in a ball by the side of the canal, and the noise that is twisting out and spiralling up towards the sky is from me. I keen for all that is lost: for Pippa, for my dad. For the world of the summer, for myself and for all that might have been. I have been holding it inside for a very long time.

A man with a spaniel walks by on the opposite bank. He turns his head as he passes. The dog runs ahead, spotting something in the undergrowth and jumping on it with all four feet at once. I watch the dog as if, by not letting him into my field of vision, the man will cease to exist. Somehow Victoria is next to me.

"My dad disappeared." I turn to Victoria. "Did you know?"

Victoria plucks at some grass.

"I didn't, no." She sprinkles the grass stems over the water and we watch as they bob and separate. "That must have been hard."

"He said something about negligence." I close my eyes, trying to recall his words. I hear the sound of the ice cubes rattling in my drink, of Dad's voice coming out of the darkness, and I start to cry again. "I thought he was talking about me . . ." My voice cracks as the memory continues to unroll.

Victoria is a stillness beside me.

"And before, when you said about him taking you in, it made me remember how he didn't want me around. I never understood why" The words come out in jagged clumps, as painful to produce as they must be to listen to. "But he meant the petrol bombs, didn't he? That he was responsible for not getting them out of the way?"

I am rocking, my knees pulled in to my chest so that I won't fly apart. "I always knew it was my fault he left." This is the abyss. This is the knowledge I have been avoiding for the whole of my adult life. I say the words for the first time. "He killed himself. And the very last thing I said to him was that I never wanted to see him again."

"Helen, you were sixteen." Victoria speaks with absolute conviction. "You were hurt and confused and nobody was telling you what was going on."

I feel the weight of her hand on my shoulder.

"He was the one who rescued Will, you know." Victoria draws up her legs and wraps her arms around them, resting her chin on her knees. "They all went in — your dad and Piet and Seth. The firemen said it was a miracle anyone got out." She is staring out across the water, across to where the trees hide the end wall of the cottages. "The smoke was so thick that they couldn't find the stairs. He's never got over it." Victoria's voice continues as if from a great distance. I think she is talking about my dad, but it doesn't make sense after the first words. "Losing his twin, his mother. He's only ever been half a person." Will. Victoria is talking about Will. "The fact he's the one who's alive. He can't forgive himself."

Everything around is quiet, the distant barking of the spaniel the only sound. I fill in the silent half of my mother's sentence. My dad. He never forgave himself for not rescuing Pippa.

"I can't imagine him going anywhere. Your dad, I mean." Victoria tilts her head so that she can see me. "This place, he loved it so much."

He did. I think of him, watching me go past on the bus, then walking home, untying the boat.

"I didn't believe it. Not for years. I kept expecting him to come back."

Victoria reaches for my hand. "I kept expecting Alice to come back too." She's turned back to the canal. "You wait for ever, and then realize it's not going to happen."

We sit there together. After a while, the waitress comes out from the door of the coffee shop. She is bringing me the box.

It's sealed with thick brown parcel tape that goes over and over and covers every gap; I can't find an end, and my fingernails aren't sharp enough to get through. Eventually, Victoria produces a small penknife from her shoulder bag, and I dig through with that.

The first thing I notice is the smell of home. It is out and around me and gone almost before I have realized it is there, air that has been sitting in this box since the time my father disappeared.

The contents are not a surprise, in some strange, equally inexplicable sense. I have been carrying the box since I left my mother's flat, have felt the weight, computed the empty space and picked up the tremors of how the contents shifted as I walked. My subconscious has been busy.

They are items from another age, dusty and small, with no explanation, no letter. I wonder who collected them all. Not my dad.

"She emptied the house straight away, you know." I hold my hands over the open top of the box, so that nothing blows away. "I used to listen to her telling people how it was best to accept the situation." I dredge up a laugh. "I suppose it helped her."

"Did you never come back, after he'd disappeared?" There is almost more sympathy in Victoria's voice than I can bear.

"No." I squeeze my eyes shut so tightly that red speckles dance behind the lids.

Victoria nods with understanding. "Did you find out anything about how he left?"

"Some people saw him heading down the canal." I nod my head to the right, downstream, away from the cottages. "And the lock keeper said he seemed normal when he went through."

I wouldn't listen at the time. The sight of my mother with her head next to the liaison officer used to make me want to scream. And if I didn't believe it, then he would come back. It was simple.

"Which lock was that?"

"It's about five miles down." I nod in the direction I mean. "Not the one we found, the broken one. He only had one way to go."

The lock he went through led into the river, and from there, eventually, to the sea. I found the bare details years ago on a microfiche in the library of the local newspaper. There was a high tide on the night of the last sighting, followed by several weeks of calm and unseasonably warm weather.

"Nobody ever saw the boat again. In the end, Mum told me she'd throw everything away if I wasn't prepared to help. So I told her to go ahead, and I didn't speak to her again for about a month."

"I can see why." Victoria's hand closes around one of mine, and I grasp it tightly.

"I was never going to talk to her again, but, you know . . ." My voice trails off. "And then I ran away. I never wanted to see her again."

"And here you are, she kept all this for you."

I lift my hands away and we bend our heads to see inside. There is a diary, letters, the box I kept my earrings in. One sheet of paper is a faded purple, and I know before I unfold it that there will be a printed cartoon rabbit decorating one corner. I hold it out. It is our book list.

Victoria snorts. "Bloody *Ulysses*. I don't think I read any of them properly, you know." She shakes her head.

"I read them all." I fold the paper up and drop it on the ground. I doubt I'll be reading them again now.

In among the scatter of papers are some pencil sketches, and I pick them up with the delicacy of a bomb disposal expert. Most are Piet's. He spent an afternoon trying to teach me, and his drawings hold so much life that my heart aches: Seth bending over his guitar, Pippa on her tummy, reading a comic, Alice sitting. One or two are my attempts, crude, cack-handed, but, even so, there is the odd line that makes the moment recognizable.

Victoria leans across my arm to look. "I forgot about you doing these." She takes one from me. "You always said that Piet was a cowboy."

Piet is standing with his back turned, slouched with one shoulder against a wall as if he's thrown his Stetson down on the ground.

"You lost all of your photographs." I have the briefest sensation of smoke passing in front of my nose. "When I went back to the cottage, that's all I could think about. The photos and the records . . ." A sob rises in my throat as I remember how much else was lost. "You should have these." I hold the papers out. "Take them."

"I'll be seeing them tomorrow." She has tears in her eyes. "Piet hasn't changed at all."

I have a flicker of a thought, the briefest image. I could go with her, be part of it. It's what I've always wanted.

"What does Seth do now?" I study my hands, aware of the old feeling of giving myself away.

"He's a psychiatrist, would you believe."

"What really happened to your dad?" After all this time, the question feels simple but somehow unimportant.

"Which version did I tell you?" Victoria is shaking her head. "There were drugs, a fight. He died. All a bit sordid."

"I heard Piet talking to Seth once." I remember the heat, the roughness of the apple tree beneath my fingers. "They didn't know I was there, but I imagined all sorts. Murder. Intrigue."

"And you never said." Victoria's voice holds a ghost of a laugh.

"I thought Piet might be the twins' dad as well."

"Nah." She examines the sketch. "There wasn't ever much of that between them, if you ask me. Piet's pretty good at stories as well."

There is one more sheet of paper in the box, folded into four, and I pick it up and open it out. It is Seth's sketch of me, my hair tumbling down from a loosely knotted bun. I fold it up again and hold it tight between both hands. I don't think I can manage any more memories. But Victoria is reaching into the box. Half hidden under the flap in the base of the box are two photographs. She eases them out, and I take them from her despite myself.

In the first, I am a small girl in a blue cotton dress, and I am holding my father's hand as we crouch on the bank of the canal while he points to something on the other side. The other is upside down, but I don't need to turn it around to know what it is. It's the square white of a Polaroid snap, and on it, Pippa and I are smiling for the camera, and in the background is the boat.

"You should have this as well." I hold it out to her, keeping the snapshot of my father and me in my other hand.

As I feel the Polaroid pass out of my grasp, I stand up and step on the sides of the box to make it collapse. The sky is rich with sunset now, the rain clouds from earlier gone completely. Victoria stands as well. It's as if we've changed places. For the first time, I am leading the way. She follows me back across the footbridge.

"Helen —" There is a shiny four-by-four parked in the lane. The Victoria who drives that feels like a stranger. She doesn't know what to say.

"It's been nice seeing you again." I hold out my hand. I need her to go, right now.

"Helen, are you OK?"

"Yes," I say. "Yes, I'm fine." I rub my hands up and down the sleeves that cover my arms. "Say hello to the others."

I walk away from Victoria, along the path that leads to the sea. I feel her eyes on the back of my neck, and it takes all the strength I have to keep walking. Pippa once told me I was like Helen of Troy. I used to think, if I tried hard enough, I would be as beautiful as my namesake, as desirable and desired. I forgot about Helen's main achievement, destruction.

You're never far from a canal. Often you don't know it. Canals don't shout out. They're flat and self-effacing and, once they get away from the flourish of a lock flight, they hide behind factories or disappear at the far end of fields. Sometimes you catch a glimpse from a train, or they slip past the corner of your eye as you drive over a bridge. But once you know, once you begin to look out for them, the slow bends appear around unexpected corners. This canal has been waiting for me to come back.

I follow in the wake of a white lifeboat's stern, which disappears behind the bend of the willows before I can catch it. I force myself to keep at a walk as I, too, follow the curve of the bank. As the sun begins to spill sunset red across the horizon, I feel the breeze in the rough ends of my hair. My dad isn't there. He is never going to be there. But I cany on following the ghost of an old lifeboat, watching as she swings out for the turns and drifts down the straights with her engine throbbing slowly, and a faint twist of diesel smoke curling up from her far side.

What I didn't tell Victoria, in that last moment as she stood by her fancy car and I saw the lines of age on her face, is what I have remembered. It came out of the box, the final link with the night of the fire. It wasn't triggered by the smell of smoke and ashes. It was triggered by the smell of the past.

I remember seeing Seth, made naked and reeled in by Moira. I remember the feel of Victoria's cheek underneath my hand, the raw and crawling shame as she rejected me. I remember Mick in a deckchair, snoring, Piet walking past me as if I didn't exist. I remember bending to feel down the back of Seth's tea chest for the bottles and I remember lighting the rag in the neck of one and I now see myself tossing it down the path by the side of the house. *That'll show them.* My voice echoes in my head.

I turned around, laughing in joy and in pain, and Alice was standing there watching me. She was so beautiful. She was the one men went crazy for, she was the one they crossed oceans to find. She was laughing too. She took my hand and we danced, the bonfire throwing its flickering light over us. And when we fell on to the ground, we could both see the same stars, and she held my hand as if I was keeping her from floating up to join them.

Beautiful girls. I hear her voice, husky and bewitching. Her fingers are squeezing mine. I squeeze back. She is telling me something, she is giving me a piece of wisdom that I can hold in my hand and take out like a jewel. I strain to hear her. It's something about the universe. *We have to do what the universe wants.*

She is saying it wrong.

"Universe." I try it for her. "*Yes, that.*" But she's not happy now. I hear her voice wobble, see the tears that are making her face shine as the light from the flames catches them as they run.

I want to make her happy again.

"Don't cry." I'm holding her hand between both of mine now, shaking it up and down to make my point. "You shouldn't cry."

"He left me." Her eyes are holding my gaze. "My Jakob. My Jakob. Why didn't he come back?"

332

It's so easy. Alice is my friend. Not Victoria. Not Seth. She wants to know. I can help her. I have the answer. I hold her other hand, and feel the smile cross over my face.

"He didn't leave you!" I feel a surge of joy. I am taking all of her troubles away. "He's dead. I heard Piet talking about it." I give her hands a shake, and let my own version of events take me further. "He always loved you, he would never have left you alone."

Vows of secrecy crumple like paper before a flame, words turning to the grey of ash after the burn and the flare.

I'm not even sure Alice has heard me. She has the traces of a dream on her face. I wonder if I should tell her again. I close my eyes.

My hand is empty, lying on the floor with nothing in it. And someone is moaning. I can't turn my head, though, and I don't know what is happening any more. The moaning is almost like words. *Myjakobmyjakob.* I turn my head and Alice has her face next to me, her mouth drawn back from her teeth in a snarl. And I feel her anger, I take it for myself. This is what the universe wants. I am holding the last bottle, and yellow flowers grow out of the top as I press it into Alice's hand. She is throwing it for me, for all of us who have been lied to.

In slow motion, I watch as Alice's arm goes back, and then there is the blossoming orange, and then I know nothing.

My name is Helen, and I destroy people.

I stand by the canal with the ghost of a boat sailing away from me, and see what I have broken. Rain is falling again, in cold lines that slide across my head and run down my neck and I want it to keep falling, to make the water rise until it laps at my knees, at my chest and finally covers my shame. And yet I am standing, and the canal stays where it is, where it has always been. Somewhere, in among the ruins, is a small clear space. It is a space with no secrets, no hidden memory. It is a place where I might be able to start again.

Another shred of memory floats back. I am lying on my back, smelling smoke, too much smoke, and feet run past me. All I can see is the feet, but I hear a voice, a high voice full of panic.

My special things! I have to get my special things!

And I don't stop Pippa as she runs by, and I don't reach out and tell Will to catch her more quickly. They disappear into the darkness and in my hand it is as if I can feel the shape of a tiny spoon.

My dad and Piet never managed to get around to putting glass in the window holes. The boat was launched with plastic sheeting stapled across the gaps in the plywood, thin wooden battens covering the raw edges. Plastic sheeting gives a cloudy cast, makes vision tricky, so I wouldn't have been able to see him clearly anyway. He would be a dark shape standing at the back of his boat, leaning into the tiller arm and looking forwards to where he was going.

The boat travels at a walking pace, and we carry on together, the boat always out of sight, until we reach a small, grey humped-back bridge which carries the towpath over to the other side of the canal. I don't go down the other side. I stand at the tallest point, and I watch the light from the setting sun as it shines on the water beneath me, opaque and dappled with circles of gold. I let the boat go.

Acknowledgements

Debut novel = a lot of people to thank.

For instance, grandmothers. In my case, Doris, who passed on her love of books, and Bridie, who told tales and read me *The Tale of the Flopsy Bunnies* as often as I asked. Then there's my mum and dad, who let me grow up with my head in a book, and have always seen writing as a positive thing. Happy childhoods are a gift, and I'm very grateful for mine. xx

I've got amazing friends, especially Jo Sutton, who saw more than one false start; Katy Quayle, who has given unending support; and Esther Batchelor, who kept on at me until I sent my MA application form off.

That leads on nicely to my cohorts and tutors from the Creative Writing MA at Manchester Metropolitan University, where the serious stuff began to happen. You, especially, Steve Galbraith.

To the maniacs from Moniack: you rock. Those writing weeks saw me through to the end of the first draft, and I always wrote better after spending time with you all. May the Gimtos never run dry!

The writers in the North West are an incredible bunch. The spoken-word nights and festivals and the overall solidarity and friendship have all been a tremendous encouragement, and an essential part of Keeping Going.

My second official edit happened mostly on Anglesey with the Ann Atkinson Writers. They're another amazing bunch, especially fellow boater, Jo Bell, who has been unfailingly generous and generally splendid.

I'm so happy to have moored up at Conville & Walsh with my fabulous agent Carrie Plitt: many thanks to Jo Unwin for the introduction! Working with Transworld has been a delight, also, where I've had two incredible editors in Katy Loftus and Bella Bosworth. Thank you all so much for making this a better book than I could ever have done by myself.

Is this the first official acknowledgement aimed at the Prime Writers? You're a writing support network extraordinaire, and I can't wait to see what you all come up with next.

Graeme Shimmin, you fit into more than one of the above groups. Maybe I'd have done this if I hadn't met you, but I don't know. I'm glad you were alongside. Thank you for everything.

To Ged, for having the boat, and Penny, for having a Ged. Love you both.

Fuchsia, Hatty and Gabe: you're at the beginning, and it only seems right that you're here at the end. Love you guys so much.